LOVE, SICK PUPPY

A TALE OF UNREQUITED L__

M CLAYDON

Contents

Dedicated to
Jerilee

Wren - Ophelia

Cape

Humphrey

Without you all, I would have finished

writing this book much sooner.

Prologue

There is the odd occasion when I find myself wishing away time, pondering my existence, questioning the point of this infuriating life. At other times, like this splendiferous moment right now, I feel pretty significant: I have it all; the looks, the wardrobe, the money. I am one of life's winners, a man on top of his game.

It is most likely a Wednesday or a Thursday and I am doing my thing. Currently there is an extraordinarily drunk twenty-something waiting in the lounge. She is keen and I had better get out there before she sobers up or slips into a drink-induced coma.

A taxi from the West End to my home – my space in Shoreditch, my East London bachelor's pad with its gritty, urban exterior and well-considered, sleek interior – was just shy of 30 English pounds and I want a return on my investment.

I stand here naked. Now I know I have definitely come into the bathroom for a specific purpose – aside from, of course, admiring my magnificent Moorish tiling and the lavish roll-top bath that I rarely use.

The colognes are evenly spread on shelves. Most have been specifically created to partner my natural masculinity. I have one in a bottle no bigger than a thimble that was developed by a little-known perfumier from Antwerp who mixed the musk of the London Underground with the intensity of a boxing gym to create a unique and powerful scent; a scent that I have yet to find an appropriate time to wear.

1

The latest body hair trimmer perches above the toilet basin, the remains of my earlier trim irritatingly entwined between the razor blades. Hairs stuck to the inside of the basin, hundreds of individual strands scattered in the sink. I don't recall being in a rush; I must have had other things on my mind. A mild dose of disgust and self-loathing creeps in – nothing I can't handle, mind you. I will not have this evening ruined.

A smallish cheap wicker bin sits slightly hidden between the sink and the bidet, very aware that he does not really fit into such luxurious surroundings. A gift from a colleague who clearly does not know me well, or perhaps Katia, my loyal cleaner, was attempting some kind of initiative and got it horribly wrong. Peering from the top shelf are two shampoos: different brands, similar promises – similar broken promises. Both guarantee a thicker head of hair, but to date the results have been negligible.
On the floor a heavily thumbed copy of *Men's Fitness* and what looks like an old photo album.

At least five minutes have slipped away, penis in hand and my bladder apparently empty. I know why I am in here; it's just slipped my mind. Sometimes I overthink things. Come on, brain – give me a bloody hand. Think straight; do not let unsightly pubic hair get the better of you. I am further distracted by my resentment of the tatty-looking photo album and the déjà vu that comes with it.

I hear a clattering from the kitchen, which nudges my brain into gear. The girl – the girl who looks just like her. I must make sure she uses my ensuite and not the bathroom, where a crop of my dark, tightly curled pubes line the sink.

2

Then I notice it: my flaccid, lazy, unmotivated, work-shy penis that has not being playing its part recently. I will need to knock back a Viagra – or, to be specific, a Kamagra, Viagra's black-market, no-prescription-needed counterpart. There is no need for a prescription as there is no need for a doctor, as there really is no issue. It will sort itself out in due time. I am an athlete of sorts and all good athletes need supportive supplementation. Besides, I am so busy: big plans, crazy busy and stressed out. Forty-two per cent of men under the age of sixty suffer from erectile problems at some point in their life, according to several online studies.

I pop the pill, taking a swig from the bottle of bubbles I must have just cracked open. I splash cold water onto my face and then cup and tip some into my nostrils in an attempt to ease the congestion. Instinctively, I drop and get eighteen push-ups out on the bath edge, creating a rush of blood to my chest that adds a fresh pump to my continuously developing pectorals – known as chest muscles to Joe Average.

I am ready to head back into the arena.

The clattering was the result of the drunk, maybe too-drunk, guest opening a cupboard door that she should not have been touching and pulling to the floor hundreds of pounds' worth of Le Creuset. I step around them, anxious that they may have chipped the imported tiles.

Taking somewhere between a deep breath and a sigh, I approach her confidently from behind. I allow her one bite of the wholemeal pitta with crudely spread peanut butter that she seems to have made for herself. I take it out of her hand and toss it onto the marble work surface. I encourage her past the love seat that is too expensive to soil and onto the sofa. I unzip her little black dress, which looks reasonably expensive but feels decidedly cheap. This is starting to feel wrong. I am having second thoughts, but it's too late to change my mind – she will be so disappointed.

Then, to my dismay, I notice her stubby fingers. I notice her stubby fingers tightly gripped around a protein-boosting cereal bar that she must have pillaged from my dwindling supplies.

"If I do not hit at least 150 grams of protein a day, I am at risk of muscle depletion and this will impact my potential gains," I mumble to anyone who cares to listen.

I loosen one dwarfish finger at a time and replace the snack with my hardening penis. I reach around and knead her breasts firmly and a little carelessly. I note her blonde hair, her dyed blonde hair, and compliment her peach-like bottom. With the dimmers on low and the mix of expensive champagne and cocaine blurring my vision, it could almost be her.

I smile. Not a happy smile; more of a knowing one. Before the end of the year it will be her and everything will be significantly better.

Now, it is important to focus on the task at hand. I cup her mound. My soft, well-manicured hand skates across her soft, well-cared-for pussy. There is not a bristle to be felt; we both came prepared.

My mind drifts to the mess of pubic hair in the bathroom that really needs to be attended to. Love making should take around forty minutes and I normally do not allow guests to use the ensuite. Could I get the cleaner in at this time of night? Or a street hooker who knows how to polish ceramic?

I ease her over. She is talking gibberish in a nasally, colloquial accent. I would much prefer silence, as the two of them sound nothing alike. I dull her incessant noise by pushing her face into the scatter cushion. I manage to loosen her grip on my cock. I stroke my pulsating tool up and down like an artist working a brush, from front to her neat arsehole and back again. This should be enjoyable, yet I am so distracted.

First the incident with the cereal bar and then the talking, the unbearable chatter. Even when dulled by tasteful cushions it is so off-putting. Please stop, you really must, it is ruining the ambience. The reflection, it is all so wrong. What stares back at me from my impressive floor-to-ceiling mirror is just not accurate enough.

Even through the haze, through the drugs, the tequila, the champagne, the sleepiness, my increasing disgust and confusion, I can see her reflection and she really is nothing like her. Her face could be pretty, her eyes a similar blue, her skin the same tone in patches, but every feature is just so far apart, spaced out on her unusual head.

Just get through this. Tomorrow is another day. I should have searched for a hooker; I could have been more accurate and perhaps she could have cleaned up the mess.

I angrily thrust against her, finding some temporarily satisfying moisture. I glance over at my Swedish but certainly not Ikea-ish bookcase and get caught in the gaze of one of the many books I have yet to finish.

"Just be present, enjoy the moment," it suggests, in the most patronising of tones.

I catch a breath and appreciate the sudden silence.

Pausing there motionless, a hippo comfortably wallowing in warm waters. The Kamagra has bought a fiery heat to my cheeks and forehead, my nose is running, my nose is streaming.

I risk a glance at my own reflection: my frantic, sweating grimace, my flushed face, a dilated pupil in my one open eye. All side effects of the dick hardener that I really wished I had not taken. All side effects of the grade-A cocaine whizzing around my veins that I cannot imagine life without.

"Quitting is for quitters," an upbeat book hollers at me from the shelf. So I keep going. I continue to thrust in and out, I tense my just-about-visible abdominals, I attempt to force open my welded-shut right eye, I plan my attire for Friday. It is such an important day; she is always in on a Friday. A crisp white shirt open at the neck.

With every push my boredom escalates, my mind wanders away from the job at hand. I squint at the date on an unread copy of the *Financial Times* carefully positioned on my centre table. Three months until the end of the year, that's three months to wrap things up.

"Just make a plan and stick to it," The book whispers repeatedly in a reassuringly assertive manner.

The talking has stopped, her eyes are shut and her frame motionless. A sad-looking row of eyelashes hangs from her face and tickles a Baja-inspired Jonathan Adler cashmere throw. I am surprised at the surge of excitement I feel as I reach for her pulse and challenged by my disappointment when there is one. She is not dead; just sound asleep. I kill some time half-heartedly masturbating, with no relief, over her crimson buttocks.

I roll her onto the sofa, removing the brand-new cashmere throw and placing it a safe distance from any potential vomiting. I then escort my still rock-hard dick to the bedroom for a few hours of lonely contemplation.

Chapter 1

A horrendously blissful chime penetrates my eardrums and only seems to be getting louder. For the first couple of days the bohemian beat would go off at 7am, I would be up out of bed, showered, fed, medication taken and in the back of a taxi to the office by eight o'clock.

Today it is closer to 9. Normally four and a half hours' sleep, a crippling hangover and a twinge of guilt would persuade me to take way over the recommended amount of Nurofen, one of the Amitriptyline left in the bathroom cabinet and close my eyes to the dullness of the working day.

Not today, though, Oliver; no way. Today you get up and you get dressed and you start to put the wheels in motion.

I pull myself upright. The pain pulsates from my now-open left eye to the top of my spine. From the side table a neat paperback that I had once started to read calls out to me:

"Failing to prepare is preparing to fail."

Today and every day for the next three months I need to be prepared, focused and energetic. I am going to need a note pad, the cleaner to up her game and a hell of a lot more cocaine.

I hear a single floorboard creak. The house guest is leaving. I envision her quietly shuffling across the hallway.

I appreciate her gently tiptoeing out and considerately closing the front door. She didn't mention her name or where she lived and I certainly did not bother to ask. The copious amounts of fake tan I hope she has avoided spreading onto any of my possessions suggests Essex – a pitfall of living east I failed to consider.

No doubt she will rush to tell her friends, update her social media, maybe even call her mother. The penthouse, the thick pile rugs skimming solid oak flooring, the exquisite tiled kitchen, the rock-hard cock and the expertise in how he handled me. Then she will think back to earlier in the evening: the smile across the bar, the approach, the expensive-looking shoes, I think they were handmade, the champagne. "You know me, I never do this kind of thing, but he was well, just so charming."

She will not remember dozing off near the end. Anyway, on reflection, I am fairly certain her last few groans were an intensely satisfying orgasm.

Still unable to face the hair-filled horror show of the main bathroom, I pull myself out of bed and opt for the en suite. I rock under the almost scalding water and squint down at my uncomfortably erect penis. There is a tight pain in my scrotum and the recognisable sensation of seasickness. I make a brief attempt at ejaculation using my hand and an Aesop scrub much more suited to the face. I give up. I take a seat and flip the shower to freezing cold.

The tag from a new pair of crisp dark blue jeans comes off easily in my hand. They are a combination of cotton and cashmere and were very expensive. I like to buy several pairs in one go. The salesperson tried to discreetly hide her smile at the till; we both knew what a difference the commission would make to her pay packet.

I procrastinate over which shirt to wear. The white Tom Ford is certainly of better quality, but the stretch content in the Neil Barrett helps accentuate my improving physicality. I toy with the idea of wearing a tan Hermès belt before putting on the subtle and frankly more sophisticated Prada. I change my mind about loafers and no socks after remembering we are well into autumn, opting instead for oxblood socks and a deep brown brogue; a deep brown brogue that just so happens to be handmade.

In London, wealth is everywhere; everyone who is anyone has money. Bankers, lawyers, techies, old money, dirty money, Arab and Russian money, drug money. However, it is rare to find wealth and style, true style combined.

Today is an important day. Day numero uno. It is time to try something new. I take the tiny bottle from the shelf, doing my best to ignore the hair. I spray it into the air and let it lightly land on my neck and shoulders. I had once read that this helps leave a subtle, long-lasting fragrance rather than spraying directly onto the skin. Although my sense of smell is somewhat dulled, this was definitely the correct choice.

I grab my door key and both iPhones from the outrageously expensive coffee table that took four deliverymen to carry up the stairs. I must have had to mention its antique status near ten times, as their energy sapped and so did their conscientiousness, but somehow it remained undamaged and of course I still tipped well.

More than one motivating book highlights the importance of giving back.

I slip on last night's Saint Laurent blazer. Instinctively I check the pockets for any remaining powder. The wrap is damp but manageable. The sensation as it hits me right between the eyes is sharp and delightful.

I head over to the windows to pick up my wallet from the sill on which I always leave it. I see dust – an unexpected level of dust – and no mottled leather Saint Laurent. I recheck and then I see it, scraped in the muck, scrawled in the grime, is the word "LOSER".
I spend several minutes contemplating exactly what has occurred before realising that last night's lovemaking session was a relatively expensive one.

I drag my finger through the dirt and slowly etch out the word "whore".

I head into the bathroom, run the taps and smear any remaining hairs across the sink. I care little about the money; the cards are replaceable, the wallet last season's, and I have certainly paid more for sex in the past, but the wording hurts.

"LOSER".

Wanker, prick, arsehole, bastard. I have been all of those, but "LOSER" just does not feel appropriate.

Chapter 2

"1234, 6969, wait, wait, I remember – it is 1999. Well, it would appear I do not fucking know, do I. The account name is Danbrook. The company name is Danbrook and my last name is, guess what...DANBROOK."

My dust-induced rage has led to a complete blank of the Addison Lee password. I rip the empty wrap into as many pieces as possible.

"I am sorry, sir, I will need the correct four-digit password before I can confirm the car. Alternatively, you can pay by cash or credit card."

I picture the monotonous-voiced bitch waggling her badly manicured finger right in my face. She is probably on her third Nescafé and feeding her foul mouth with some kind of tuna melt in between breaths.

"Right, well, fuck you then. I will be cancelling our account at the earliest opportunity, so well fucking done, bravo, you've lost yourself a loyal customer. I will be switching to Uber, so explain that to the board." I clench my teeth together furiously. Why can't I recall the four-digit password, four single numbers? On Monday I will make it my mission to find out who authorised the password being put on the account and they will be out. Let's just get today out of the way. Breathe.

"Okay then, sir, sorry for not being able to help further, and I do hope your day improves." She manages to harmoniously merge patronising and considerate into one tone.

It is desperately unfortunate that the iPhone does not have a receiver, as I would have slammed it down. Instead, I just press the little red button and while taking a deep in-breath walk back to the windowsill and scrawl "FUCK YOU" into the dust. Katia oh Katia how did you miss this. I stare at the bookshelf for inspiration while pointlessly downloading the Uber app, which I cannot use without my debit card. I look around the apartment one last time. I look at the safe, I stare at the numbers, I kick at the door. Since when did I start locking it?

I catch the gaze of an Oyster card looking up at me from behind an empty fruit bowl. How it got there I do not know. Maybe it belonged to Cate from the office, I kind of recall having dull sex with her a few times in the spring. Could she get public transport? I cannot be certain.

"Sometimes with risk comes great reward," states a book in a particularly matter-of-fact American manner.

So this is the chosen path for me: today is the day I take the bus. I remove the Sea-dweller; it isn't appropriate for a bus journey. It would be cruel for the locals to see their annual salary peering from underneath the cuff of my shirt. I put it back into my initialed Aspinal brown croc watch box and clasp the much more affordable IWC to my wrist. The hallway mirror was a moving-in present from my mother. Today, a swirling concoction of anxiety, excitement and fear looks back at me. My skin looks overly dry and tight to my skull; my eyes are in a hurry, darting backwards and forwards, side to side. I cover them up with Tom Ford and leave the house.

13

The sun is low in the sky and even through three hundred pounds' worth of UV protection I feel the need to squint. They glance me up and down. I am clearly not one of them. The men are unable to hide the aggression in their poverty-stricken faces. The women do not attempt to mask their desire while edging closer, creating an uncomfortable moat of lust around me. The baying mob pushing me forward, I attempt to hold my position. The contracts were in the hands of the solicitors, three million for a mews in Westbourne Grove, when I changed my mind. It was too small, stuffy, claustrophobic. How could my creative juices flow in such an environment? Dad was furious. "What a waste of money! Can you even contemplate the legal fees?" She was more supportive. "Let him be independent, stand on his own two feet for once, perhaps it will be good for him."

So here we are.

The hoards grab at me, pushing and pulling. Although physically I may well be in the best shape of anyone here, I feel completely out of control. A sharp pain in my back, a bayonet encouraging me to my execution.

"You need to buzz your Oyster – the card, push it against there," something snarls at me.

The warmth is unbearable. Surely someone is gagging me, forcing a towel into my mouth, cotton wool into my nasal passages. I yank my arm upwards, hand to throat, firstly to remove the chokehold someone must have on me, secondly to check I have not accidentally done up the top button on my shirt. Something is pulling at my legs, taking me to the floor.

"Sit down, love; you look a bit peaky." A kind but common voice comes to my rescue.

I catch a short breath. I attempt to steady my trembling hands. A small wrinkled claw pushes a bottle of water into my palm. It isn't a recognisable brand, but I take a mouthful and catch a slightly longer breath.

The bus starts to empty out. The condensation on the windows slowly clears. I wipe at the window with my sleeve. Liverpool Street Station, the heart of the financial district. Red-cheeked men in badly cut suits dash across the road, barging past anyone in their way, rushing to their unfulfilling jobs, slaves to their wage. Not a creative cell in their stress-soaked brains.

I hear them first. She screeches. The only decipherable words are "fuck" and "fucking" and "fucker". Then I see them; the mother with greasy, scraped-back hair and cheekbones only seen on catwalk models and crack addicts. She yanks her grubby-looking child down the bus and passes me in the aisle. Even with my sporadic sense of smell I take in the dampness of her quilted jacket, dog kennels, cigarettes, deep fat fryers. He is swamped by school uniform, head shaven to the bone, with visible nicks from the clippers. A can of Monster energy drink in hand, almost as tall as he stands. The boy bogs at me – it's the only word for it – our eyes meet and we share a moment of pure desperation. He breaks stare first and takes a gulp. His teacher is in for one hell of a day when that caffeine kicks in.

You've got no hope, kid.

My upbringing, on the other hand, was one surrounded by privilege.

Not exactly old money; there was no trust fund, Hunter wellingtons, shooting weekends, rosy cheeks, secret handshakes, acres of land or little rings on little fingers. New money, but with just a touch more class: the holiday home wasn't in Marbella; there was no need for brash designer logos on every item of clothing. I cannot recall a time when it felt like the money might run out.

The family home was, and still should be, in Esher, Surrey, a huge sprawl with several bedrooms, tennis courts, spa and pools. It seems a long time since I have been back there. The "little apartment" in Marylebone was far from little. Mum stayed there for a while, but I think that was sold during the divorce. There was a holiday home in the south of France, not quite St Tropez but only a stone's throw away. School wasn't Eton or Harrow – similar money, but without the ancestry. As an only child I got exactly what I wanted. Well, for a time, anyway.

The bus has yet to pull away. I look out of the window to see Cheekbones and a guy with the same barber as his son arguing. She pushes the boy in the chest towards him. He looks towards me. Just for a moment our eyes meet again. I drag my finger through the remaining condensation. "U R Fucked Kid."

He breaks a smile.

As the bus pulls away I have the urge to make a change.

"We R Fucked Kid."

Mum always said he had a touch of Del Boy about him. He would tell you he was more of a Richard Branson. By sixteen he was selling whatever he bought for one pound for two. He was born in South London – Lewisham, to be precise, although the cockney drawl is long gone. A right spiv, always in the finest cashmere jumpers and mohair suits, perfect spit-and-polish shoes, he stunk of charm. Always quick to make the point of telling anyone what a ladies' man he was, especially if Mum was in the room. Had the pick of them all.

He met her near the end of his first career. Didn't have a house but did have the Jaguar and the Rolex Daydate. Hadn't queued for a nightclub in years; always the best table for Jimmy Danbrook.

He was starting to push his luck, though, skating on thin ice with the law, knocked-off goods, slightly grubby money. Then, just in the nick of time, Mum walked into the right West End club. Apparently, they were inseparable. He introduced her to the high life and she introduced him to the better life; real money.

She introduced him to straight living. He took a job in sales with an old family friend, an ageing family friend. He excelled and then he slowly took over. Within four years he was head honcho, invaluable to the firm. The old boy was ready to step down and James "Jimmy" Danbrook was ready to step up. Within a decade he had built one of the largest recruitment firms in Europe and I was just about old enough to enjoy the fruits of his labour.

Mum was beautiful, stunning. She modelled for a while, mostly catalogue stuff. Fake smiles, blank eyes and perfect blow-dried hair, in a multitude of camel-coloured rollnecks and matching skirts. She packed it in the year they got married, the same year I was born. Ten years later she would always point out what could have been: Milan, Paris, New York.

I wondered what that kid's dad did for a living? The occasional bit of cash-in-hand labour? Out of work due to the influx of cheaper foreign workers? Angry and resentful, unsure of how he was going to pay the rent.

The three of us did everything together for a time.

Years and months are a bit of a blur at the moment. However, I remember the days of sun-filled holidays, never-ending coastlines, the clear blue seas, the breeze from the deck, the anticipation as you would hit the cool water, bobbing up against the waves, squinting in the sun looking up at them both waving down to me. This was before the seasickness started.

Oh, how they loved the newest restaurants, initially in awe; everything looked so shiny, everyone was so friendly. Their background chatter was enough, soothing, offering me security as he would talk and she would laugh. I would people-watch; different venues but always the same clientele.

As time passed, he would still talk but she wasn't laughing anymore. I would look up to see her fake model smile and someone else laughing; the waitress or a gaggle of fresher-faced girls squeezing past to their table. The restaurants seemed to get louder, shinier and the dinners longer but quieter. Whispering and what seemed like snarling replaced the comfortable conversation I was so used too.

He started to come home later at night. The company was expanding and often he would sleep at the office. I would sit in my den playing computer games and checking the clock every fifteen minutes. I couldn't sleep until he got home. She would leave me to it. Most nights she would spread out on the biggest leather sofa you can imagine – it reminded me of a snake weaving across the room – feet raised in the air, shoes still on and a full face of make-up. Hands always full, a huge bowl-like glass of white wine in one hand and the telephone in the other. I would hear her on the phone to her sister: "I know you warned me"; "I can't, I won't do that," as the bottle of wine emptied, and her voice would get more animated, followed by tears. Often I would stand in the room and watch, wait for her to notice me. Often she wouldn't notice until the key turned in the front door.

When it got to midnight, I would climb up onto my desk and watch out of the window. A taxi would pull up at the gates, or his car would wind down the driveway. He would stumble to the front door. I remember him always looking so tired. I would run down the stairs and normally made it for a hug before the shrieking would start.
How many of those wine glasses she broke I could not keep count. Patiently he would clean up the mess and then go to sleep in a spare room.

Perhaps that kid isn't so unlucky.

He would take me to tennis lessons every Saturday. I am not sure I genuinely enjoyed being made to run around the court for two hours, but I always managed to fake a smile – something I suppose I should thank my mum for. I did, however, always enjoy the drive home, whether it was in the Jaguar, the Range or very occasionally the 911.

Fuelled by all of the gifts Dad was buying me, I started to make friends at school. Not real friends, not the sort you can rely on or trust – more the sort of friends who would use your outdoor pool in the summer, who would borrow your "cool stuff" and take their time to return it.

That was just fine with me, though.

The same strategy secured me my first kiss, grope and sexual encounter; and my second, third, fourth and fifth. Losing my virginity conveniently coincided with receiving a convertible BMW on my seventeenth birthday. We did it in the garage, awkwardly on the back seats. Luckily it was over swiftly; luckily the seats were leather. It would be another six months before I could drive the car without my dad in the passenger seat.

I had developed quite a collection of timepieces by my twenty-first birthday: Pateks, IWC, Rolex, Audemars Piguet. Watches never seemed to impress girls, but they did impress boys, leading to me being invited to spend Dad's money in the better clubs that inevitably let to more interest from women.

This is around the time I was introduced to my powdery white first love.

I really do feel for that poor, hopeless kid.

I look in the glass, hoping to see his little face one more time, but only my reflection stares back; only the stench of her jacket lives on.

The knowing of being watched distracts me.

Cautiously, I swivel my head to the right. My most likely dilated pupils meet the dark brown eyes of a young black girl. She has an inquisitive, cute face. Her school uniform looks professionally pressed and her hair is meticulously plaited. I look long enough to see her inquisitiveness merge into a frown.

"Why are you talking out loud to yourself? Are you mental, 'cos if you're some mentalist I am moving downstairs," she says fearlessly.

I find myself sitting firmly upright in my seat.

I do not feel threatened; of course not, she is a child. She has just caught me unaware. Anyhow, I am damn near sure I wasn't talking to myself, but feel the need to make an excuse.

"It's called positive mental assertion. I was preparing for the day ahead. Have you heard of Danbrook International?" I want to say in a convincing tone.

"Your breath stinks of alcohol. I'm going to move away from you. You're a bit odd," she says, moving out of the seat without breaking eye contact.

I feel relieved as the top of her well-cared-for hair disappears out of sight and down the stairs.

The bus pulls into a stop by Oxford Circus. The seat next to me has remained empty and I assertively nudge people out of the way to exit the vehicle. I decide to give the impression that I am in a hurry, most probably for a senior-level breakfast meeting. I imagine I appear very important indeed, although crippling anxiety is starting to weave its way through me once more. I touch my left arm just above the watch. My skin is clammy, toxins evacuating out of my pores.

The frown and those judgmental eyes watching me. She shakes her head. Her uniform so pristine, my uniform stained with the murkiness of last night. I push past whoever is in my way.

The mistake from last night… what if, just what if, perhaps she is a mutual friend of a mutual friend? She has my wallet, for Christ's sake, she knows my name. She could mention the falling asleep while fucking, the filthy windowsills, my cock being too small for her. I sent her to sleep, for Christ's sake. This could get back to Poppy. It would be a devastating setback on day one. I rack my brain for a motivational quote to get me through this. I draw a blank.

I really wish I had started the day with the slow-releasing energy of porridge rather than the remains of last night's chang.

Chapter 3

The Danbrook Global sign gleams garishly from the back wall of the reception. It is a modern eyesore. I would not be surprised if the old boy came in early and polished the damn thing himself.

The building itself is prestigious; W1 surrounded by funds and embassies. Just imagine the cost per square foot.

Danbrook Global, the leader in its field. London to Hong Kong via Dubai. The partners in India, China and South America. James Danbrook the founder, the Managing Director, the CEO. The last time I was paying attention, I heard rumours of a flotation. This would be fantastic for my aspirations of getting the hell out of here. My exact role within the company has never been defined. I try to find time for thirty hours a week and a decent-sized pay cheque appears in my account at some point every month.

I seem to be given the scope to make minor decisions about the aesthetics of the communal rooms in the building, and as I am highly presentable I am occasionally wheeled into meetings with foreign clients. I sit there, sometimes nodding enthusiastically and sometimes, more often than not, pretending to make notes on my phone while actually scouring the web for fitness tips.

As I exit the lift I see Theo something-or-rather, a big earner at the firm, making small talk with a plump receptionist. Her giant breasts make up for her exaggerated face. Eyes, nose and mouth all tightly packed in the middle surrounded by pounds of firm but fatty flesh. I am sure I was very clear with HR that the first face any potential clients must see is one with cheekbones, or maybe I just put a reminder in my diary. I make another note of this on my iPhone and then immediately delete it. I simply do not have the time.

"Good morning, Oliver. Glad you made it in today. The place isn't the same without your valued contribution." Theo is a smug prick and his string-like lips drag a grin across his pompous face.

"Not that it's any of your concern, but out of choice I am happy to keep you in the loop. This morning I had a high-level breakfast meeting at Dean Street; great poached eggs, not-quite-ripe avocado. Potentially it will bring some major business your way, help pay that hefty mortgage I presume you have like a noose around your neck. Let's hope the interest rates don't go up."

Theo knows, I know and somehow the tubby receptionist knows that I have been nowhere near Dean Street this morning.

"Glad Daddy's making you work for your pennies, Ollie. I might suggest that we open an office in Columbia or Peru. You could shoot over to South America, head up the operation and get paid a wage in your favourite currency – cut out the middleman, if you catch my drift. Anyhow, I am off to earn some money for the company. Claire, sweetheart, it was good meeting you. If you need anything, my extension is 221." Theo winks at the blushing receptionist while just about disguising his resentment towards me.

At the last minute I refrain from shouting across the foyer that I actually pay near to wholesale anyway; it is simple economy of scale.

Theo, oh, Theo, last name most likely something double-barrelled and wanky, he cycles into work every day. He is tall – my estimate puts him at around six foot two – slightly hunched and slim with dark wavy hair. Apparently he has classic good looks, although I am not convinced.

Last year, Danbrook paid him £400,000, which quite frankly turns my stomach. This is surely way more than the average wage of a London worker and therefore I am baffled as to why the fuck he cycles in.

On one occasion, at some point last year, I arrived at the office very early. Actually, truth be known, I had stumbled out of an all-nighter by Kings Cross and got an Addison Lee straight here.

It certainly wasn't my intention to be present at the crack of dawn; I was just looking for a little boost that I was sure was hidden at the back of my office drawer. There he was. I watched him hop off his racer bike, his slightly reddened cheeks the only indication of any physical activity. He took off his helmet – his helmet with a camera on – and pushed a hand through his bouncy, seemingly unruffled, hair. He wheeled his bike effortlessly into the building while whistling a vaguely familiar tune; if I had to guess, maybe something by the artist
Bruno Mars. He held the door open with his foot and slapped me on the back as I slithered in.
Hatred isn't a strong enough word.

He is everything I despise in humanity: stiff, upright, corporate, a sheep, a follower, always there to help, nothing too much of an effort, "if you need anything, call me on extension 221". The only thing she needs, Theodore, is a fucking gastric band.

If I had my way he would be gone, and therein lies the problem. The old man likes him. Apparently he comes from good stock and would be almost irreplaceable. I recall putting the phone down to my father that day uncertain of who he preferred: his own flesh and blood or this well-bred twit on a bicycle.

Out of the lobby windows I can see the sunshine breaking free of the cloud, a rare sunny day. The temptation to spin on my heels and walk back out of the building is proving quite the battle.

"You made such an effort to get here this morning, keep going Oliver, keep going," I say in Claire's direction.

Eyes from the open-plan office harass me as I greedily glug several cups of water from the machine. I gasp with satisfaction as water spills from my mouth. I wipe the wet residue from my chin and weave between the irrelevants. I look for that smile of admiration, a respectful nod hello, hoping, begging that someone will make a desperate attempt to impress by vying for my attention. They do not. They never do. Surely having my last name on the door commands some respect, or at least one of those fake smiles. It could be that they do not recognise the Danbrook jawline under this stubble, or it is a case of simple intimidation.

The morning hit is wearing off. I cannot face trudging back to the water machine, so I drag my tongue around my gums trying to collect moisture.

I keep walking, staying focused.

"Hello Oliver, how are you" She says once, maybe twice

"Fine, busy and heading into a high-level meeting Cate" I reply and keep moving.

There it is, his office. I have never understood why he needs his own office, but Dad insists that he deserved the promotion and "has senior management potential". I read the text reply back from my father several times that evening and couldn't help but wonder if I had senior management potential.

I root around in my pockets. That familiar confidence starts to kick in as I push open the shut door. He is going to just love hearing about last night's conquest.

It must have been early when he left, maybe midnight, something about meeting a friend, so he was fortunate enough to avoid seeing her face. It's good I can embellish her features slightly. It feels necessary to mention her friend, who was definitely game; I mean, she was pushing a six, which in truth is an eight by Clarke's standards.

Tell this tale with enthusiasm, Oliver; forget the bitter disappointment, the theft, the loneliness.

I pause, take breath in through my nostrils and expel from my mouth. I visualise the unloved street urchin on the bus. I snatch his energy drink from him, I gulp it down. The sugar, the caffeine rushes through my veins. This is my Popeye moment. I have a winning mentality. I stand upright, smile, actually smirk. I march in. There is a zone and I am in it.

"Let me tell you about this sort from last night, the tightest little body…"

Forget the face; do not mention the face.

"Looked just like a young Cameron Diaz."

Jesus, his office has a familiar smell. Perfume – Tom Ford Neroli Portofino.

Unprepared, so unprepared. It is warm in this office. Make a mental note to turn the air con up a notch. Shit, Oliver, smile, look impressive, stand upright, scan for some glass or a mirror. I need to check my hair. Stop wringing your hands. Why am I so damned clammy? I am disgusting.

Perched on the corner of his desk in all of her perfectness is the main reason for today's attendance and potentially the sole reason for my questionable existence.

Okay, Oliver, pull yourself together, pivot. The meeting agenda just needs updating, that's all. Now take a breath.

Poppy had first appeared in my life some time ago, when her whore of a mother decided to seduce my father. According to him, the affair had lasted only eighteen months. They had met on a work weekend away; she was a secretary for an old golf friend of his. Looked like Mum, dressed like Mum, yet he still did it. Maybe she was just slightly less fake.

The history I have shared, the holidays, the restaurants, the tennis and the watches; consider them as highlights. The overbearing memory from my childhood, the tale I have reeled off to several psychotherapists and the odd psychologist, the pivotal moment that helped create the man I am, is this one.

Everybody we encountered would remark on how noticeably chilly it had been. She pulled my coat tightly around me, zipped up to my chin. I tolerated the scratchy wool hat covering my head and ears. It was two weeks before Christmas and rumours were circulating that it was going to snow. I was excited, as this year we were not heading to Barbados. I would be here for my first white Christmas.

We were meant to have gone to Hamleys to look at gifts for me; we detoured via Selfridges looking at gifts for her. Mum was dressed up in towering high heels and a fur. You could actually see the little animal's face. I would look into his glazed-over eyes and wish he would come back to life. I had always wanted a pet. I hadn't let on, but had overheard that I was getting a kitten for Christmas.

I remember repeatedly asking Dad when we were going to get my stuff. He just kept saying, "as soon as your mother has finished buying more shoes than she could ever possibly wear."

I bet he wishes he had hurried her along. I zoned out as they bickered. The clattering of shoes hitting the floor grabbed my attention.

"Mum, look it's Uncle James," said the scrawny-looking girl in neon leggings and an unzipped anorak that was not suitable for winter. Her voice reminded me of one of the poor kids from the stage production of *Oliver*: *"please sir, can I 'ave some more?"*

She sounds so different now.

I looked at this bony bag of pasty-grey skin with curiosity as she tugged on her mum's sleeve. The arguing I could hear going on behind me seemed so distant. I couldn't avert my eyes; I was intrigued.

The sound of open hand hitting face snapped me out of my trance. I looked up at Mum. She was pushing my flustered father in the chest. The other woman looked slightly younger. She stood uncomfortably and in silence; the intriguing girl seemed oblivious to the argument, trying to show my dad her new friendship bracelet, like there wasn't a care in the world.

Finally, after what seemed an age, Mum's focus changed. She turned away from Dad and started swearing at this other woman – a few impressive new words I had not heard before. Now in tears, the other woman dragged the curious girl away. As she was being marched off, a young Poppy turned to me and poked out her tongue.

A security guard attempted to calm my mother while the sales associate collected the scattered shoes from the ground. I remember her flustered face like it was yesterday, obviously worried about the fracas and the potentially lost sales.

The next thing I knew, the three of us are sitting in somewhere new and expensive, Dad and I on one side of the table, and three pairs of shoes in bright yellow bags and my mother on the other side.

They pointed at the menu. She downed a huge glass of burgundy red wine; she pushed scallops around her plate. Dad cut what looked like black ravioli up with the side of his fork and took the occasional bite. He went to speak and then stopped himself. He just sat there, the lines on his forehead deeper than usual, head bowed slightly. He picked up a garnish and twiddled it between thumb and forefinger. Still silence. Mum kept making a retching sound, like she wanted to be sick but was empty inside. I looked at her with spite in my eyes, unable to understand why she had caused such a scene.

If Dad were her uncle then we must be cousins. Hopefully I would get to see her again.

The waiter took away their food. I had managed to eat my fries but did not attempt the raw-looking beef burger. My appetite had been replaced by butterflies. What was her name and why hadn't we met before? Why wasn't she at those awful family get-togethers I was forced to attend?

The separation dragged on. They lived apart but still in our family home, but when the divorce came it was swift. "It will be a blessing in disguise," she told her sister, her voice heightened by the bottle of Pinot Grigio consumed. She moved on, moved to Spain to live with a "bearded fucking spick," according to Dad. She didn't argue for custody; "Let's not pull him out of school, he has taken this the hardest."

31

They had stopped mincing their words. Hushed became blunt and to the point. It became clear that the scrawny brat was no relation to me at all and that I was about to see my mother a hell of a lot less.

A decade of therapy, medication, stern talking tos, and upbeat fatherly chats. Then it just happened. I saw her eleven years on. We didn't pass on a busy street, catching each other's eye, unable to place how and where we had met. She stuttered into the reception of Danbrook. There was only one floor at the time and half the number of employees. The plaque on the wall was smaller but just as shiny.
I do not know what made me look up from the copy of *Vogue* I was perusing. I do not know why I hurriedly tossed it onto the table and edged behind the office door, taking several breaths before peering over at her.

She awkwardly hurried past desks, married men arching their bodies to see her pass. Women shaking their heads and pretending not to look. A clap, a slow clap that looks like it might have fazed her. She pauses, takes a deep breath, adjusts herself and continues.

A business administration degree and an unexpected email, that is how, apparently, she ended up back in my life. Dad had mentioned someone new was starting. I do not recall; maybe I was busy, maybe I blacked out. It happens sometimes.

I followed her to his office and squeezed through the door before it closed. I saw her face, I saw shoes dropping to the floor, I heard arguing. I felt a hand on my shoulder and my father's voice.

"Oliver, this is Poppy, my new PA. I mentioned her starting at the briefing last week. Was it anything urgent? If not, can we catch up later?"

The light seemed to sparkle from her shimmering blonde hair. Her blue eyes caught your attention and then playfully skipped away. Five seven but long-legged and on the healthier side of skinny. Her eyes; why won't you hold my gaze? Her breasts, keen to clamber out of her crisp white shirt, pushing out of her not-completely-appropriate-for-the-office bra. Her cheekbones high and elfish, her skin more golden than I recall. I catch that remarkable blue and see not complete certainty.

For the first few months I watch as she sheds her skin. The mistake of the trouser suit, the price stickers left on the sole of her shoes. Finding the balance of excessive and just the right amount of make-up for the day; how many buttons to leave open on the blouse.

It was not long before she glided along the floors of Danbrook, not a price sticker in sight on the red soles of her high heels. Her handbags suddenly seemed seasonal and expensive. Female colleagues compliment her on the way she could put together an outfit; male colleagues would appreciate her input; any leering became more considered and subtle. The Cartier watch surprised me; it was stainless steel but still a considered purchase. Perhaps after my father gave them a taste of the high life her mother had married rich. Occasionally, but not very often, I would consider whether my Dad was still in contact with her mother. Perhaps not. It would have been easy for her to have found Uncle James Danbrook all by herself.

I had searched for my stainless-steel Cartier for hours, desperate to wear it around the office as an icebreaker. An icebreaker that after six months was well overdue. Every drawer was emptied onto the bedroom floor. I frantically typed random numbers into the mini-safe in the hope that it might open. I jammed a knife into the side and hit it with the heel of a handmade shoe, but still it would not budge.

After hours, maybe even days, of searching my father's sprawling house, it hits me. Several women to choose from; the one who led me to the grubby room was not my first choice. She tried everything, but the more she tried the softer I got. Her accent grated on me. Her pimpled skin and dirty nails. She sits on the edge of the cheap mattress that dipped in the middle and watches me as I hurriedly get dressed. I pull several notes out of my wallet and push them into her open palms. I pick up the stainless-steel Cartier from the pine side table, momentarily fiddle with the clasp, then, for reasons unknown to either of us, toss it towards her.

Every stair squeaks as I try to make my exit. A monster of a man with the same accent as every cleaner you've ever met opens the heavy front door for me. He asks if I need a taxi. I ignore him. He wishes me a good night. I start to run.

I spend two hours in Wempe on Bond Street; two hours seriously considering purchasing a replacement Cartier. The sales associate's skull remained faceless as I retold the story of how I lost it. I expected more than a blank expression as I regaled him with my reason for re-buying such an unspectacular timepiece. In fact, the only time the milky-skinned, auburn-haired charmless bean of a man utilised any of his facial muscles was when "authorised" appeared on his little machine. I left that day with a much more suitable Rolex Daytona in white gold and the realisation that I would need a new icebreaker.

He never thought to mention that I had met Poppy before. Maybe he just hoped I would not remember.

Destiny is a funny old thing. There seems to be no measurable timeline, no real way of nailing down an exact date. You know it's coming, but the waiting around is a bitch.

Over the years I have turned up at various West End nightclub gates crashing a "girls' night out". Splashing the cash on champagne, bringing a little coke, a bit of MDMA, anything that might get me noticed. I would sit alone surrounded by Grey Goose or Ciroc and watch with dilated pupils as she gyrated on the dance floor, letting anyone's hands aside from mine brush her torso, pulling away just as they went in for a kiss.

I studied her type. I would see them at the bar, well heeled, seemingly successful, in tailoring or dressed down with cashmere and loafers. They would not break eye contact. He would be talking and she would nod, smile, occasionally frown and then always lean in, placing her hand on his forearm while letting out an appropriately timed giggle.
There I would sit unnoticed from a distance; well heeled, seemingly successful, and always immaculately dressed, and never did she seem to notice.

Helpfully, hopefully, I would organise taxis. However many times I mentioned the after-party at mine or the hotel suite I had booked, the party never actually occurred. She would always squeeze into another car, or jump in with the identikits of me to head to another party, always on the opposite side of town. I couldn't bear to watch her leave, smiling and laughing, blowing kisses to the crowds as I helped one of her less attractive friends high on my drugs into a taxi.

The Monday mornings should have been awkward. I would apologise for the inappropriate texts I had sent. "I was so drunk."

"Oh, they were from you? Now that is so funny. Don't worry, I was drunk too; I barely even read them."

"Oh, that is your number. How rude of me; I am so sorry, Oliver, I would have replied; I presumed it was that hedge fund guy who was boring me at the bar."

"Have you changed your number, Oliver? I don't seem to have this one saved, otherwise of course I would have replied."

Poppy and I have never spoken about the past. Why would we?
"Forgive and forget," that's what they say, isn't it? Besides, she was just a child, how was she to know the damage it would do? Let's focus on our future, fate, destiny.

Her perfume snaps me out of my daze and my focus returns to the present moment. Their eyes, although entirely different, both portray a look of utter confusion. My vision is too blurred to make out the time on the watch.

"How long have I been standing here?" I mumble.

I notice the high heels first, near five inches, an open rounded toe, patent leather. Tights cover those smooth tanned legs, or are they stockings? Shit, I think they are. My eyes make their way up the slit on her pencil skirt for confirmation. Her white blouse crisply pressed, there seems to be little room between where her waist ends and her perfect breasts begin. Matte black glasses frames tug down on the open neckline of her blouse, exposing more breast than she should be comfortable with.

No drastic changes in uniform to report.

I dread to think how many hours I have spent trawling porn sites for "secretaries getting fucked" or "PAs getting pounded" only to be left weary and unsatisfied. I drag my eyeballs away from her chest and attempt eye contact. She is facing Clarke and they have continued their conversation.

Clarke, oh Clarke, he is my closest comrade in the office. Brimming with confidence, a considerable earner who apparently brings a lot of new business Danbrook's way. This is all the more remarkable considering his surely debilitating ailment. He is of Scottish or Irish ancestry, a vivid shade of ginger, every hair on him, the quiffed mess on top of his head, the occasional sculpted beard he seems to grow with ease, the finer hair on his knuckles and shins. The freckles are in the same burnt orange Pantone, accentuated by his weekly visits to the tanning salon.

We train at the gym the same number of times a week, sometimes four, often five. Although I would suggest Clarke's routines are more focused on power, I also have my suspicions that he takes a lot of injectable steroids. His jaw is heavily set and even if he didn't train he would have a large frame. His waist looks around thirty-two inches but his chest is definitely closer to forty-two. I have overheard girls in the office refer to him as Clarke Kent. This is remarkably inaccurate. There is not one rendition of the Superman stories where the heroic lead has undesirable orange as his hair colour. Secondly, although Kent is not exactly the linchpin of style, he does manage to wear tailoring that enhances his well-built frame and carries his change of clothes around in an expensive-looking, even if a little dull, leather briefcase. This Clarke, on the other hand, utilises a nylon overnight bag that I can only imagine came free with a bottle of Ralph Lauren Polo aftershave at his local Boots. If this Clarke was in fact a superhero he would be taken down by Lex Luthor very early on in his career. I have pondered whether any comparisons have been made between myself and a full-headed version of Lex – the intelligence, the power and, without meaning to sound crude, the wealth. On further consideration, I expect the most likely comparison would be Bruce Wayne.

Clarke's suit trousers often bunch at the waist, pulled in with a not particularly tasteful Hugo Boss belt. Hugo bloody Boss. His jacket is always too tight; the fabric strains awkwardly under the pressure from his pecs and upper back. The ill-fitting nature of his suit is not what will end up getting him killed; it is much more likely the colour combining. No superhero could remain incognito with Clarke's wardrobe. When you have hair the shade of a bonfire at its most vibrant the key to colour is soft muted tones. Not Clarke; he will find the boldest stripe in pink and red or, like today, opt for a matching fuchsia shirt and tie. It would be nigh-on impossible to get changed into his cape and leggings without being spotted. It would not take long for Lex to note the large man in garish clothing stripping off in a phone box and then he would make the call, and one of his many henchmen would put an end to his life. Fact is, he wouldn't be able to leave his change of clothes anywhere in public.

From my investigations, I have him earning circa half of what Theo does, which has to burn. Still, it is a good wage, yet he still sports a pair of cheap tan shoes with a pointed toe so heavily worn that they curl upwards, the inside of the heels almost worn to the ground. If it wasn't for the fact that he left senior school over nine years ago I would suggest he had been playing football in them at lunchtime; as soon as he went off to fight crime, a do-gooder would stick those god-awful shoes in the bin.

I scan his workspace. Paperwork, contracts, printed emails semi-neatly stacked next to his twenty-three-inch monitor screen – who signed that off, I wonder. I gulp at Clarke's screensaver. He looks so much better in just swim shorts. I mean, they are still a suspect choice of colour, an almost iridescent turquoise blue, but his body fat must be sub-eight per cent. The fullness of his deltoids more than impressive; thick arms and calves without looking chunky. I say this out of admiration for a well-defined body rather than any homoerotic tendencies. Clarke is posing on a cabana with an attractive-looking hostess in the background. I cannot help but wonder who took this picture. To the left side of his screen two mobile phones sit stacked on top of an open copy of September's *Men's Health*. For no obvious reason I feel panicked that he may have taken it from my office drawer. I edge myself back towards the door, unsure of why I entered in the first place.

39

"Urm, yeah, hi, Oliver. Any chance you could say something? It's a bit creepy you just standing here," Poppy says in her bemused tone.

Caught off guard, I think on my feet.

"Morning, Clarke, morning, Poppy. I hope I haven't disturbed the morning gossip? Subject, whether Oliver has been really hitting the gym recently? I can confirm the answer would be yes. Now get back to your work." I squeeze my chest muscles as I speak in a tone of playful authority. An authority that seems to have almost completely diminished.

I have immediate regrets.

"Spot on, bud, Poppy was just enquiring whether your hair loss and noticeably tiny balls could be down to the horrendous amounts of steroids you pump into your childlike frame." His face wide like the Cheshire cat as he says this, and then he immediately pulls a sterner face.

It is truly remarkable that an employee gets to speak to the owner's son like this.

"On a serious note, Ollie, Pop's had some big news." Clarke pulls a strange pout and adjusts his necktie so it sits underneath his uncomfortably large Adam's apple.

"Is it blowjob Friday, Poppy?" I enquire hopefully.

Innuendos had never previously worked; perhaps today is the day.

"Ugh. It is only just ten in the morning and already you have managed to repulse me. No, my fantastic news is that Theodore has proposed; we are to marry in the late spring." Poppy still has a confusing look of disgust on her face as she tells me her amazing news.

This piece of remarkable news stings; it burns. Clarke seems uninterested and spends the hours, the years, the fucking century that passes as I attempt to digest this nonsense by placing one iPhone perfectly on top of the other.

"Ugh, Poppy, it is only just ten in the morning and already you have managed to repulse me," I quip, desperately looking around for the escape route to my office.

Theo and Poppy, Poppy and Theo. Now, in my defence, I genuinely despised him way before their inconvenient alliance formed.

They have been dating for the last thirteen months. Thirteen months and nine days, to be precise. Although I estimate an additional three weeks of friendship that led to a drink, a drink and dinner, a weekend in the Cotswolds, a kiss in the rain outside of Yauatcha. I have pencilled in late November for the end of this facade.

It needs to be done and dusted by at least the second week in December, to give me adequate time to plan for Christmas.

Yes, of course the gifts will still be expensive, but more than just a price tag they will be well considered. Not just a £3000 Tiffany bracelet that anyone could pop out on their lunch break to pick up. No thought put into it at all; he just strolled in and took the first one the Egyptian-looking girl behind the counter suggested.

I start to back out of the room, but neither of them seems to be getting further away.

I can feel the vibrations of words rattling up my tightening throat, picking up pace. My tongue curls towards my teeth in an attempt to act as one final barricade.

"For fuck's sake, Poppy, when did this all happen? You are rushing into things, snap decisions, the allure of a sparkly gem temporarily eroding your brain cells. I mean, seriously, Clarke, tell her, tell her, mate, he cycles into work, for fuck's sake, he is, he is not suitable for you, he is just an awful, terrible cunt."

Although the severity of the word has softened over the last decade, it does seem to have left my mouth in a somewhat aggressive manner. Clarke has put down his phones. His massive jaw is practically resting on his massive shiny desk. I feel her stare but opt out of eye contact.
The stolen wallet was a sign. The thieving whore, she was an angel, my guardian angel; I was meant to stay at home. She will have changed her mind by Monday; this heartache could have been avoided.

"All I mean is, he is not for you, he is not your type. Now, Elaine in accounts, with the really pretty, really symmetrical face, always in leggings, she is much more suited. I am sure she cycles. She has the calves, now she would be a much better match for Theo. I have seen them flirt, I am sure of it. Clarke, you agree with me, right?"

Clarke's chin has forcibly been lifted back to his face by the breadth of his smile.

"All I am trying to say is that you are better than that, that is all."

Her face is furious but in her eyes, I am sure deep in her eyes, I can see some indication that she agrees with me.

"Just be happy for us, Oliver; stop being a twat. You could always come to the wedding with Sarah; she really liked you, she's going to be a bridesmaid." Poppy's face is not filled with joy.

I make no attempt to recall who Sarah might be.

"Early engagement drinks tonight to celebrate. I am going to get wasted," Clarke remarks without really opening his mouth.

There is a familiar pulling in my jeans, that moment when the hangover creates an appetite in your groin. I stick close to the walls, attempting to track my way to the washrooms.

My skin is often tanned, my eyes alluring, perched high on chiseled cheekbones, helping create a very attractive face. My smile self-assured, my teeth once described by a South African dentist as quite beautiful. His head is almost tubular, his chin like an elder gentleman's scrotum, sagging away from his bottom lip. The colour of his eyes indistinguishable, hollow-looking, set close together and buried deep in his face. The mirror cannot answer my question of why. Maybe it is his hair? He does have great hair. The chill of the cold water cools my temples. I splash it into my nostrils to help clear my airways, to ease the congestion, allow some oxygen to the old brain.

43

"Are you ok, there?" says Glen in a voice that normally would not catch my attention.

"All good Glen, all good. I just have a lot of cocaine residue in my nasal passage and it's bothersome," I say without really thinking.

We have very little in common. I consider whether his name is Glen; it could quite comfortably be Andy. I do recall his first day at Danbrook; I really questioned the decision to bring onboard a man with such a limp handshake.

I raised the point with human resources and typically have yet to hear back.

As Glen relieves himself he makes a monotonous sound, "So, great news about Theo and Poppy, huh?"

I feel obliged to pretend I have not heard.

"It is just really nice to see the Big T settling down after all these years. Seems unimaginable really, huh. I suppose he has had a good run, a good ten years of spreading his oats, huh. Can't be many he hasn't had his way with. Still, Poppy has bagged herself a ticket there, a real high flyer." Glen finishes.

I watch his dark, toxic-looking piss hang around in the urinal.

"You need to drink a lot more water, Glen; at least two litres per day."

Glen looks up, confused.

"Now tell me," I say, passing him a thick wad of paper hand towels, "What the fuck were you just waffling on about, Glen? I mean, Theo is hardly the international playboy, is he?" I load the question with surprising guile.

I mull over the information Glen has fed me. Theo is not as dull as I had presumed; the hookers in Thailand, the escorts in West End nightclubs; the threesomes with French students in East London and the handjob from the intern at the Christmas party. This ridiculous proposal next to the Trevi Fountain in Rome seems somewhat out of character. I look at Glen, hoping for something, an indication perhaps that we could become closer friends. I try and look past the boot-cut trousers and see perhaps another ally. If Theo was to be fired I am fairly sure Poppy would make her excuses immediately; she has to be looking for a way out.

"Glen, mate, tell me something. I find this whole wank from the intern thing a little bit too much, bloody disrespectful. If I wanted to lodge a complaint, would you back me up?" I say, for the first time actually looking at Glen's dry skin and cheap frames.

"Theo is a thoroughly decent bloke, great work ethic. I would not dream of dropping him in it. He is, however, taking me for a bit of lunch at the Chiltern next Tuesday, though, so I will be sure to mention it," Glen says as a matter of fact.

"Okay then, Glen, perhaps I will take it up with the head of HR."

"That would also be me," Glen says, in exactly the same tone. "And Ollie, for the last time, my name is and always has been Andy. Make a note in that iPhone of yours, will you?" Glen's voice raises a notch.

As he leaves I have a better understanding of why my weak handshake complaint was never acted upon.

After locking the toilet door, I lay near half a roll of paper over the lid and take a seat. The hangover horn has long departed but has left a sharp stabbing pain in my groin. To-do lists bump into each other as they stumble around in my head. Unanswered questions raise themselves; ideas, some plausible and others frankly insane, bounce from one side of my mind to the other.

A quote, a ray of positivity shines through.

"The greater the obstacle, the more glory in overcoming it," or something along those lines.

I smile, maybe smirk and whisper to whatever irrelevant member of this corporate cesspit has just sat down in the adjacent cubicle.

"I have to have her," I repeat, louder than before. "I have to have her."

And then I get up and I leave.

Chapter 4

It is 12.30 according to the iPhone and slightly later on the worthless hunk of stainless steel currently irritating my wrist hairs. I have spent three hours trying to find the thieving whore from last night on Facebook, Twitter, Instagram and Snapchat. I scream THIEVING WHORE at Siri. She too ignores me.

I get sidetracked. Similar-looking females gawp at me from well-practised profile pictures. I zoom in; the majority of them look just so familiar. I send several friend requests and follow another twenty or so; not literally, of course. I scan my friends list; not one of the men who is "in a relationship" is better looking or as engaging as me. I count the number of my three hundred and eighty Facebook friends I could call today and meet up with. I cannot help but feel underwhelmed. The burning sensation in my groin causes me to wince and I am struggling to create any moisture in my mouth.

A body-building forum weighing up the pros and apparent cons of steroids distracts me for a moment or too. Balding and anger issues. Balding and anger issues; these are a side effect of life.

I wince with pain once more, undoing the buttons on my jeans to release some pressure. I consider if anyone would notice me masturbating under my desk to Poppy's Instagram pictures. It seems unlikely. I decide to get some lunch. I do not bother logging out; the cleaners, myself and

Clarke, when invited, are the only persons who frequent my office.

There are plenty of food choices around here: trendy market stalls, hipsters selling burritos from modified camper vans, a Pret on every corner. I cannot queue today and I do not want to see any of those disrespectful irrelevants from the office. I need high protein and low carb, or it might be the other way around. I decide on Earth Deli and Google "twelve-week beach body" as I walk. It is the new kid on the block, a smug-looking café serving overpriced salads, organic wraps, tiny snacks and juices while paying its smiley staff just about minimum wage. I wonder how much hatred is masked by welcoming grins.

According to *ES* magazine, it is also now the place to go. It's packed to the rafters and already I spot three irrelevants. I smile and nod. They do not seem to recognise me. I freeze as I see Theo and Poppy awkwardly huddled in the queue. They look ridiculous, like a stepbrother and sister maybe. Hating every moment together but keeping face for Mum and Dad's sake.

They seem to be having a mumbled but heated discussion. This seems the perfect opportunity to say hi.

"Hi-ya, Theo, congratulations on the engagement! Kept that quiet. I suppose you were quite occupied with the large-breasted receptionist when I saw you last!" I manage to mask the spite in my voice.

He turns to face me.

"I know, it's hard to believe a couple can be so in love after such a short time – pure lust maybe, but LOVE, it is a rare and beautiful thing."

He pulls her close.

The queues in this place are so damn unorganised; managing a conversation while vying for position is quite a challenge.

"Man, I am hanging today, last night was a wild one, not a cheap table in the Cuckoo and then back to mine. Not much love, but there was some seriously intense lust going on," I say. My quick change of subject should take him off guard.

I had momentarily forgotten Poppy was present and immediately regret blurting it out.

"Sounds smashing. Well, as long as he was gentle and you enjoyed yourself, then there's no harm done."

Theo has smashed a verbal custard pie in my face. All in one sentence the smirk that has formed drops from my face. My eyes meet hers. The look of pity she gives me is humiliating. Surely she knows that I am only into women. One woman. I consider mouthing the words "there is only you," but I am not convinced it would have the desired effect. As I prepare my retort, the overtly camp Earth Deli team member disturbs my trail of thought.

"Hiiii there, what can I get for you today?" sings Sergio from possibly Brazil or a sunny part of Eastern Europe. He has a great even tan, let down by a pierced eyebrow and highlights in his thick hair.

"I think he would like a cuddle and some tender kisses," sniggers Theo.

Nobody seems to pick up on this dig aside from me. By now my skin is flushed and I am desperate to get away from the pair of them. I am feeling increasingly claustrophobic. I can feel another wave of tequila nausea coming.

"Can I get a chicken avocado wrap, extra chicken with NO aioli, a side of Lebanese flat bread with hummus and a kale explosion – wait, no, an iced green tea to go." I say this with a tone of urgency.

"Okey-dokey, that will be eighteen pounds and ninety pence, please," Sergio says with a huge grin and excited eyes that seem to dance, rhythmically, side to side.

I wonder if Sergio might actually be Australian and heterosexual. He clearly goes to the gym; maybe we could buddy up. No time to think. I grab at the bag of food and reach into my pocket for the wallet that is not there. The heat in this fucking hell-hole intensifies.

"Err, sorry, I haven't got any money. I mean; I have forgotten my money. I personally have a lot of money, plenty of it, but my wallet, it was stolen." I tap all of my pockets. My mind is choking my brain, stopping logic from going about its work.

Why is this happening to me? Not now, please. I try to organise my thoughts and weigh up my options, but before I get the chance I hear the voice of the man I want to

50

die. Actually not die, just fuck right off. Move on. Get over it.

"Don't you worry yourself, superstar, I'll get this one. You read about it in the trashy papers, dodgy male escorts running off with their wealthy clients' belongings, terrible business," Theo says.

His performance indicates a certain level of empathy, like it actually might be true. I envision the crowd, the hungry, baying mob, raucous laughing and jeering – enjoying me being pulverised by the enemy. The emperor signals thumbs down. Theo the gladiator is about to end this battle.

My testicles retract inside my body, pretending not to know me. The counter server must know I'm not gay, and even if I was I wouldn't need to pay for the services of an escort, for Christ's sake.

Theo's smile could not have been broader. Even with the mix of embarrassment, self-loathing and hatred running through my veins I couldn't help but notice how white and polished his teeth are.
I remind myself to look up teeth whitening as soon as I escape this onslaught. Perhaps I have overestimated his unattractiveness.
Every mouthful of the food that pompous prick paid for tastes disgusting. I will not eat there again. I consider going back and complaining.

Instead I leave a very negative comment on the Earth Deli Twitter feed including a subtle hint about Sergio's customer service leaving a bad taste in my mouth.

It is late in the day, 5pm maybe, and I am sitting in the toilet cubicle masturbating furiously, with little resolve. I can hear an irrelevant taking a noisy dump in the cubicle next to me. I can only presume he can hear me too.

My balls ache and my wrist is tiring. Every time I am close to completing, I see those sunken eyes and those glistening white teeth. He is laughing and pointing. She is laughing too. They hold hands and their laughter slows and deepens.

I wake up, head on the side of the cubicle door, jeans around ankles, pain in groin, dried tears on face. The watch tells me it is 6pm. I want to close my eyes again. The one thing I do not need is to be going for celebratory fucking drinks. There is very little to celebrate at this moment in time.

However, "I must persist".

"I must persist," I say to the irrelevant, who actually looks up from their desk as I pass.

I shut down my PC. I notice the five emails received today, none of which I intend to reply to. I seem to be receiving fewer than ever, and this suits me down to the ground. Twenty reminders appear on my screen. I need to get more organised. I consider getting a PA and then remember that some of my to-do list might be frowned upon.

Chapter 5

"Were you knocking one out in the toilet, you grubby little bastard?" Clarke passes me a wrap.

The pub is incredibly busy. Due to global warming it is a claustrophobic evening and the drunk are spilling onto the streets. A doorman struggles to keep the chattering crowds within the roped-off area. There isn't much room to move. Most men are in suits, lawyer-looking types, boring as hell.

Women of all ages who left the office a minute before five and have already drunk two bottles of Pinot Grigio swarm. They try to attract the attention of any hellish bore who might consider impregnating them, taking them away from their destiny of answering the phones.

Before I have a chance to warm to my surroundings we have moved on, further downmarket it seems. I can see the bright lights of Piccadilly Circus, tourists everywhere. European teenagers with huge backpacks egg on a young tanned guy beatboxing for money. Clarke pulls me away as I cheer him on; it is great to see someone follow their dreams.

I intentionally walk in front of two separate couples trying to have their pictures taken. I try to look at the gritty face of a homeless girl as I pass, just to see if we could make it work. We could not. I pat at my truly empty pockets. She forces an understanding smile.

I am caught off guard by an Indian trying to shove a free newspaper into my midriff. I jump back like he has a blade and then continue walking.

This terrible dump has two doormen, one extremely tall and very black, the other shorter, very white, almost translucent, head shaved down to the bone. I find something about his face very unnerving. The girl with the clipboard, which I am sure has no names on it at all, ushers us inside.

It hits me almost immediately, the stale smell of sweat. Jesus, how strong must the stench be to those with fully functioning nostrils. I am not two metres inside the venue and someone has spilt beer or vomit on my shoes.

The tequila girl bounces past. I am sure I have slept with her but cannot be certain. She looks like a very unattractive version of the unattractive one from that popular girl group. I contemplate catching up with her and letting her know, just to dampen that upbeat spirit slightly.

Clarke directs me to our sectioned-off area. There are four balloons and several congratulations cards. Theo, who doesn't appear to be drinking, has put his card behind the bar. I am surprised he chose this shit-hole. Surprised but pleased.

"Right, quick speech. Thanks to Andy for organising this place at such short notice, there really was no need, and thanks to Poppy for making me the happiest man alive," Theo shouts above the din of recklessly loud music.

I am desperate to drink as much as possible. I am nearly as desperate to see if it is his company or personal card. A piss-up to celebrate a doomed engagement – that has to be against company policy.

There are sixteen of us sitting around two tables. I buy twenty shots on Theo's tab and give five to the babbling gaggle of fours standing by the bar. They seem to ignore the drinks and continue their yawnsome chatter. I consider starting a conversation, realising in the nick of time that not one of them has a single redeemable feature and move away.

"Time for Patrón, people," I announce with little effect.

I forcibly pass all fifteen out.

"I'll do a shot with you" says Cate.

I stay focused on Theo.

"Sorry, Theo, I must have miscounted, mate; have mine," I say, keeping my drink well out of his reach.

"Not a problem, Danbrook. You party animals enjoy the tequila. I'm going to leave you to it, got a big Taekwondo tournament in the morning." Theo takes an inappropriate karate stance as he speaks.

"Going for your white belt? Don't worry if you need a bit of protection for Poppy; Clarke and I will keep our eyes on her. I'm benching one-ten nowadays." I push out my arms and tense.

I can't be sure if I have actually been to the gym this week; it really has been a blur.

"You're benching ninety on a good day," Clarke helpfully chips in.

"Ninety-two. Anyway, Theo, safe cycling home. Watch out for those street gangs." As I speak, I imagine Theo sobbing as a crew of hoodies steal his bicycle and the skinny, vintage 1960s Rolex watch that his type tend to wear. This leads to an intentionally strained grin that I do not attempt to hide.

"We don't have any gangs in my part of Notting Hill anymore, Oliver; they're all confined to your way nowadays, I believe. I'm actually mentoring a group of kids from troubled backgrounds tomorrow. Just want to have a clear head so I can give them my undivided attention."

As Theo says this I realise my use of the word "cunt" to describe him earlier in the day was, if anything, a bit generous.

"Come on, Poppy, put your coat on, I've booked us a car," Theo says bullishly.

"I'm going to stay for a while. Seeing as it's our engagement drinks I thought one of us should," Poppy says under her breath, looking anywhere apart from at Theo.

I watch the coat drop to the floor.

"Right, you guys, I want all of you to enjoy our special moment, but please, no vintage Dom P on my tab – I imagine I have an incredibly lavish wedding to pay for." Theo waggles a finger at me and cocks his head.

Temporarily I am blinded either by his white teeth or my pure hatred as I watch him march away.

The evening passes, maybe an hour, maybe longer. I am struggling to stay focused. I watch colleagues, irrelevants, make conversation with anyone aside from me. I count at least twelve remaining tequila shots on the table. I decide to make my way through them. I get up, and as they get closer I notice all five of the non-tequila-drinking girls at the bar. All five now look considerably more attractive.

I look around and cannot see Poppy anywhere. I decide to flirt. Anyway, what does it matter, it's only a bit of harmless fun.

"Which one of you was the attractive brunette who I was contemplating taking back to mine?"

My open eye is struggling to focus and I can taste chemicals from the line I can only presume I have recently snorted.

"For the hundredth time, just pick up your jaw and fuck off, will you, before I call the doorman over," maybe one of them, maybe all of them say.

"One vodka cranberry and five more shots of tequila, Patrón tequila," I slur at the barman.

"I would love a glass of bubbles" Says Cate apparently appearing from nowhere.

"One vodka cranberry and five more shots of tequila, Patrón tequila," I slur at the barman.

"That'll be £75," the bartender says.

He really does remind me of Sergio, the Earth Deli employee.

"Put it on the tab, his tab, Theo's tab." I down the vodka, hoping to wash away the foul taste of whatever chemical has been used to cut the coke I have at some point ingested. I half-push the tequila the way of five now departed girls.

"That tab's closed off, mate; you'll need to settle the bill." The Brazilian barman suddenly seems very English and slightly aggressive.

I tap my pockets, raise my eyebrows and point towards our seated area. Sergio's attentive gaze averts momentarily and I hurriedly push past people and head towards the exit.

"Clarke, I'm outside, had to make an emergency escape. That tequila girl was staring at me and it was freaking me out. I think before, you know when I fucked her, I may have accidentally done something very bad. It's time for us to move on, buddy."

"Ok, cool, there's only five of us coming, so let me just settle up the bar bill you just avoided paying and we will be out." Clarke says this like he has heard it all before.

I crouch down behind a car and watch who enters and, more importantly, who exits. Sergio does not appear.

"Clarke, bud, do me a favour; I left my wallet at home. Can you lend me a couple of hundred until the morning?" I shout up at him from my position behind the passenger door of a bright yellow smart car.

I feel confident that I didn't tell him my wallet was stolen by the girl with the angular head.

As he queues at the cash machine I stare at Poppy, the way she moves. Helping fucking special-need delinquents do karate, what a wanker. I consider telling her my suspicions that Theo is probably a sexual predator with a penchant for young boys.

She is not yet drunk enough for me to explain how I feel. She glides across the uneven pavement in her high heels with not so much as a stumble. Her hair bounces with such confidence, knowing it is attached to a perfect face. She picks up pace and skips towards him.

"Hurry up, muscles, I want to get more drunker," she fake slurs while playfully punching Clarke on his surely tensed bicep.

I stop staring. I breathe in through my nose. Very little air has made it into my lungs; my chest feels tight. I hold my breath while removing a door key from my jeans pocket. As I breathe out through my mouth I too tense my bicep and scratch a heavy line through the yellow paint of the innocent smart car.

"Clarke, where the hell are we going? I need a drink. I'm fully charged over here. Let's get a taxi – my calves are hurting from that lunchtime gym session."

Both of us know I haven't done leg training in a long time. Earlier today a reminder to research calf implants appeared on my phone. I remember hitting snooze and the disappointment hitting me. He chooses not to answer; he isn't even here. I see them both emerge from behind an overspilling recycling bin. He tilts her chin up with one hand and wipes away the powdery residue from under her nose. She giggles and I cannot help but smile.

I jump into the back seat of a well-worn, burgundy – actually more oxblood – shitpile of a car. It smells of oily food and cigarette smoke.

"I called an Uber. My name's Oliver Danbrook. I need you to take my friends and me to an extremely good nightclub."

"You don't call an Uber, you do it through the app, you understand? Please now get out of my car; I am not a taxi."

I have no idea what he is talking about and stay put. He reaches over to his passenger seat and wipes a thin-looking naan bread around the inside of a Tupperware bowl.

I patiently listen to him chew and swallow.

"My friend, I am not a taxi, I am just on my way home, but tell me where do you want to go," the taxi driver says.

I lean out of the car door window and call out to Poppy and Clarke. They are making conversation with two irrelevants and Cate and clearly cannot hear me.

I shout louder, but still they choose not to hear me. Poppy's arm appears to be interlinked with Clarke's. A car door slams. I watch the driver slowly, more slowly than he chewed, amble over to the five of them. He points to his car, he shrugs and points to the queue of black taxis on the other side of the road.

The two irrelevants, one of whom is most likely Glen or Andy or whatever he's calling himself nowadays, walk off in the direction of the black cabs. Poppy, Clarke, Cate and the driver head back towards the car.
Rap, tap, tap, tap, rap. My hands hit my thighs, faster and harder. Rap, tap, tap, tap, tap. I try to massage away the pins and needles. My eyes close and I attempt to slow down the rhythm of the drum. Rap, tap, tap…

"Ollie, what the fuck are you doing? There's a queue of perfectly good taxis less than ten metres away, and you're sitting in the back of – no offence, mate – a shit wagon.:

Clarke appears agitated. I remain focused on slowing everything down.

"Fifteen pounds I will drop you in Shoreditch, very good clubs, very busy," says the definite taxi driver.

The breath, in through my nose and out through my mouth. The pins and needles have spread to my chest. RAT, TAT, TAT, TAT, RAT, TAT, TAT, my heart bangs against my ribcage.

Poppy's hand is on my shoulder. Just maybe she caresses my upper arm.

"Move over, you twat, I suppose I should sit in the middle," she says.

I reach for her fingers but they have gone, replaced by a shovel-like mitt, potato picker's hands. Clarke forcefully edges me across the leather- looking seats.

"I'll sit in the middle, probably for the best," Clarke announces.

The car lurches away. This guy's driving seems as painfully slow as everything else he does. Before we reach the end of the road, Poppy has opened her window and Cate does the same in the passenger seat. I just lean my skull against the glass. Turning to the side, all I can see is Clarke's head, completely obstructing my view of her.

I yank at the door handle, an attempt to spill myself onto the road. Even at this speed it should get me noticed.

"That door is broken, my friend. Please wait until I stop before exiting the car," the driver says. For the first time I fully appreciate his thick Indian accent.

I can see Cate staring in the off-tilt cracked rear-view mirror. She likes me. She watches me when I am in the office. I find it a little eerie. We fucked at some point this year; I don't recall when or how, but I do recall it being a real struggle to get rid of her in the morning. I also recall sitting on the toilet in my en suite crying, knowing that without doubt she would tell Poppy what had happened. All I wanted was for her to leave, and all she insisted on doing was asking if I was okay, if it was something she had done.

"Yes, Cate, it is something you have done."

Our eyes meet and before I can avert them she smiles. I do not smile back.

The car lets out an asthmatic wheeze and attempts to pick up pace. While my face is pressed against the glass I note Glen giving me a double thumbs up as he whizzes past in a Hackney carriage.

I slump back in my seat, twitchy, intentionally rocking forwards and backwards, hoping to catch Poppy's eye. Unfortunately, there is a cumbersome ginger blockade in the way.

"Are you okay, Oliver? Do you need to pull over? Are you having a fit?" Cate asks.

I do not think I reply. I just try the car door handle one more time.
My hands explore all eight pockets twice over for the highest purity chang that I am sure I have on me and find nothing but lint.

Is he ignoring me? I tap on his turned-away shoulder again and again.

"Dude, Clarke, Clarke, mate, dude, Clarke-mate." I tap repeatedly, rat-tat-tat-tat-ta.

"What, Ollie? What on earth can you want? Can't you see I am having a conversation?"

"Dude, let me do a quick line; Cate must have done all of mine."

He pushes a baggy into my hand, eyes firmly on the driver in the rear-view mirror. Greedily I pinch and sniff, I push it around my gums. I make little to no attempt to be subtle. I spill around half a gram onto the leatherette seating. Wetting my fingers, I scoop up as much as possible. It hits my tastebuds and, even with the overbearing chemicals in the coke, I can taste the smell of this grubby little car. My pupils, specifically my pupils, start to take in the surroundings at lightning pace.

Cate's captivated eyes are locked on me in the rear-view mirror. Glen somehow passes by again in his black fucking cab, at first not noticing me, but I see the irrelevant sitting opposite him joyfully tap his knee. He turns, he smiles, he does a double thumbs-up. He then taps at what looks like an entry-level Tag Heuer, shrugging his shoulders and appearing to sigh.

I hear Clarke's voice, Poppy's voice and my own. I don't know what I am saying or if I am part of their conversation. I lean at the hips and peer around Clarke's back. Poppy is furiously tapping at her iPhone and simultaneously muttering to Clarke. Clarke attempts to further block my view by twisting away and flexing his broad lats. It works. I am equally frustrated and impressed. Cate has turned around in her seat. I lean in behind Clarke in an attempt to hide.

"Oliver, please put the seatbelt back on; I don't want you to go through the windscreen and spoil that pretty face."

I momentarily imagine that these are Poppy's words.

"Oliver, please put the seatbelt back on, I don't want you to go through the windscreen and spoil that pretty face," Cate repeats herself and punches me hard on the kneecap.

Through the windscreen, at fifteen miles per hour, seems unlikely. It takes us somewhere between fifteen minutes and a lifetime to get off the Old Street roundabout. The Silicon Valley of London, the home to the "booming tech industry". In that time I attempt to open the car door twice. I also contemplate reaching around the driver's headrest and squeezing his scrawny neck until he goes limp.

I snort some more coke in an unorthodox manner from the palm of my hand, licking at the crumbs that hide in my trench-like creases. I impatiently bang the hide of my head against the glass. Their chatter seems to have died off and silence fills the car.

We pass dirty-looking kebab houses and dirtier-looking strip clubs. Eastern European girls with pinched faces and superbly skinny bodies chainsmoke outside as young men eagerly and as soberly as possible pass by the doormen.

We crawl past a group of homeless people huddled up in matching military-coloured sleeping bags. A well fed dog lays beside them. A queue has formed outside of an inviting-looking bar, its rainbow flag adding colour to the drab scenery.

"Guys, should we maybe just pop in for one here? I'm gasping for a drink," I say unintentionally.

I watch Clarke's face as he turns towards me, his chin contorting and eyes wide.

"You're gasping for something, mate," he struggles to say.

The car grinds to a halt in a side alley by what is most likely Hoxton Square. I poke Cate in the back of the head, somewhat playfully.

"Pay the man. He will accept thirty pounds cash or twenty-eight and a blowjob." I say this humorously.

Our safe arrival and the last sprinkles of coke I lick from the bag have lifted my spirits. Confidence soars. Let me sow the seeds tonight; let Poppy know my intentions.
The driver opens my car door and I athletically leap out. I pull the crisp night air in and it tries its hardest to clear the blockages in my nostrils. I pace up and down the pavement, avoiding Cate. An age has passed and still Clarke and Pops haven't evacuated the vehicle. As Cate walks around the front of the car I jog around the back and bang on the glass.

"Driver, can you help me open the goddamn door," I plead.

He does so, at his own pace, of course. I lean in and tug at Poppy's arm.

"Hurry up, you two; I'm sure whatever work-related topic you're discussing can wait," I shout in an inconveniently high-pitched tone.

"Clarke, let's do a quick livener here before going in. The toilets are a disgrace in this place. Poppy, you may have a small one but please don't start getting touchy-feely with me; I know how that coke makes you horny; hornier."

"If you were the last man..."

She looks at me with bored eyes and speaks in a bored tone.

Clarke passes Poppy a tightly constructed wrap.

"Less chat, more sniffing. Clarke, keep your eye on this one. If she touches me 'here' I will be going to HR first thing Monday." I feel powerful right at this moment, a bloody great drug; thank you, South America.

She neatly folds the wrap back up and passes it to me. Our hands touch fleetingly.

"I'll keep my eye on her. Shit! Fucking bollocks! I've left my phone in that cab! Fuck! Fuck! I won't see that again!" Clarke shouts and punches the wall.

I smile, content in knowing that his grazed knuckles will be stinging now but will feel even worse in the morning. My smile disappears as I hear her trying to calm him down, nurturing the wounded.

Upon entry I immediately feel out of place: overdressed, too contemporary for my own good. A segment of the Square Mile has turned up in their reasonably expensive suits, watches and shoes but worn with very little panache. There is the out-of-town contingent, all scoop-neck tees and quiffed hair, up to London on a mini-bus. Then, of course, you have the local Shoreditch mob. This bunch of photographers, fashion students and artists are slowly moving further East, hopefully taking their tiny moustaches, skateboards and gaunt appearances with them. If everyone has them it does not make you an individual! I scream inside. I want to punch myself, but change my mind in the nick of time.

"Where is Cate?" I ask myself. "Not that I care, probably went off with the taxi driver, but I hope not. It was a joke, Cate."

"At the bar, you drunkard. You asked for a Ciroc Cranberry and she's getting you one," Glen replies.

"Where is Poppy? Where is Clarke?" I ask, this time actually directing the question towards Glen.

"Don't know, dude. Why don't you go and have a little sit down?" Glen replies.

Fuck you, Glen.

I walk behind Cate, pick up my drink and walk off. It is heaving. Nobody seems to squeeze past; they just walk into me. I try and move around them and head towards the music. My drink drops to the floor. I crunch the glass under my shoe and move on.

The beat is repetitive. Faces race past me. Everyone is in such a rush. Rather than my body moving I can feel my eyes straining, trying to escape the evil clutches of their sockets. I go to this small bar and order a vodka cranberry and three shots of Patrón. Clarke and Poppy must be looking for me. Stay put, they'll find you. I briefly wonder if they have a tannoy system in here; that's how Mum found me the time I was lost in Peter Jones. I lean down and take a generous pinch of what I hope is coke.

Some time passes. I drink the shots and give one to Sergio from Brazil behind the bar.

"Thanks for the line, Sergio. Drink up, man. You're a good guy. So many women in here tonight; easy pickings."

"I told you, my name is Peter. Yeah, so many great-looking people, great vibe in here, I am glad we met." Sergio is talking and wildly gesturing with his arms behind the bar.

I am starting to wonder whether this time Sergio or Peter or whatever his name is might be homosexual.

"I've got to find my girlfriend and Clarke; they'll be looking for me. See you later, take care of yourself." I am no longer feeling in control.
I buy a pill from a white teenager in the corner of the room. Within seconds I have either taken it or dropped it. I feel like I forgot to pay him, so head back to where he no longer is.

Some black guy aggressively explains he does not have any drugs, so I back away.

I stumble into the bathroom, shoving money onto the grinning attendant's collection plate. I swipe an arm out at his repulsive collection of fragrances.

I watch the last of the coke turn into mush as I chop it on the wet toilet seat. The banging on the door makes me lose concentration. I keep my heel firmly against it, applying some pressure as the door starts to give way.

When did I stop having a good time?

My stomach is bubbling. I yank down my jeans down and sit on the wet toilet seat. The diarrhoea feels cleansing.

"Time to go, sir. There's a strict no-drugs policy. Pull your trousers up," the doorman says in a weary voice. He is well built but carrying some excess weight. Some high-intensity cardio would help. He isn't in the mood for advice. Strangely, given the current situation, I feel a little bit sorry for him. This is a rough job; he is probably just trying to put food on the table.

As I am escorted out I snarl "traitor" at the bathroom attendant and try to grab my fiver back. He knows the rules.

The city workers, the out-of-towners, the fashionistas, the ravers, the indie kids, the workmates out for just one quick drink are knocked out of the way like skittles as the heavy-handed doorman puppeteers me out of the building.

The night's icy breeze wakes me slightly. I pick at the inside of my nose and squirm uncomfortably, trying to escape my unwiped buttocks. My fist bounces off the bonnet of a passing car. I sway onto a side street confident I can make my way home. I chuck the five-pound note at a spotty homeless kid. He has endearing puppy dog eyes but lank greasy hair.

I see them; they do not see me. He is putting her into an Addison Lee, making sure she gets home safely. It feels like I call out. I definitely wave, but perhaps they do not see. My knuckles are bleeding and it doesn't hurt anywhere near as much as I had hoped.

Chapter 6

It feels like a Sunday morning. My head is clearer than before. The previous day had disappeared, taken up by soul-searching, planning, plotting, masturbating.

I further investigated my missing wallet, finding very few clues, but noticing that I have lost three Facebook friends since last checking. I have to consider a possible connection.

My hand is swollen, my knuckles raw. I do not recall what happened; could it have been caused by too much masturbation?

A phone rings for the seventh time. I eagerly look, hoping it might be her. It is not. It is my father, the old coot. I decide to answer.

"Hi, Dad, I was in a meeting, what's going on?" I glance at the wall clock to see how quickly I can get through this.

"Oliver, we need to talk," he says in that no-messing tone of his.

I can imagine the stern look, those heavy lines on his ageing forehead, ridged like corrugated iron.

"Oliver, as you know, or I hope you know, I am working eighteen-hour days to push through the IPO so we can finally take Danbrook public. Again, I hope you understand what this would mean for the company, for me, the family. Now, these guys are thorough, they are leaving no stone unturned. They are looking at every cost, the structure of the organisation, our assets and, more importantly, our liabilities. Does this mean anything to you, Oliver? Are you still there?" Dads asks, aware that perhaps I wasn't.

I surprise myself, as I am paying full attention. He must want me to have a clear-out, remove the dead wood.

"Yes, Dad," I say, licking my sore knuckle.

"Ok, good, you are still there. So tomorrow morning, let's discuss it. I have had quite some feedback from the office on you, I… Well, let's leave it and talk in the morning, 8am sharp," Dad barks.

After putting the phone down I browse the internet for suede desert boots in seal grey, with little success. I then peruse Poppy's Facebook page, followed by Clarke's. I am unsure exactly what I am looking for, but the entire episode leaves me frustrated.

I smother far too much cottage cheese onto gluten-free rice cakes. I am not surprised when a heap of creamy protein-filled mess spills onto my impossible-to-clean sofa. I am more surprised when I rub it into the fabric with my fingers and for the first time in a while I feel an almost euphoric level of satisfaction.

That tone of voice: "Oliver, we need to talk." I can count on one hand the number of times I have heard it directed at me. The time I lost the Patek; why I bothered mentioning it to him, I do not know. The occasion I clocked into the office at 1am pissed and high with a hooker I had met by sheer coincidence passing the building outside. We didn't have sex; I was past capable. We kissed and she helped me search a few of the irrelevants' desks for drugs. He was just furious because I had been violently sick on the peanut suede reception chairs. The time I run away from home after Mum left.

My heart palpitations are worse than normal as a knowing anxiety sets in. I set the alarm on both phones for 6.15. Anxiety is joined by annoyance as I spot the 8am Brazilian ju jitsu beginners' class in my diary that I must have scheduled in at some point last week.
I will not cancel the class just in case the old fool changes his mind.

After a few hours of procrastination and an unsuccessful tug, I head out to the corporate, soulless gym I am dedicated to. The weekends are so quiet in here. I count twenty people working out. Nine of them men and only one has anywhere near the dedication I do. He is lifting more but sacrificing form. He catches me looking at him and I just know to stop staring. I decide to move to the cardio area.

There are three women on the cross trainers, all chatting and burning very few calories. They have set up so the only spare machines are in between them. They are not particularly attractive and their conversation will most likely be draining. Besides, too much cardio will have a negative effect on my muscle gains.

I stand in the warmdown area, looking at myself in the mirror, imagining I had no reflection. Hoping that my thoughts and behaviours are excused by the fact I am a vampire. All that looks back is disappointment.

I lie down and feel sick. There is no 4G or WiFi and I urgently need to check her Facebook page. I try to call Clarke, but he doesn't answer. I regret not finishing my workout. I am sure she would like me if I had a thicker chest.

Just around the corner from my apartment, with its drab exterior but expensive interior, there is a spit 'n' sawdust gym called Hercules or Masculines or something similar. A month or so ago I nearly joined. I am kind of certain that a doorman who has removed me from several bars hangs out there. I wonder if we could train together, become the best of friends. I enter the steamroom in my T-shirt and shorts, hoping that someone will ask me why and I can explain that I am trying to sweat out the final few pounds before my big fight. Nobody does. There are just two men who must be in their late seventies, legs akimbo as if they almost want me to see their sagging sacks hanging down low towards their knees, which look about as healthy as my knuckles. They stop their conversation and one asks me a question that isn't about my choice of attire, so I get up and leave.

The girl at the counter is cute but she doesn't seem to understand my need to cancel my membership with immediate effect.

"It may well be that I will need to start training in the middle of the night. I have specific goals, specific gains I need to make within the next six weeks and I just do not believe that your gym has the facilities to support this. Besides, two ageing homosexuals harassed me in the steam and sauna area."

"Unfortunately, Mr. Danbrook, you are only two month into a year's membership. I did explain this to you last week also. My manager Neil is in on Monday; perhaps it would be best if you called back then." Her cuteness evaporates as she speaks.

I am momentarily distracted by what I hope is a text message, but it is nothing more than an ever-more-occurring calendar reminder. I leave, choosing not to cause a scene.

Laying down on the fresh sheets, cold and crisp against my skin, I push my legs up against the wall and pull the pillow over my face. This has always been my go-to position.
If I closed my eyes tight enough and clenched my jaw hard enough, I could just about drown out the arguments, the slamming of doors, the smashing of glasses. It does not seem to work anymore. I am sure Clarke got into the taxi with her.

I type a text.

Hope you got home okay on Friday. I saw you and Clarke. WTF. See you Tues X

Delete it. I retype. Delete again.

I scroll through my address book.

Mum Spain mobile

I call. The international dial tone rings out and goes onto voicemail. I disconnect and retry three more times. She must be busy. I text instead and spend most of the afternoon checking my phone for a reply. I drift in and out of consciousness.

The alarm goes off at 6.15am. I am already awake. Ten reminders appear on my phone:

Calf implants
Call bank, order new cards
Poppy, Clarke observe?
Buy *Men's Health*
Contact Mum
Take medication
Google testosterone boosters
Cancel gym membership
Buy cat food
Protein

I snooze them all and decide I will get the bus to the office. Maybe I can give advice to the kid's mum, before it's too late.

The seven o'clock crowd is oh-so-different. The fashionistas are still sound asleep; I am surrounded by junior-level irrelevants and the immigrants on the way to or from less-than-minimum-wage cleaning jobs. No sign of the kid. What was I thinking? His mum has probably only just got in. He is scratching around in the cupboard trying to make some kind of breakfast to help get through the day. I know the estate they no doubt live on; it's a fucking eyesore. Maybe I will pop over there later, just to make sure he is okay.

Alone on the upper deck, I feel alone on the upper deck, but then there is someone else. He is dressed in what could be a good suit and looking effortless in an open-necked shirt with a natural-looking tan. I want to look at his shoes but what must surely be a gym bag obscures my view. There is an indication of a classic timepiece flickering from behind his cuff as he repositions. The expensive brand of headphones suggests that behind his corporate attire is a creative soul. I consider approaching. A bold move, networking on the bus, but opportunities can appear in the rarest of places. Before I can he has headed downstairs. I watch out of the window to see where he walks but he doesn't appear.

We pause at traffic lights for some time, roadworks holding up the hellish traffic. I glance at my watch to check the time. Surprisingly, I am not wearing one.

I look out and see an uninspiring box of a building, stained by pollution and creatively limited graffiti. A smattering of people leave via an open fire exit. Two high-cheekboned girls and a guy with a V-neck tee almost down to his navel stand around smoking. His hair is stuck thick to his forehead with sweat. Both arms covered with tattoos, he struggles to put on his just-back-in-fashion circular sunglasses. One of the girls, in denims that seem to start just under her breasts, stands on tiptoes and pushes them onto his face. She then puts a hand through his hair and it immediately sits upright. I want to check out my own hair but I am too close to the glass.

The sweaty faces, their glazed pupils, their exaggerated gesturing; they have had a good night. I take a picture of the sign and then the girl in high-rise jeans.

The offices are quiet. A cleaner who I believe was on my bus flicks a duster around the edges of the revolving doors. A security guard sits bolt upright at the reception.

The whites of his eyes divided into a thousand bloodshot pieces, his suit cheap and too big even on his broad frame.

"Good morning."

He seems wary, perhaps intimidated by a businessman calling so early in the day. I am taken back by how well spoken he is.

"I'm Oliver Danbrook. You will know who I am. Are you new, as I am normally a stickler for a face?"

The reality is that we haven't met, as I have never frequented the office before 9 – unless he was there that one time with the hooker. Before he has a chance to answer, James Danbrook marches through the glass doors.

"Morning, Paul, hopefully a quiet night last night? Did you get to listen to the Arsenal match? Terribly dull affair," Dad says, walking right past me.

He shakes the security guard's hand and grins.

"Yes, Mr. Danbrook, quiet night. I managed to listen to it on the radio. Very disappointing. The papers seem to think it's time for a change."

"Jolly good, Paul. This here is my son. Have you met before?"

"Just the once, Mr. Danbrook – you know, that time when he had to collect some important documents from the office in the middle of the night."

"Ah yes, that's right. Well, that is why we are here today, to put a stop to that sort of behaviour. Come on, Oliver, in you go."

Dad ushers me past. Paul gives me a knowing look; his face suddenly becomes very recognisable. I recall banging on the glass and then slumping against it on the floor. I remember he helped her carry me in.
At some point Dad has overtaken me. I cannot see his face to decide whether he is talking or not.

I look at myself in the glass as we pass several offices. With each reflection I appear more grotesque. My suit, which I do not recall putting on, lacks panache.

I pass Theo's office. Looking in, I see Clarke and Theo arguing. They stop when they see me and point. I pick up the pace. The glass is the only thing separating their outstretched fingers from my face. They merge into one. They start to shake the door handles. I hide behind another office and peer around the corner. They are out of sight, and so is my father. I take a moment to catch my breath. I hear giggling. I am pressed so hard against the wall I feel like I could step through it. The giggling is Poppy's. I recognise the panting, the noise of a man trying to get that last repetition out in the gym. I cannot see either of them but I know they are there. Clarke's fuchsia necktie lies tossed on the ground. I grip the door handle for support as Poppy lets out an ear-shattering orgasm. I skulk into my office and close the door firmly. Hands over ears, I collapse down on the floor behind my desk. Cautiously I remove a hand. Surely she must be done. I bravely get to my feet. On the desk is the newest edition of *Men's Health* still in its polythene wrap, a banana and a small desktop calendar. The month of July. Poppy's birthday written in capital letters and underlined. What did I buy her? I want to remember.

I eat the banana and chuck the skin into the bin. It lands half in and half out, two segments of its peel desperately gripping to the rim, screaming for help.

My attention is drawn to the corner leg of the desk. A perfectly folded piece of card, a wrap. Surely it is empty. How did the cleaner miss it? Maybe she left it there for me; her skintone could easily be Columbian. Who knows; all I know is that whatever is there will certainly settle my nerves.

"Oliver, what the hell are you doing down there?" The annoyance on his face is apparent from his tone.

I do not look up. Like a Tom and Jerry cartoon, I only see a pair of shoes centimetres from my face. In this episode they are tan John Lobbs and light grey Kilgour trousers rather than grubby house slippers and tights.

I reverse out from under the desk, leaving the solid little package where it is. The excitement of coming back for it makes me eager to get this meeting out of the way.

"Sorry Dad, dropped a vitamin D tablet down here somewhere. Lack of natural sunlight and all that. Not to worry." I hurry him out of the room and try to ignore the tight grip he has on my arm.

"Let's hurry this up, Oliver. For your sake, I want to get this done before anyone else arrives today," he says, adding to my confusion.

Now, James Danbrook's office is large, to say the least; most certainly Theo's, Clarke's and mine combined. A huge corner desk, bookshelves lightly scattered with hardbacks and evenly spaced industry awards. In the corner of the office sits a comfy-looking leather chair, and an expensive but disappointingly tacky globe-shaped liquor cabinet. In this exact corner of my office, I have an empty mini-fridge and a Swiss ball, used to crunch out mid-afternoon abs. In the opposite corner sits a much smaller desk. A cocktail dress hangs on a coat rail behind and several pairs of designer heels are neatly placed on the floor ready for a suitable occasion. Her perfume still lightly fragrances the air.

He has three large framed pictures perfectly placed on his antique desk. One of him in Japan grinning ear to ear with his arm round the shoulders of a short, equally happy, Asian man. He must be about forty in the picture and has a full head of mousey-brown hair. Next to it another picture from around the same time. I am proudly holding up the only medal I ever won at the Sunningdale summer tennis camp. Dad has that same beaming smile, both hands on my shoulders. My mother looks immaculate, tanned and expensively groomed, but her face is lonely and distant, exactly how I remember her. Dates aren't so much my forte, but I feel certain this is the summer before I met Poppy.

The third picture is in a smaller frame and much more recent. It is of Poppy. She is wearing the dress hanging behind her desk. It shimmers under the flash of the camera and accentuates her eyes. The same cleaner who left me at least half a gram of coke on my office floor has also put her picture back on the wrong desk. I pick it up, unsure whether to place it back where it belongs or in my jacket pocket.

A tanned, well-cared-for hand comes into view. It looks like an expensive glove. Before I know it, the picture is out of my hand and face down on the desk.

He is talking to me, lifting the lid on the globe, taking out a drink. An alcoholic drink at what can only be 8.30am. I am struggling to focus, listening out for key words: promotion, pay rise, praise.

I thank him for the kind words; I accept the exec-level promotion. I offer my hand, he grips it proudly, genuinely smiling like he did with that security guard, and then he pulls me in closely, a manly hug, one of respect. In Italy he would pull away slightly and kiss both cheeks. He tells me how he believes in me; how I am the future of the company. He wants me to clear out the dregs, explore new opportunities. "You are going to need a PA, though. Pick one, your choice. Poppy? Of course, great match." I give my speech, appreciative of my award. Looking out at the crowd, I see him, hands on my shoulders. Poppy no longer a PA, now my wife. She has no need to work – maybe a project of her own, to keep her motivated. My mum is present. She is immaculately dressed, she is…

A combination of a glass slamming on the desk, the clashing of ice and an overbearing smell of straight whisky brings me back into the room.

"Oliver, how are you? Outside of work, I mean. Any girlfriends? Any new hobbies? Any idea on what you want to do with your life?" His tone starts firm and edges towards desperate as he finishes.

He takes a gulp of fine whisky. I wish I was allowed my indulgence.

"You know, Dad, I would not know where to start. There is the dedication to my health; currently I am upping the amount of high intensity interval training, or HIIT, into my workouts – you have probably noticed the change. I am also spending an increasing amount of my day evaluating the time-versus-money equation while nurturing a blossoming relationship. It is early stages though, so please do not get ahead of yourself."

"Oh, and, of course, work's busy, always busy. How are you doing?" I add in unconvincingly.

Dad's face is frowning, crows' feet around his eyes, patchy brown skin from too much sun, his lips thin as if he is really contemplating what to say next.

Hours pass or maybe less.

"I am disappointed, son; that is how I am doing. Surprised, not so much, but disappointed, yes. I am disappointed. It is my fault; I ignored the warning signs. It was mentioned in passing; it was mentioned via senior management, in emails and even posted in the suggestion box, but I refused to face the reality. The float changes all that, son. There is no room for costly errors."

I go to speak but all that comes is out "Theo."

"We knew this wasn't for you; your mother told me you didn't have it in you. You were missing the focus, lacking the acumen, struggling to adapt to adulthood. Her words,

Oliver. They sounded harsh to me back then, but hell, it seems she was right; she was just trying to protect you. I wouldn't accept it – my son must be a chip off the old block. Perhaps I spoilt you. Maybe it is my fault. What a waste of an education. Are you even listening, Oliver?"

I am.

"Your only focus was to support Theo's team and be front of house for the company, smile, occasionally pick up the goddamn phone and check if our clients are still breathing. Sometimes, just sometimes, turn up for a bloody meeting just to give the impression that you are actually an employee of the firm and not just here to hinder others and pick up your inflated bloody pay cheque."

His nose is two shades redder than his rosy cheeks, sweat slaloming through the ridges on his brow. He takes a pause. The speech is building up to a climax. Like a thriller that drags in the middle I am paying attention, waiting for the finale.

Maybe a heart attack; maybe that is the answer. He drops down, I administer life-saving treatment, call the ambulance just in time, the meeting is forgotten and the only focus is on my heroics. As he raises his voice, I am hopeful. How quickly can I Google "what to do in the onset of a heart attack"? I presume Theo is the office first aider and I will not be calling for his help.

"Arrives after 9.30, leaves before 5, lets phone ring out rather than answering, especially if an internal call, spends at least thirty minutes a day planking, whatever the hell that is, in his office, watches porn on work computer, although does have the decency to put headphones on, any meetings Oliver does attend he spends the majority of time on Facebook. Two definite counts of masturbating in the bathrooms, one possible sighting of masturbating in my office, drug taking in office hours, one complaint of sexual harassment and finally a habit of chucking away other people's food from the fridge based on your opinion of whether it is suitable for the owner." Dad stands up as he says this, speaking more quickly as he reels off my list of apparent dishonours.

As he finishes, he seems exasperated. He is breathing heavily. He leans one hand on desk edge. Is this the moment?

It doesn't happen. He pours himself a glass of room-temperature water and looks directly at me.

"Well?"

"Dad, not one of those accusations is true. Theo is making all of this up as he wants me out. He sees me as a threat. Did you know he slept with hookers? I very rarely do drugs; if I do it's only to fit in with the other employees, a team-building exercise." I speak and convince myself simultaneously.

"STOP lying Oliver, for your own sake. For a start, Theo has not said a damn thing; lots of the team mentioned these things to me, and Clarke, with a little persuasion, confirmed it all. He can see you need help. He wants you to get help. Perhaps it is time to go back to the therapist." Dad says this, looking calm and composed and increasingly unlikely to have a heart attack.

I remain unconvinced that the therapist – what was her name? – would have me back.

"I cannot have you in the business, in these offices, anymore, Oliver. You understand; I am sure you understand. Do you have anything to say?"

I close my eyes and envision Clarke and Poppy getting into that taxi. I focus on the hand in the small of her back gently guiding her into the car.

Chapter 7

I am wearing £500 trainers, but they look like a pair of cheap New Balance to anyone who is no one. Black lightweight sweatpants and a gym tee that is oversized aside from on the biceps where it tightens, accentuating my freshly pumped arms. A sweater is tied around my waist. I toy with the idea of nonchalantly yet strategically placing it over my shoulders, to look as relaxed and as in love with life as possible. What is this world aside from perception?

I watch the three of them. Theo standing uncomfortably close to her, his grip on her arm less affectionate than you would expect from two soon-to-be-married lovebirds.

Clarke has placed an extra, a decoy, possibly Glen or Andy, in between himself and Poppy. Their smiles are almost identical, teeth on show and seemingly genuine.

Clarke seems to have gone all out on his shirt and tie combo: the shirt is navy, I am sure of it, and the tie a shinier black with pink flecks. An especially offensive get-up for my final day.

"So, I would like to thank Oliver for his commitment over the last few years. He has overseen new projects and helped Danbrook Recruitment to build market share within new sectors of the industry. His efforts have helped position us ready for our imminent flotation. He leaves the business in a strong position to move on without replacing his role. Oliver, Ollie, I thank you." Dad says this with a look of relief on his face but embarrassment in his eyes.

I cannot be certain whether the embarrassment is due to my leaving or due to himself for the clear-to-everyone-in-the-room bare-faced bullshit he has just spouted.

Their smiles broaden to an almost face-splitting level. There is clapping. Fucking sea lions.

Theo manages to make the loudest clap with his right palm against his thigh, if anything tightening his grip on her arm.

There is a pay-off. I am not sure how much I agreed to. I am not sure if the company is paying or if it is Mr. James Danbrook himself, but some more money will appear in my account at some point.
I am free. Free to focus on my travelling, my working out, my business plan, perhaps some philanthropy. Afterwards, of course, after I investigate the circle of deceit, then I can focus on all of these things with my soulmate.

"I do not want leaving drinks, Clarke. The very idea of leaving drinks repulses me, Clarke."

I read the text back, unsure as to how this has occurred.

I wanted to slip out of the office quietly. A quick visit to the gym – missing chest day is unacceptable – then straight home to continue the investigation.

Clarke must have insisted.

"Drinks at the Charlotte Street hotel and a club afterwards. I will bring some very good product."

He shows me the text back. I must have been too occupied to read it.

There would be no drugs for me this evening. I say to myself repeatedly. Focus, believe and achieve. I say to myself repeatedly.

Clarke mechanically chops up a lump of pure in the back of a black cab. I look at the screensaver on my phone. Focus. Believe. Achieve.
I imagine her dancing on the beach, cocktail in one hand, more tanned than usual, smiling – a real smile, not like those at my leaving do, or the smile of my miserable mother in her camel cashmere rollneck.
I bring my scabbed knuckle with the molehill of coke close to my nostril, as close as it could possibly go without ingesting it. Perhaps I should just do a little pinch. Maybe just a minute amount will help maintain focus. I manage to flick it away with my left thumb. Clarke isn't paying attention.

I start my lines of enquiry.

"Some great cocaine you've got there, Clarke, lethal stuff. What did you pay? Do you reckon you'll pull tonight?" I say routinely, hardly looking up from my phone.

"Not very much; I have a very good relationship with my dealer and yes, I expect to pull every night," he says, just as routinely, flicking through pictures of himself on his phone.

I do not recall Clarke's last name. I think he is twenty-six years old, twenty-six years old and still living with his parents in Hertfordshire. I don't know where – Watford, Barnet, somewhere provincial and dull.

His dad had been a relatively successful footballer, played a season or two in league one for one of the London teams, but it doesn't sound to me like he made any money.

His oldest brother followed in his father's footsteps but up in Scotland. The middle brother has been selling property in Dubai for eight years – doing well, but he is stuck in the desert. "Doing well." What does that actually mean? I don't suppose he has a penthouse apartment in the hub of London's start-up district.

Anyway, with sons in Scotland somewhere and Dubai, his mum insists that the youngest kid remains at home. I am of course sceptical about this and think it's much more likely that Clarke spends too much of his pay packet on drugs, drink and inappropriate tailoring. If I do ever meet the old girl, which seems unlikely, I will be probing her on the topic.

Every Sunday Clarke plays golf with his dad. They both play off a four. This is of no interest, but Clarke has mentioned it several times – not specifically to me, to Theo, but I picked up on it.

Maybe hanging around the office would have been the better idea; surely that's where clues will unravel. I could call the old coot, ask if his decision is final. Maybe I could work part-time on a consultancy basis.

Clarke once told me he has a Range Rover at home, all black. I do not care enough to ask but presume it's the

Evoque. I haven't seen it; if I had to take an educated guess I would say it was his mother's.

They do stuff as a family. I would not go as far as to say they go to church, but they definitely have a roast dinner on a Sunday. Then they go for a stroll, the mum walking up front, son and old man walking behind talking about mortgages or something similar. Then reliving his past glories. Clarke laughing and eager to hear the end of the story he must have heard one thousand times. "You played at Wembley, Dad? Dad, did I mention I am playing off a four nowadays?"

He attended no university of relevance. He had fallen into recruitment after studying some kind of physical education. His body fat was low, like eight per cent low. Good genes, sportsman's genes, played rugby for a while but then hurt something; a knee maybe, or an elbow. I saw him sitting waiting for his interview. I went over and introduced myself as the owner's son. I offered to get him a drink of water, quench his thirst, ease his nerves. I seem to remember getting sidetracked, but the intent was there. I wish I had sent him on his way now, told him the vacancies were filled. Maybe it would not have come to this.

Chapter 8

The taxi pulls up in Fitzrovia. I feel high, but it must be a sober high, excited in the knowledge that I am one step ahead. Clarke pays as I tap my pockets. Well-heeled drinkers spill out of the hotel entrance. I catch the eye of a wealthy-looking older woman, wrinkles woven into her tanned skin. Her eyes twinkle and I get a glimpse of her mischievous past.

For the first time today I notice a change in the temperature; not cold but cooler. I cannot be certain, but it feels like November. A sense of urgency surges through me; Christmas is only around the corner.

I expect the world to look different through my sober eyes, but it does not. I still have a disregard for the people around me; I still feel anxious and alone. They were drunk but smiling, enjoying the company of friends. I can't recall a time when I felt joyous in the company of others. I look for the playful older woman, but she is nowhere to be seen. I hold the phone close to my ear. My mother's voice is being drowned out by the noise of the Friday night crowd, so without speaking I put the phone in my sweat top pocket and take a deep breath.

I have fallen behind Clarke, who is already at the table. As I get closer I can hear them talk. I wouldn't focus on the words but more the tone. Analyse the situation from the eyes of an outsider. Like Attenborough watching a group of chimpanzees assessing who would be the dominant ape.

"Hey T, wasn't expecting to see you here? How come you're here? Thought you may have swerved it, stayed at home, chilled out," Clarke says to Theo with genuine surprise at his attendance.

I am not surprised that Theo has turned up. He must have been dying to see me get pushed out of my own family's company. He is also very unlikely to leave Poppy with me; it is going to be an emotional night for us both. Anything could happen.

I sense that Theo – his name is not T or Big T, it is Theo – just ignores Clarke's, or the Big C, as I might start calling him, question.

"Congrats on the new client today, Clarke, a real big hitter. That's the kind of deal that could well help you buy your own little bachelor pad." Theo's eyes were focused solely on Clarke as he says this. The words came out playfully; there doesn't seem to be an underlying spiteful tone, but surely it was laced with some malice.

"Thanks, T. I might just look at getting myself a little place in Kensington or that side of town. An investment more than anything."

They clink champagne glasses.

It looks like Clarke murmurs something in Theo's direction. I can't make out what and write it off as an early-evening, drug-induced involuntary spasm.

Poppy is nodding and smiling, her slender fingers seductively twiddling the straw in her mojito. Her eyes are focused on Theo, but I am sure I see them flitting towards Clarke.

Nobody seems to have noticed me yet.

A place in Kensington; Jesus, how much was that deal worth? I casually type a reminder into my phone. On Monday morning I will find out where and try my hardest to gazump him.

"It was touch and go for a while though, T. I had to go on a major charm offensive this last week to get it done. Thanks for the advice." Clarke leans into Theo as he says this.

On the word "charm" he definitely looks across the table to Poppy. Theo may have missed this subtle piece of interaction. I did not.
Just watching them, looking for clues, for indications, I hold my iPhone low and casually check that it is recording.

Two hands appear on my shoulders. A middle-aged group all in black tie squeeze past. I shove the phone into my pocket.

"Earth to Oliver, are you in there? Why…don't…you…go…and get…a …round in."

Clarke's heavy arm weighs down on my shoulders. His words ring in my ears.

"And stop filming me, you freak."

I shake my head, blinking and stretching my pupils, as if I had just come around from concussion.

"Good idea, Big C, I will get us all some potent cocktails. Poppy, Theo, what can I get you? My treat." I almost shout this. Certainly there is a confidence in my voice. Suddenly I feel extremely significant.

I know something others do not, I am fucking sure of it.

"PS, Clarke, that flat you want to buy in Kensington. The investment property you were looking at, I might make a call to Savills and buy it in cash."

I am unsure whether I say this aloud. Clarke doesn't notice, as he is now back in a deep conversation with T. I mean Theo. These two could easily be homosexual. The kind who get up at the crack of dawn, brush their perfect teeth together, Theo dressed in all white and Clarke in something horrifically gay, rowing on the Thames. Their broad backs forcing the oars to cut through the water with ease.

"Two times whisky sour, one very strong mojito and one double whisky soda." The words roll off my tongue in a commanding manner. I speak with such resounding confidence that even over the noisy bar chatter I do not need to repeat myself. So far, so good.

"Here you go, that's £42. Enjoy, let me know how you like it." The barman seems cocksure with the drinks he has prepared. He smiles at me as I hand over my brand spanking new debit card. I feel like I recognise him. Maybe from the most recent Burberry advertising campaign.

I am ready to confide in him, let him in on the secret, the plan. Before I have a chance he is gone.

I have to take two trips back to the bar for the drinks. Nobody gives me a hand and nobody notices my return. Oh, except for Cate, of course, who has now appeared. She has made an unnecessary effort to look pretty. She taps all three of them on the shoulder and they turn to face me.
I bring the drink to my mouth, wash it around. Shit, the whisky burns, eroding my gums. It spills down my throat. The majority I slowly dribble back into the glass.

It doesn't appear anyone has noticed. Aside from, of course, the watchful eye of Cate. Jesus, she makes me uncomfortable. I need to escape Medusa's stare. The only thing she couldn't turn to stone is my penis.

"Right, I am off to the bathrooms." I had been practising the line in my head for the last five minutes.

It didn't sound quite as poignant as I had expected.

I feel a hand pushing into mine under the table. It's Clarke and of course he is passing neatly folded paper into my palm.

"Good man, good man, I knew you'd liven up. Take your time in there," Clarke whispers in my ear.

I enter the bathroom. Out of habit I put four pound coins in the attendant's tray. In the cubicle I lock the door. Carefully I undo the wrap. For reasons unknown I scoop some up with my brand spanking new debit card, Coutts debit card, and pass it under my nostrils, wanting to just take in the aroma as if it was a vintage Bordeaux.

With my right middle finger I push about a quarter of the smooth white powder into the toilet water. I do the wrap up, and before flushing pour half of the pricey whisky sour away.

Take my time. Why would he want me to take my time? I know why, you terribly sneaky bastard.

As I walk through the bar, I practise trying to hide the knowing smirk on my face. I notice a handsome reflection in a mirrored column and am convinced it was mine. I am desperate to hurry back. Catch the two of them flirting while the gormless Theo looks on. My heart pounds with irregular excitement.

As the group gets closer I rub my nose, looking directly at Clarke.

"How do I look? Clean?" lifting my nostrils slightly so he can check for any powder residue.

"All clean, buddy. Listen, I think you should just go and chill by the bar for a while, or pop outside, chat to Cate. I need to make a call," Clarke says, slithering off.

I glance down at my vibrating phone. Dave. I drop the call. A text comes through.

Returning your call, bro. Call me back. I presume you have my paper.

Dave is my local dealer; by "local" I mean he most likely lives on that eyesore of an estate nearby. I know it's not his real name but it's damn easy to remember at 4am on a

Wednesday morning. Anyway, I won't be needing him anymore; I cannot recall for the life of me why I called him. It seems unlikely that I would go to that length to settle my bill.

Leave. Chill out by the bar. I don't think so, Clarke; I think I will stay exactly where I am.

I look over to Theo. He is tightly holding Poppy's hand. Her fingers overlap; they look somewhat uncomfortable. As I look directly at her she averts her eyes. There is a definite sense of discomfort, poor girl.
The silence is bordering on unbearable.

"So, Poppy, how much on a scale of one to ten are you going to miss seeing me most days?"

Another pathetic attempt on my part. I really have nothing to say to either of them right now. Sticking with the unbearable silence was the better option.

Nervousness is overcoming me. It must be all of the toxins leaving my body. Kicking a habit was never going to be easy. Unsurprisingly, Poppy doesn't smile. Theo doesn't smile. Clarke doesn't smile; in fact, he is nowhere to be seen. The atmosphere is worsening and I cannot fathom why. There is an unnerving tension in this place.

"Ollie, you complete fucking idiot. My suggestion would be that you put your drink down and step outside before I decide to embarrass you in front of the six people who could be bothered to attend your leaving do," Theo snarls further, crushing her perfectly manicured slender fingers.

He is seated but pushing the balls of his feet into the floor. He looks animalistic, predatory, like he is ready to pounce.

My natural instinct is to look at her. She looks down, then turns her head so her nose is touching Theo's cheek. I am certain she cannot look me in the eyes.

My brain feels like it is grabbing for oxygen. I cannot assess the situation. Even if they are onto me, he should be pleased. He is being made to look a fool. Do I retort? Have I done something worse than normal? I scan through my memories from the last few days. I need to check my diary.

Without moving my head I catch a glimpse of Clarke in the reflection of a reflection from a beautiful wall-mounted mirror. He is peering through the hotel window. Where is Cate? She could lighten the mood.

"Glen, how are you doing? Appreciate you coming." I attempt to bond.

"It's Andy," says Glen.

I am hot and wishing I hadn't worn fleece.

"Theo, I know it's a big week for you this week, your mentor leaving the workplace, but seriously, chill out, man. Poppy, maybe you should give him some action tonight just to help him rela…"

I do not get to finish my sentence. I see the small round table fall. I see Theo release her hand. I notice three or maybe four drinks fly left off of the table. I admire the

99

power he harnesses pushing off from a seating position. Then it all goes very quiet.

Chapter 9

The sharp, echoing pain starts at the top of my spine, sprinting from the nape of my neck down towards the bottom of my back. Which is strange, as Theo's fist definitely connected somewhere at the front of my face.

Noise and smell become apparent. An authoritative voice, which I instantly recognise as a doorman, rings in my ears. The first smell I note is sickly and sweet, possibly expensive but cheapened in some way. My eyes open without my command and I see Cate's chin and long cleavage in front of me. She is touching my face.

"It's okay, Oliver, just keep lying down. The ambulance is here. They just want to check you over." The doorman has a calm and caring tone.

I appreciate his calming voice. I thud my skull back against the floor.

"Oliver, you brave boy, I am so glad he missed your perfect nose. Don't worry, I am going to take good care of you." Cate leans into me to speak. All I can engage with is the smell of the foulest of fermented grapes on her breath. I thud my head backwards onto the floor once more and decide to stop breathing.

For a moment I feel a light in my eyes, questions directed at me. I have no idea what I am saying but it seems satisfactory. They get brighter, sporadic, blurred eyes, movement. The doorman helps me up, or perhaps it's the barman. I try to give him my number, to tell him what I know. They all look at me, I float, a car door is held open. I disappear.

Back to consciousness. I want to hear the soothing voice of my new friend; we have much to discuss. My body feels so comfortable, relaxed and yet confined. I feel a tugging at the top of my waistband. I feel a toxic wetness on my mouth. I open my eyes as wide as possible to fully grasp the horror. It is like being at the front row of the Imax, instead it is not a close-up three-dimensional action scene I see but a crazed look on Cate's face as she bombards my lips with unattractive kisses.
I push my hips forward to allow my pounding head to get some distance. Unfortunately this gifts her the leverage she required.

"Ohhh, there he is. Little Mr. Danbrook isn't so little," Cate slurs as my semi-erect penis is forced into her relentless grasp.

"There's an upside, there is always an upside," I recall, as Cate doesn't seem to be able to slobber all over my face while squeezing the life out of my member.

I say nothing, and try to work out where we are and how we got here.

"Facking hell, love, put it away, I'll lose me license. Anyway, you'll be home in five minutes, lucky fella." His voice grates worse than Cate's handjob.

I have a feeling this moment will end up in his wank-bank, the talk of the local snooker club: "you'll never guess what happened in my cab last night."

102

I want to frown, but it hurts under my right eye, a heartbeat-like thumping.

We pull up. I recognise my surroundings. I have been here before. I recall being impressed. I recall refusing to acknowledge how impressed I was.

Cate has a stunning apartment overlooking the Thames. Daddy pays for it; this is a presumption on my part. I have no idea what role Cate plays at Danbrook or her salary.

We do not even make it through the front door and my sweatpants are around my ankles. The pounding at the top end teams up with some discomfort in my groin as Cate drags my disobediently hard cock out of the leg of my boxers. She is working it like a skinflint cake maker trying to squeeze the last of the icing from a piping bag. I grimace at her frankly insane smile and shudder as her mouth heads south. I do not have the heart to tell her I am not really a fan of blowjobs. Her teeth scrape at the flesh. I try to make my yelps of agony sound like cries of enjoyment.

She removes her wine-drenched hole from around me and spends the next few minutes fumbling around with her door key. As it finally swings open I am dragged and pushed onto the bed. During the front door fiasco my cock has shrivelled. I imagine most of the blood has left my genitals and is making its way up towards my pounding face.

Cate clearly sees my shrunken member as a challenge – how quickly can she force it hard again. She pulls my shirt over my head, tugs my sweats and boxers off – I should have worn jeans and a belt, terrible error. I close my eyes as she pushes her breasts into my face. Her hardening nipples are not welcome against my tongue, but her flesh helps cool my swollen cheek. Rubbing up and down on top of me, a thoroughly unenjoyable experience, one of my testicles is caught against her hip bone and I have this terrible feeling it is going to be completely ripped off. A balding, beaten up, unloved, unemployed eunuch.

"Cate, you're going to need to stop that. I am in a little bit of pain." I am completely sober, I think, but my words are slurred due to what feels like a fat lip.

How big was Theo's fist? Or do I have a particularly small head?

"Poor baby, I understand, I know exactly what will help; you need some of Nurse Cate's medicine to ease the pain."

She sounds a little out of breath talking and simultaneously manoeuvring herself around into an ambitious sixty-nine.

I have no energy to crane my neck to even contemplate eating her, feeling very aware of a tiny fleck of toilet paper stuck to that thing bridging the vagina to the arsehole. I lay back with two pale but friendly-looking arse cheeks wobbling in front of my one open eye.
Whatever she is doing to my cock is much more relaxing than against the front door so I let her get on with it and contemplate what the hell went on earlier in the evening.

The conversation between Clarke and Theo; I need to know what was said. Unable to move, I swipe my hand out to the bedside. Surely my phone recording will have the answers. It must be out of reach.

I do not cum, but Cate appears to have. She shoves my annoyingly rigid dick inside her and rides up and down for what in pissed terms seemed like hours but was in fact just shy of one hundred and twenty seconds. After one minute eight seconds she was panting so badly that I lifted my head to look at the bedside table for an asthma pump. I make the executive decision to let out a shuddering groan and fake orgasm, unfussed as to whether Cate notices the lack of male bodily fluids inside of her.

The energy expelled from faking orgasm makes me sleepy. I feel my right eye closing.

I awake in an empty bed feeling drowsy, separating the soft cotton sheets, sliding my feet into bedside slippers. Without touching my face I walk straight into the bathroom. I have been here before, perhaps more than once. The white Chanel watch on the floor by the bidet shows the time as late morning. I stand in the wet room. The steam from the shower clears my swollen airways, the near-boiling water slightly distracts from my pounding head.

Although I do not mind Cate taking advantage – I mean, I am considerably more attractive than her – I make a mental note to Google whether a man can technically be raped by a woman. I at no point remember consenting.

My mind drifts and I feel a happy moment as I look at the huge variety of products Cate has to hand.

I wash my body using an abrasive mitt with some almond and coconut body wash. I put some Moroccan argan oil shampoo and conditioner in my hair. I follow this with the exact thickening shampoo I use, which is pleasant but surprising as she already has a thick head of hair.

I avoid the temptation of an oil-reducing deep clay mask and gently pat at my lumpy face with slightly more tepid water. I wash my cock and balls thoroughly for a second time with the exceptionally creamy soap. I then take a deep breath, get out of the shower and take a look at my battered features.

The steam wipes from the mirror with reluctance and somewhat dramatically. Oh what horror shall I see?

I have to blink, refocus and look again. There on my left cheekbone is a bruise the size of a pound coin and my lip appears slightly swollen.

The damage is minimal: knocked down by a sucker punch and hardly marked.

"It's not how hard you get hit, but how hard you can get hit and keep going!" I shout at my smirking face in the mirror.

I feel great, like finding Cate, bending her over the sink and sodomising her. I am a scarred Roman soldier, damaged in battle but not defeated. After conquering the city's army I am ready to conquer the brothel's most experienced whore. However, I pine for my wife, in a place far from here. How long has it been? Just to feel her warmth, the stroke of her soft fingers against my chapped skin. Oh, Poppy, how I yearn to see you again.

My longing is interrupted by a light tapping on the bathroom door and an ever-so-irritating sound.

"Hi, big boy. Want to shower together before I make you a brave boy's breakfast?" Cate's voice is even more high-pitched than usual, a chihuahua in an animated Disney film.

I open the door and my disobedient penis hardens all by itself yet again.

Chapter 10

Cate's refusal to let me put it in her backside is bothersome, especially considering the controversial way she molested me last night. However, putting her over the bath edge and aggressively slamming in and dragging myself out for the thirty seconds or so it takes from start to finish satisfies the centurion within. I watch my army march in unity from her rouged bum cheeks and fall to their death on the bathroom tiles.

As we lay on the sofa, our bodies awkwardly entwined, I eat grapes and drink tea. The breeze blows in from the French doors leading onto what is a quite impressive terrace. I feel happy, playful, relaxed; a feeling I cannot wait to experience with Poppy.

"Yes, Oliver, of course we have fucked before as you so delightfully put it. It started last February, after someone in IT's leaving do. You had been following Poppy around all evening like a sad, unwanted little puppy, so I took you home and gave you some attention. Anyway, you know this; stop fooling around."

As always, I feel a distinct annoyance whenever Cate mentions her. It almost feels – well, like cheating.

"Ok, I take your word for it, although I must have been very, very pissed or high on each occasion as I have zero recollection. Oh wait, do you have an Oyster card, per chance?" I ask.

There is an unplanned pleasantness in my tone. I squeeze or maybe even caress her fleshy but oddly attractive love handles and then, for reasons unknown, lean up and kiss her on the forehead.

Before she has a chance to respond I add, "By the way, just for your peace of mind, I won't be lodging a police complaint about the rapey nature of last night's lovemaking, on one condition: tell me everything you know about Theo. Tell me why on earth he felt the need to sucker punch me."

I open my phone up, ready to take notes. As soon as she has spilled the beans I will go into the bathroom and watch back my recording. Piece it all together and formulate it into a dynamic plan of action. I am now sitting upright and facing her, a fitting set-up for an inquisition.

"Rapey, wow. At one point I thought I wasn't going to be able to get your little winkle hard, so you should give me some credit for persistence." Cate laughs and indicates an inaccurate measurement of around two inches with her thumb and forefinger.

I feel pleasantly at ease. I reach for more tea, and am taken aback as I pour a cup for Cate also.

I turn off the relaxed and switch on the stern face, the "down to business face", the "reason I am sitting in your living room while I have better things to be doing on a weekend" face.

"What happened last night, Cate?"

"C'mon, seriously, you don't know? You can't think of any reasons why Theo might be slightly peeved at you?" Cate is wide-eyed, looking directly at me. She is smiling, waiting for my realisation.

My blank stare struggles to deal with her surprised expression.

"Nope, no idea. The odd sexual innuendo directed at his current partner? My good looks and considerably better body? My confident workplace persona? Surely these are qualities to aim towards, rather than resent me for?"

"The messages, you fool. Theo saw the messages between you and Poppy – the messing about last Christmas when he was away."

Cate's apartment is really very well done, contemporary yet warm, minimalistic but full of charm and consideration, hardly a piece of Ikea in sight.

A large side unit that I nearly purchased from LuxDeco is the feature piece in the room. Adorned with carefully positioned, varying sized frames. Floppy hats on golden beaches, muddy boots at festivals, a male stripper with killer abs and greasy hair struggles to contain the five or six women hanging off him. She is smiling in every single image; in fancy dress, holding babies, drinking champagne with her girlfriends, a selfie stick picture from a swimming pool, no one looking their best or appearing to care. All indicators that she has a life outside of her obsession for me.

I feel a sense of disappointment.

110

In pride of place, larger framed pictures of her and what must be a mum and dad, a sister, on an imposing drive. I count ten floor-to-ceiling windows. It looks Georgian.

The fruit bowl is overflowing with those small hard-to-peel oranges and firm-looking nectarines. A smaller adjacent bowl is jammed with brightly coloured festival wristbands and backstage passes. I can just make out the screen on her MacBook: some kind of blog. The open plan allows me full view of the kitchen: a spiraliser, the Vitamix, a Bose sound system – all the hallmarks of a relatively acceptable human being.

Through the swelling of my right eye, I catch a glimpse of an animal skulking across the worktops. It drops down and then scales the sofa side, perching behind Cate. It looks like a Persian. It is; it's a blue Persian. Memories come flooding in. We were inseparable. Jesus, I loved that cat. He would follow me out of the house, jump the gates and watch the car pull away. I would swivel round on the shiny leather seats and wave goodbye. I would open the car doors before the driver had a chance to and sprint up the drive, dropping my school bag and clambering up the stairs. Everyday, there he was, waiting on the bed. We would sit there sharing cheese and crackers. He would even eat red grapes and apple if you sliced them thinly. I would rub his tummy and his purr would make everything else sound – well, just so much quieter.

Rocky left around the time of the divorce.

It just stares at me. She doesn't even acknowledge the poor little thing.
I blink and it seems to take this as some kind of victory and averts its eyes from mine.

I sense another set of eyeballs on me and cough up my words.

"I had a thing with Poppy at Christmas." It comes out of my mouth as a statement, which I am sure is unintentional.

"I had a thing with Poppy at Christmas?" This time it sounds much more like a question.

I catch a brief moment to close my eyes and begin to weave truth into this dream scenario.

It is short-lived. Her firm hands slap down on my thigh.

"I KNOW! You mucky pup, all that chasing her around finally got you somewhere. It turns out both of us are persistent." Cate shuffles her hand up to within inches of where my dormant penis rests.

I shuffle back further into the sofa.

"I mean, I should mind, but I don't. It annoyed me when I found out, but the way I look at it she had her chance with you and now you are mine. Did it happen though, Oliver? I would like to know," Cate says, with a hint of menace.

I scan the room frantically looking for the little fella. He is nowhere to be seen. I don't blame him; there is an unavoidable awkwardness forming.

I try to recall the last time I saw Rocky.

Cate moves next to me on the sofa.

I was pretty high most of December. Maybe it did happen.

While Poppy's weasel of a boyfriend was most likely skiing and shagging chalet girls at some terrible European resort, I was wining and dining his soon-to-be fiancée at Zuma, Nobu or possibly even the Chiltern. The food keeps coming although neither of us eat, both suffering from nervy butterflies in our stomachs, the anticipation almost unbearable.

I am buying very expensive champagne. There is a vintage red and white on the table. For hours we sit deep in conversation. I keep waving the waiters away, "do we look like we are ready for the bill?"

Poppy heads off to the bathroom as I finally settle up. I leave a large cash tip and to my annoyance they take it before she gets back. It feels like an age. She is adjusting her hair, applying lipgloss, perhaps freshening up.

As the waiter brings her jacket I feel compelled to push a fifty into his hand, his appreciation marred by a level of confusion.

We are both silent in the taxi back to Claridge's. It could have only been Claridge's. The taxi driver starts to talk so I lean over and turn off the intercom. When will they learn? Nothing they have to say is of any interest to me.

In the room I open the mini bar. Before I can pour the miniature Grey Goose onto ice, Poppy has taken it from me and places it to one side. She takes both my hands and leans in to kiss me.

Cate's voice breaks my enjoyable, plausible recollection.

"Oliver, answer me, please. I really do not mind if you did. I know you like Poppy; she is a good-looking girl, if not a little bit screwed up."

Cate is looking for reassurance, hoping I will say that my love is for her, that Poppy was a brief infatuation. That by some unknown act of God I would be willing to give up on the main reason for me still existing, concede defeat and spend the rest of my miserable days watching and listening to her noisily gobble away at my bored cock, waiting for the inevitable moment I keel over from disappointment and die.

The blue of his eyes seem so familiar as he saunters back through the door. Without breaking step, he hops up onto my lap and nuzzles my hand.

Cate seems like she still expects a reply. I thought I had answered; perhaps I was not clear.

She ignores him. I have decided that pretty soon I will, we will, make our escape. Reaching for my phone I send a text message to myself:

Remember to buy organic cat food.

"Cate, I think first it would be best that you tell me what you know."

I stare directly at her, stroking the cat from head to tail in a villainous manner. His fur is so soft. Cate seems to ignore my question and looks at me with a level of confusion I have seen before.

"Cate, I need to know what is being said. Tell me every detail."

"Ok, here goes. So, as you must have noticed, there has been some real tension in the office between Theo and Poppy. His leaving the engagement party early with the hump, the obvious flirting with receptionists, clients and office interns, his checking up on her every moment she is out, escorting her to lunch. In fact, even the marriage proposal itself was all about control." Cate is whispering as she tells me this.

"Yes, of course I had noticed, who hadn't!" I think my tone of voice covers my complete surprise.

"Well, a while back, I found her, Poppy, crying in the bathroom, and she told me nearly everything that had gone on. Her therapist was out of town and I was the only person she could confide in. Which shows how deranged and desperate she actually is."

I nod.

"Well, apparently, her and Theo were on the verge of splitting up when he went on his ski trip. She just could not stand the constant flirting with other women, the rumours of his infidelities. However, he comes back an apparent changed man, says that Poppy is the one, etcetera, etcetera. I know this is all bullshit, mind you, as Andy from HR told me that Theo had taken one of the chalet maids 'off-piste' the day before he came home. Anyway, so a few days later, Poppy gets up early to go to a spin class, anorexic bitch. She's on and off living with Theo, sometimes living at an old friend's house. She

115

accidentally leaves her phone on the kitchen centre unit." Cate takes a breath and pulls me to face her.

I am desperately trying to quieten my racing mind so I can actually absorb every detail.

"Please continue, Cate, and just for complete and utter clarity when you refer to 'off-piste', do you mean anal?" I use the same tone and take the same posture as the therapist that I haven't seen in some time used to.

The cat lets out a noisy miaow as he slides from my knees to the carpet.

"So a text message comes through and Theo, being the controlling character he is, has no qualms reading it. Apparently it just said, 'I hope you enjoyed emptying my Christmas sack, winking smiley face, I've got a NYE firework for you to let off, double winking smiley face, double kiss.' Poppy tells me Theo went ballistic, turns up to the Notting Hill Bodyworks and literally drags her out of the class. She said he really grabbed her, bruised her arm, standing in the middle of the street at 7.30am demanding to know who the fuck Saskia Davies is and how Saskia could not possibly have a sack or a firework."

Cate is struggling to keep her excitement to a whisper, her voice picking up in pace and pitch. It must have been all too much for Rocky, as he has disappeared from sight.

I take a deep breath.

"And then what happened?" I say, purposely frowning and resting my chin on the points of my fingers as if I was deep in analytical thought.

"Well, Poppy lies through her teeth, tells him that Saskia was an old college friend, hadn't seen her in years, thinks she'd moved to Amsterdam and that she must have got rid of her mobile number and this mysterious text must have been from whoever had the phone now – a practical joke, maybe. She knows Theo doesn't believe her, but what can she do? He seems to calm down, he takes her home and makes her call the number. It just rings out." Cate has real excitement in her voice, stopping only because I interrupt.

Poppy's lies excites me. It makes her cheating on Theo with me all the more feasible. The texts do sound like the sort of thing I would send – a fun play on words – but it is not clear to me why I would be saved as "Saskia".

"Hold on one second, Cate. So Theo thinks it was me who spilt my sack over Poppy's ever-so-pert breasts. You also think it was me. So from this I only presume Poppy told you it was me. Maybe she was confusing fantasy with reality?" I say this in a chirpy manner, pleased that Poppy credited me with such snappy innuendo.

"No, no, Poppy didn't tell me. She says it was nothing, a nobody, just a fling; a one-night stand with an over-eager guy she had met in a bar. She got really drunk after not being able to reach Theo, did not believe he had no 4G. She ended up doing shots with a cute city boy and then going home with him. She says it was just one small mistake. So anyway, Theo forgives or at least seems to forget about it all. In public he is overly nice to her, at home not so nice. He makes her move in with him immediately and watches her like a hawk.

"Poppy gets used to it. I mean, Theo is quite a catch. It all seems forgotten until the other week, the night of their engagement drinks.

You probably won't remember, Ollie, but Theo left rather early."

"Correct, Cate, I have no recollection of that, why would I?"

"So Poppy gets in late. She is drunk, desperate for a wee. She dumps her bag down – you know, the light pink Céline tote."

I nod.

"It is a really great bag but open at the top, contents on display. She goes into her bathroom to shower. What she does not realise is that Theo had waited up, livid that she hadn't gone home with him earlier in the night, so as she drunkenly showers he gets her phone from the bag and with absolute certainty types in her passcode." Cate's arms are wide open, her eyes darting from side to side. This is the most animated I have seen her. Her voice quickens to extremely yappy dog level. No wonder Rocky had gone into hiding.

"I reckon he finds an inappropriate text," I say, fairly certain I sent one to her that evening.

"No, no, Oliver, I know you know it was much worse than that. A text comes through as he picks it up. No name this time or innuendos. Just a message from a number saying something like, 'cab firm can't find my phone, bunch of crooks, thought I would just text you sweet dreams off this number, I wish I was with you now'. Now, Theo is

118

switched on, cool as a cucumber, I bet. He waits for Poppy to get out of the shower, then as she is going up the stairs he appears with his phone and hers. He shows her the message and before Little Miss Liar can even concoct a story he goes to his phone and looks up the number for that old college buddy Saskia Davies. Turns out that cunning old Theo had saved the number. He now knows Poppy lied before and, keeping both phones, tells her they will discuss it in the morning. Can you believe it!" Cate shouts the last few words as she gets up and heads to the bathroom.

I can't believe it. Firstly I admire Theo's thoroughness, logging the telephone number just in case. Then I feel disappointed that he did not have the foresight to check the number on WhatsApp – there was sure to be a profile picture. Then I feel sadness and anger that Poppy could be so promiscuous but not interested in me. Why the fuck did Cate have to tell me this? I wish I could forget it all and just go back to snuggling on her sofa. There's also a niggling broken memory in the back of my mind – the lost phone. Fuck, it will come to me.

Cate finds me in the bedroom, looking under the antique wardrobe, painted in a light duck egg, trying to tempt him out from underneath with a piece of clementine.

"What on earth are you doing, Oliver? If you're looking for drugs I have none here."

She helps me up from the floor and with her knee closes the top drawer on her bedside cabinet.

"Another cup of tea? I have green or how about a nice chamomile?" Cate is keen to continue the conversation.

119

"I will take a green tea, but do not leave the bag in for too long. Do you have a protein shake? I have a headache coming on, probably caused by low blood sugars."

Sometimes I have a very dry mouth and am convinced I have diabetes. Considering I didn't touch a drop last night I am starting to feel very hungover.

Cate sits back down. She puts my green tea on a woven coaster that looks like it might be from Missoni. She has not made me a protein shake. Instead she places five sugar-laden jaffa cakes on a small hand-painted plate.

"Cate, the grim details of Poppy's mishappenings are very intriguing to me. However, I really want to know how my good name got dragged into this." I take a sip of a perfectly made green tea.

We have been sitting here talking for near two hours. The cat has reappeared by the window and seems to be toying with a noisy bluebottle.

"Just kill it and stop that damned buzzing," I might say out loud.

"Yes, so that's the weird part. So according to Poppy, Theo slept like a baby that night, like he did not have a care in the world. In the morning the interrogation starts. Apparently he says he knew she was seeing someone else, he wanted to know who it was, it was going to end today and that they would be moving the wedding forward to the following spring. Poppy tells me she didn't even want to marry him but felt she had no way out. She needed to settle down, needed financial support, needed security.

There had been another man before Theo but he kept going hot and cold, something about making sure she didn't follow in her mum's footsteps. Seriously, I should have charged, having to listen to her pitiful sob story," Cate says in a somewhat spiteful manner.

Yes, I do remember the engagement night. Theo did leave early, so if he was interrogating Poppy in the morning he almost certainly did not make the Taekwondo for troubled kids he was supposedly mentoring. This delights me. His fiancée cheats on him and he lets down our delinquent youth. Then I remember who the cheating fiancée is and feel quite distraught.

"Cate, can you please head towards the climax of your story? I need to get to the gym and then clear my name of this injustice."

"So she tells Theo that it's some guy she used to go to uni with, seen him a couple of times, slept together once, she bumped into him last night, nothing happened but he texted her. Of course, this time the lie doesn't quite match up. Theo knows she is bullshitting, gets up, takes her car keys, tells her she needs to come up with a better answer by the time he's back from Taekwondo."

My shoulders sink. Of course the absolute bastard still went to help the abused children or whatever the hell they are.

"But Theo doesn't go to Taekwondo. He decides to give Clarke a call, to go out for a brunchtime beer instead, talk about anything apart from women. Clarke happens to be in London that day, having a Nando's in Kensington. They end up boozing all afternoon. Finally, after a good seven pints, Theo starts telling Clarke all about his problems. Asking whether he has any idea who the scumbag is who has been screwing his girlfriend. Clarke says he might know something, says that this guy has been boasting, but that he's a known bullshitter so he takes it with a pinch of salt. Didn't want to mention anything as Theo and Pops looked so happy. Wasn't worth upsetting the apple cart when there was probably no truth in it. Clarke tells Theo that the texter potentially nailing his future wife is you, Oliver."

Cate finishes the sentence, takes a breath of air, then sits back deep in the sofa, almost squashing the cat that yet again she fails to notice. It scrambles to safety just in time.

My head for once isn't spinning. There is very little confusion, as, while Cate was talking, I had already seen the ending, recalling the moment in Hoxton when Clarke punched the wall. When he lost his phone. It was Clarke who was fucking the love of my life and the two-faced traitorous oaf was pinning the blame on me.

I get up and calmly walk to the bathroom. As I urinate I look around. The watch is gone from the floor and the spots of dried blood I had purposely left in the sink were missing. When did Cate have time to clear up? She will make someone, maybe Glen from HR or some other irrelevant man, a great wife one day.

I lather my palms with a gritty Aesop hand scrub that creates an aura of déjà vu and shout out: "Cate, how do you know that Theo went out on an all-day bender with Clarke? How do you know it was Clarke that blamed me? I mean it's all a bit far-fetched; I am like a mentor to him."

Cate waits for me to get back into the living room before replying. "I was waiting for you to ask that. Well, Poppy told me that Theo stormed out and that was that, end of the story as far as she was concerned. She dries her eyes, of course, reapplies make-up, thanks me for my time and glides out of the bathroom. So, I really have been busy at work, you know how hectic my department is at the moment?"

"I literally have no idea what you do," I reply, without moving a muscle.

"Well, anyway, I finally get time for a coffee with Clarke and we were chatting about life, love, you know and I felt I needed to tell someone, you know how it is. I needed to get someone else's views on it all, terrible I know, I really don't like to gossip, of course I would have spoken to you, but you were just so busy and, well, we tend not to talk at work.

"So Clarke tells me that he too was desperate to talk to someone; it was driving him crazy. Theo had been round to see him, he was really upset, it had put him in a really awkward position, he didn't know what to say, really wished he didn't know but he is not a liar, his dad always pushed upon him the importance of telling the truth. Even if it was going to hurt people, it was for the best. He told me that he told Theo that it was you, that you, Oliver, had confided in him, told him all about it. He thought it was wrong, wanted to tell you to stop, but being the owner's son he was scared to say so. He told me that he was just glad it seemed to have been brushed over, forgotten about; perhaps Theo respected your father too much to say anything. Turns out he was just patiently waiting, not wanting to beat up a colleague, waiting for you to be let go before doing anything."

"For clarity, Cate, I was neither let go or beaten up, and secondly there is a case of mistaken identity. Jeez, if I had been seeing her she definitely would have called it off with Theo."

Perhaps I did tell Clarke that I had been seeing Poppy. Perhaps I have been seeing her. It does sound kind of familiar; last Christmas was mostly a blur. Perhaps I did deserve that punch from Theo. Perhaps I did deserve to get fired from what rightfully should have been my company.

"Thanks for last night, Cate. I've got to get out of here. I'll see you around."

Chapter 11

Outside of the apartment I breathe, a gulping, strenuous breath, wanting to appreciate the fresh riverside air.

The wind is cutting, swirling left to right, the sort of wind that men with thinning hair despise. Wispy strands sway from side to side exposing naked scalp. I feel ugly and betrayed. Searching my jacket for a tissue I discover a badly folded wrap. I wipe tears from my face as the powder tips onto the floor, catching the attention of a pair of puff-chested pigeons.

I walk in the direction of the wind. The pungent smell of garlic and basil tempts my dulled nostrils. I cannot help but reminisce about our almost-date.

This particularly expensive, highly recommended, rustic yet romantic little Italian just off of Portobello.

Poppy had agreed to meet me there two years ago. If I thought some more about it I could probably remember the exact date. There were no made-up work meetings, no false pretences. I'd asked her to join me, as friends, as whatever, and she said yes. It was 8.20, and we had agreed to meet at 8. I was wearing a crisp white stretch poplin shirt, V-neck knit from Sandro and a slightly distressed pair of slim-fit Nudie jeans. I procrastinated over the Tom Ford Grey Vetiver fragrance. I went with my usual Dior Homme. I got dropped at the Ledbury and walked, just to strategise, work on my spontaneous, engaging conversation. 8.25 a text:

So sorry Oliver, some things come up, I don't think I'm gonna make it. Hope you and the others have a good night Poppy x

I am sure I hadn't mentioned any "others" would definitely be attending.

I asked the waiter to move me to a quieter table, a booth. My associate had gotten himself delayed at Heathrow. I would be conducting my meeting by phone. Yes, I will need privacy. For an hour I sat alone, pretending, playing at making a business call. Clarke, Mum, Dad, a girl I used to see occasionally, who may well have been Cate; none of them answered their damn phones. So, earpiece in, talking to no one in hushed tones, eating 1,500 calories worth of pizza, not enjoying the beer I had ordered to show how relaxed I can be, and trying my hardest to hold in the tear so desperately trying to free itself from my eye.

I look up to Cate's apartment window, hoping she would be looking down. Observing, as I am deep in thought, maybe giving an embarrassed wave as I catch her gazing at the person she desires. Right on schedule. Good old Cate. I do not wave back and walk in the opposite direction, against the wind and away from the memories.
The walk across Battersea Bridge seems an age. A young couple in layered knitwear who I presume are French walk towards me with clasped hands. They look very much in love. As they pass I give them a look that I hope will drain them of their happiness, a look that suggests I am likely to throw myself off the bridge into the murky Thames as soon as they are out of sight.

"Bonsoir," the man says.

I force a smile. The moon is half full, stars sparkle in the pitch-black sky. For those capable of happiness, this evening would be a delight.

I hail a black cab at the other end of the bridge. Climbing in, I recognise the same voyeur driver who drove us to Cate's last night. Perhaps not; the common taxi drivers always look identical to me.

The streets are busy. We pass Harvey Nichols. Smug old men and vacant young women pretend they have some common ground, probably on their way to some Russian-owned, over-priced, money-laundering restaurant for sashimi and cocktails. Hags draped in fur load their cars with Harrods bags while burka-clad women struggle into taxis with buggies and carriers, their overweight husbands catching their breath before attempting the step up into the car.

I wonder if there is anything for sale in Harrods I couldn't buy, anything in there that I might need to dip into my savings for. Probably not. What a wonderful feeling that should be.

The taxi meter accelerates past £14.

My phone bleeps twice. A grovelling apology from Theo and just "sorry, we can work this out xx" from Poppy?

No.

The first one's from my mum. What's the time in Spain? She is probably multitasking between large glasses of red and white.

Sorry I missed your calls and texts, darling, I hope you are okay, it will all be okay. Planning on coming to visit you, just looking at flights, exciting news about the company, your father has worked very hard for this, he does love you, we both love you, well I hope you're okay anyway see you soon Mum x

DELETE

Hey you, hope you are nearly home. I know how stressed out you are, I am here for you, whatever. Love you, say it back, Cate x

DELETE. DELETE. BYE BYE, CATE.

The meter is now at £19.60. Greedy bastard. No wonder he still pops out for the odd job. My tan can be misleading; I wonder if he thinks I am some kind of naive tourist who might not notice the excruciatingly long route he has taken. This wouldn't be happening if I lived in Mayfair. The Farringdon Road. There is nobody in sight. £26.80.

I bang on the glass, waving my brand new spanking debit card in all of its glory.

"Driver, can I pay by card?"

"Machine's broken, pal." He responds in the most automated of tones.
"Not my cab, pal, driving it for a mate while he's out in Spain. Nightmare. I'll pull up at this cash machine, pal." He reads his autocue.

My palms are particularly clammy; my mind is made up. The driver nudges his perfectly square head in the general direction of a grubby-looking boozer.

"Here'll do you, there's a cash machine right there, just mind that homeless, probably on the rob."

He releases the door lock. My Margielas touch the floor and I spring into life, rubber hitting pavement, oh, the thrill of the chase.

Looking behind me, the square-faced, old, older than he looked from behind, con man hasn't budged from his seat.

I take the second left turning up Coronet Street. As I pick up the pace the wind cools my face ache. Laughter appears unexpectedly upon me. I cackle, embracing a true moment of exhilaration.

I sprint past a group of teenagers on stolen push bikes. I laugh harder, my nostrils grabbing at the abundant air. A couple of cool-looking male models, scruffy beards, long hair, hang out on the corner. I speed past them and into Hoxton Square, stopping abruptly.

The cash machine and the wall Clarke punched. This seems a good place to rest. I struggle to get air into my lungs. I am out of breath. The strong, pungent stench of dried piss burns my throat. Having a sense of smell isn't all it's cracked up to be.

I open up my iPhone, desperately hoping that somehow I can undelete the texts from Mum and Cate. What did they say? There is something very warm about her, and that home on the river really is something.
It would not work. Not now, you're considerably better than that.
The adrenalin of the chase wears away. My smile disappears and is replaced by weightiness in my chest and tears. They feel so comforting and they cool the swelling on my cheek.

Sitting down, slumped, pins and needles, numbed, I pull the down-filled jacket I found at Cate's around me. It feels so familiar. I look up but cannot enjoy the peaceful-looking sky. I push back against the wall.

A taxi pulls in. I hope it's not him; I don't have the energy for another fight. Certainly looks familiar. I pull the coat up further around my face and push my head into my shell.

Perfume pierces the pissy air. Female voices. I cannot help but raise my head up to take a look.

Out step two attractive enough high-maintenance types, little to nothing on. Fashion, but not in a grubby way. Actually one, the prettier one, is not tall enough to model, glamour maybe. In the West End they would be an acceptable seven but in East London they are at least eights and right here, right now, they are perfect tens.

I look up and try my hardest to smile. Is there any chance that after a terrible few days I could snag myself a threeway? The fitter of the two, high-waisted denim shorts, slightly ripped tights showing off her tattooed thighs. Looks down and smiles back, not a flirtatious smile, more an understanding, pitying smile. She reaches out her hand and firmly pushes a pound coin into my palm.

"Fran, for God's sake, you know he'll only spend it on heroin," her increasingly less attractive friend remarks.

I gracefully accept and sink further into my wall.

Chapter 12

The days are slipping away.

£1,000 for a telescopic lens. I see them: Shoreditchers dressed up as Day of the Dead victims and children from the estate in their standard sportswear harassing hipsters for trick-or-treat money. I ignore the door buzzer, instead embracing the celebration by dropping notes, occasionally coins, from my window down to the dressed-up peasants.

From Cate's impressive terrace, I try my hardest to not watch the fireworks. I intend to switch off from the unnecessary bangs from the rockets and the unnecessary whoops from her. When I was a child we used to have the most fantastic display in the grounds. Dad would do a hog roast, Mum would serve up the accompanying chutney, accepting the praise for its delightful tang, a guilt-free face as the Fortnum and Mason jar lurked in the bin. The fireworks ended after the divorce; Dad just didn't have the bloody time.

My focus comes back. I visit the tanning salon three times, train at the gym six. Ignore twenty calls, even more texts from Mum, none from my dad and several from that imbecile Clarke. I purchase a Louis Vuitton wallet, fuck Cate more times than I care to remember, and with minimal foreplay. She is obsessed by me, often crying when I have to leave for the gym.

My muscles look pumped, inflated by the 100mg of Stanozolol I am taking and intensified by the richness of my tan. I have replaced Clarke with Dave. He's a good guy; dealing drugs is a means to an end, he's at university studying something to do with music, I expect, I wasn't really listening. We intend to start weight training together in the New Year.

I go back to the West End to purchase a variety of surveillance and spy equipment to go with the telescopic lens. Not very much change from £5,000, but everything I could ever need. The sales associate asks whether I was involved in personal security. I take this as a compliment.

Decorations everywhere, those unavoidable yellow shopping bags, reminders of that moment. I see them, the families shopping for the festive season, wearing the protective cloak of happiness in public. Oh, the smiling faces, how they hide the truth, the deceit, the affairs, the downright misery.

I have been avoiding black cabs, just to be on the safe side. It also appears that Danbrook no longer have an Addison Lee account. I point-blank refuse to pay for their services with my own money and the thoughts of me in an Uber, sober, just doesn't feel right. So I find myself sitting there, on yet another bus, with telescopic lenses, bugging devices and a Teflon vest that I am considering putting on immediately, just to be on the safe side. I don't see him, the kid. I want to help, maybe buy him a house, set up a trust fund, get him away from the dysfunctional parents.

The texts from my mum ranged from the uninterested: *hope you're feeling better*, to the intrusive: *what's wrong, please call me*.

Nothing from Dad since we parted ways.

Clarke's texts are near-identical every time: *call me, bud, maybe I got it wrong, sorry mate x; Mate, ring me back, I fucked up, come on, bud, we are meant to be mates,* etc. I accidentally delete a voicemail message.

I am studying Facebook and perusing books by business leaders, avoiding meaningful conversation with Cate and pushing my body to its physical limits. I learn how to utilise several bugging devices and buy a ten-year-old BMW 1 series from a man who looked like he was desperate for the cash and could provide very little paperwork. The rest of my time is dedicated to following Poppy, Clarke and Theo's daily movements.

The due diligence is paying dividends. I learn Theo spends Monday evenings and Saturday mornings at Taekwondo. On a Thursday evening he leaves the house with his Taekwondo bag but heads to a house in Clapham. He does not cycle everywhere; more often than not he drives a grey Audi Estate, which most Sundays he bizarrely likes to valet himself. He flirts with nearly every woman he comes in contact with, none of whom seem to live in Clapham. I need to do more of a deep dive, but I do not see any additional threat to my planned hostile takeover of his fiancée.

Clarke is an issue. He does not seem to live at his mum and dad's house in Hertfordshire anymore. After week one it was very clear that he spends a lot of time at what looks like a two-bedroom ex-council flat behind Kensington High Street. He eats far too many Nando's, double chicken pitta, and every time he has a mouthful he looks at his phone. He glances at himself in every shop window he passes. He too seems to be very focused on increasing muscle mass. His relocation and dedication to an even better body concern me. I will need to strategise.

Poppy walks to a Bikram yoga class in Kensington every other evening. Some evenings after her clammy stretch she heads up to Clarke's ex-bloody council two-bedroom flat. Not one of the pieces of equipment I bought from Samir at Spymaster gives me the angle I need to see what they are up to. I know, though. I would be amazed if Theo can't smell the peri-peri sauce on her inner thighs. She makes sure to leave Clarke's grubby den at 9 and jumps in a taxi back home. Each time she leaves I see confusion on her face and I can't help but forgive her indiscretions.

Her working day seems to involve meeting my father at 8am for breakfast at one of his many haunts in town. He always has the poached eggs, we always used to have the poached eggs, appearing to make light conversation as he carelessly empties a pot of pepper onto his dish. She only ever has a black coffee and a croissant that she delightfully dips in, never finishing more than half. On most occasions they leave together to a meeting or to the Danbrook hellhole. Whenever they part he kisses her on the cheek and a smile radiates across her face.

If truth be known, I need an assistant. This surveillance op is gruelling. The guy behind the bar, maybe, in that hotel with the whisky sours. He seemed focused and conscientious. I must have his number somewhere.

So, Cate asks me questions and I tell her lies. I wave blank papers disguised as business plans in her face and attempt to explain the complexities of fasted cardio in the morning and German volume training early evening. I throw her off the scent with cat-related questions that she can never seem to answer.

It's the evening. All I know is that the Christmas lights have been switched on at Oxford Circus. The West End is even busier with festive shoppers. Children counting down the days until their presents arrive.

I sat there on Santa's knee in Harrods, going through the motions, ticking the boxes. Yes, of course I have been a good boy, Santa. What do I want this year? Really? Come on, Santa, my Mum and Dad already know what I want and they are going to get it for me, so shall we stop wasting each other's time?

My strategising is disturbed by Cate's rambling and most likely irrelevant news. A waiter takes away the refined carbohydrates I have left on my plate.

"Are you listening, Ollie? The theatre tomorrow will need to be cancelled. Theo wants to get to Hamburg a day early to prepare for Monday's conference."

"What conference? What theatre? What are you talking about? You might need to start again, as I wasn't paying the slightest bit of attention."

I usher the waiter back over.

"I cannot see it on the menu, but I am going to need a small bowl of cottage cheese and a handful of walnuts for dessert. How can we make this happen?" I enquire keenly, fully aware of the need to fuel my muscles before bed.

Apparently we discussed Hamburg several times. I mentioned my distaste for German cuisine and my continued interest in German volume training. I pretend to look at my diary, shaking my head and frowning.

"I have nothing pencilled in, Cate. Perhaps you discussed it with one of your other occasional lovers."

The change in Cate's normally irrelevant plans are noteworthy, as she will be away for a good few days with Theo. It seems that the conference doesn't require Clarke's attendance, or my father's, and therefore Poppy will also be staying firmly on British soil.
There is a curious tingling in my groin that can only be described as the very early stages of an erection. Watching Cate greedily scoff Eton Mess soon rids me of my growing appendage.

I do not tip. I finish the Quest bar I must have brought with me and neatly fold the foil packet, leaving it in place of the fifty-pound note the waiter will have been expecting.

I put sunglasses on as we get into the taxi, just to avoid the driver potentially recognising me. The irritating hum is getting louder. A hand waves across my face. I have no choice but to pay attention.

"Baby, can I still not mention that we are a couple? Just to Theo or the girls in the office? It has been a couple of months now. We are in a happy place and I just want everyone to know."

Cate leans up to me, kissing my neck and rubbing where my cock would be if it wasn't freezing in this taxi.

"No, definitely not. Mentioning it will start rumours, confusion, get back to people, the wrong people, it could be dangerous, spoil it. What we have is so much more important than that." I top my rambling off with a spectacular lie.

"So it's not about Poppy."

"Poppy from the office? No, it is not. Fuck her, she had her chance, not at all, of course not. Poppy – that ship has sailed for her."

I push Cate's head into my shoulder. Kiss her temple, close my eyes and desperately try not to think about Poppy.

Chapter 13

I excitedly usher Cate out with her overnight bag. I kiss her on the lips, give her a playful tap on the backside and close the front door.

Immediately I skip to the window, peering through the blinds. She stands alone, in the pitch black of dark, slightly illuminated by a flickering street lamp on the other side of the road. Her Samsung lights up and an Addison Lee pulls in. Theo and the driver get out and awkwardly both try to take her not-particularly-heavy overnight bag and place it in the boot. Theo kisses her on the cheek. I swear his hand lingers.

At times I have been very dishonest with Cate. I have told her I could see us settling down; I could see us buying a place in the country and renting out the Battersea pad, renting out my apartment to a gallery owner or a successful musician. Telling the world we were madly in love and travelling to all of those places we never visited after uni. Watching the sunset. She is wearing my Ralph Lauren chambray shirt over her bikini just to take away the evening chill. Together we make a small fire on the beach, make new friends, dance under the moon, drink too much and run naked into the sea; two young lovers carefree and fearless. Of course, this is all very much theoretical, as I do not own a single piece of Ralph Lauren and due to illness could not complete university.

The rest of this fantasy is going to play out; unfortunately for Cate it is not with her.

The roads are empty. A few street sweepers, a couple jogging together, a semi-attractive foreigner who I don't bother to slow down for as she crosses the road, a pensioner trying to entice an uninterested dog to walk.

I make it to Theo and Poppy's soon-to-be-broken home in thirteen minutes. This is a record. I park up. A posse of labourers are sitting on the steps of a very impressive property. They only remove the cigarettes from their mouths to swig down their energy drinks. I look for the boy on the bus's father, not sure of what I want to say. There is no telling; they all look the same. I make sure to lock the car and then move away.

The butterflies in my stomach. Surely they would be more adventurous than before; maybe venture out for breakfast, lunch. I can get a few snaps, post them to Theo, to my dad, warn Clarke the game is up, that he should quit before he is sacked.

I re-read my notes; Clarke leaves the business, possibly punched in the face on his leaving do by Theo, cannot afford repayments on his flat, asks for my help, I say no, moves back to his parents, which ends up putting a lot of strain on the family unit, moves to Dubai to work with his brother, Middle Eastern sun tinges his naturally bright white skin, after a period of time I call him and explain that it was me who caught him out. A valuable life lesson is learnt.

Poppy and Theo split up, Poppy looks for a shoulder to cry on, leading to initial friendship, realises her feelings for me leading to more, an official couple by Christmas. Theo collapses into a state of depression, poor results at work lead to sacking, he gets his act together by mid-February but finds himself much busier at his new, not as highly paid, job and has to let down the special-needs Taekwondo kids. Goals are met.

It's the New Year and Poppy and I are dancing under the moon, drunk and just about to fuck in the crystal-clear sea. Destiny is fulfilled.

I watch the sun rise. Three children, all exact replicas of each other, same skin, same hair and same dark green uniforms, are ushered into the back of a town car. No energy drinks to wake them up. Their motivation for the day comes from the expectations of their parents, on a Saturday, for Christ's sake. These kids are fucked.

I count thirteen women in yoga leggings. Four of them do not look as if they do yoga. Not long after 8am, the fourteenth woman leaves her house. Poppy's hair is tied back into a ponytail. From the distance it looks like she has a new pair of sunglasses on, most likely Céline.
She is wearing a pair of washed black jeans, snug, and tucked into knee-high boots. Boots from autumn/winter Jimmy Choo. I was amazed that Theo had the taste to buy such timeless footwear. A soft draped leather jacket in the style of Rick Owens but possibly Zara, and a McQueen scarf to complete the look. Her classic Hermès bag, again a great timeless piece, isn't vast enough to conceal a gym kit, but the Vuitton overnight bag is. Game on.

I am caught off guard. She walks towards me – a first, a new route.
As I lean down pretending to fiddle with the glove box I get a twinge in my trousers. This chance encounter could be our moment.

A crudely folded wrap peers at me from inside the glove box, nestled behind binoculars. I ignore it, daring not to move in case she sees me. I attempt to inhale her as she passes by.

Every stealth move I have read up on comes into play as I get out of the passenger side of the car and cross the road, ducking behind a glimmering Range Rover Vogue, watching her wait on the corner.

Women number fifteen and sixteen pass; I casually pretend to be looking at the GPS on my phone, aware that in civilians' eyes I might look slightly psychotic. I am not sure my all-black outfit was necessary. The only contrast is the red and green signature stripe on my beanie hat. Do I look suspicious? Surely they can spot that a man with my good looks couldn't possibly be a threat.

My phone rings. Shit, why isn't it on silent? Dave at 7.45am. What sort of dealer is awake so early? I drop the call.

A GT Continental slows down and pulls into the bus stop. A half honk of the horn and Poppy looks up and runs over. By my quick calculations, Clarke couldn't afford to run the flat in Kensington, live his lifestyle and buy a £200k car. He must have hired it for the day.

I get back to my disappointing BMW unnoticed. I manage to do a U-turn in the road just as the white Bentley passes. I do not spot Clarke's gelled mess of ginger hair but I do notice the beautiful red leather interior and the personalised plates.

DANB10.

It looks like my father has bought himself a new ride.

They head out of London onto the M40. I am damn good at this tailing business. Cate is calling and messaging my phone. Their flight was delayed. Theo is now in a foul mood, considering rescheduling the trip.

My semi-erection is off-putting. Pushing my foot down I lean to close the glove box. The thought of my father driving her somewhere on a Saturday for no good reason was causing a retching uncertainty.

Clarke is calling me. I'm doing eighty. To add to the excitement I decide to finally take his call.

"Clarke, you calculating ginger bastard, when will you get the message?" I pull into the slow lane, dropping to sixty. Today is not the day I die.

"Listen, Oliver, Ollie, mate, no more lies, I really fucked up. She got to me. She got in my head. I let you down. I am not a good friend."

"A ginger bastard." I add the adjective and move into the middle lane, realising I am losing ground.

"Ok, buddy, strawberry blonde, mate, but yes, if you say so. Please can we just meet? I will tell you everything. Tonight? Tomorrow?" Clarke has desperation in his voice. He is probably looking in the mirror at his useless ginger mop.

"I'll call you later. Yeah, I will meet you, let's say at the Nando's next door to your secret den of deceit. I gotta go." I chuck the phone onto the passenger seat and put my foot down, undertaking a depressed-looking hag and her husband puffing away on cigarettes in their Korean car.

As I pass by I give them two fingers. I am momentarily hysterical.
He is indicating. I have no choice but to slow down. I catch a breath.
Think logically, a work event at the weekend, but where?

The Crazy Bear? In the daytime? Don't be stupid, Oliver. Cliveden House? No, he is taking the turning towards Slough. I am fairly sure there is nothing of interest in Slough, although I have never been.
Stoke Park? It must be.

We definitely held a golf day there a couple of years back. I did not attend. Ended up in Fabric at 6am; didn't get the invite, no signal in that place, so I left the hitting a ball with a stick to the others. I had heart palpitations for the next three days. I am fairly sure it would be men only and Theo is at the airport and Clarke is most likely on his way to the gym – shoulders on a Saturday. It's 2017, Oliver, perhaps the ladies are welcome now.

I am three cars behind as we pass Farnham Park. The heavens open, rain hurtles down and I pray it is a golf day. He turns into Stoke Park. I am two cars behind. Both Range Rovers, slightly better models than my one I vaguely recall. He cannot see me. I stick tight to the brand spanking new Vogue's back bumper as we wind up the road. Red Ferraris, a pair of Bentleys and double digits of Mercedes. I park up in the furthest corner and ease myself around the well-managed hedges to secure a vantage point. I take off my beanie hat, wipe my brow and enjoy the cooling splatter of rain.

There is movement from the car. I crouch. The downpour provides a little extra cover. He goes to the boot, fending off rain with a copy of the *Financial Times* weekend supplement. He pulls out a huge golf umbrella – okay, that makes sense – and then helps Poppy out of the passenger seat.

So this is the moment she holds the umbrella and he gets a set of clubs from his boot. Poppy has to use two hands on the brolly as the wind veers left to right. He pulls out what look like matching Louis Vuitton golf bags. Tasteful. No, wait: they are overnight bags. Two overnight bags. The boot slams. I manage to edge forward slightly. I can only be ten metres away. She is smiling that smile, up on tiptoes, and playfully kisses his forehead.

"You're his subordinate. A kiss on the forehead isn't bloody appropriate," I say at her.

I look round the car park for any indication of a weekend conference or for the recognisable faces of Danbrook clients that Dad might be wining and dining.

I bring my finger to my lips and usher away a nosy, elderly couple who come a little too close. Edging forward, I see the finer details of my father's face. He seems to be feigning forgetfulness. He opens the driver's door and leans behind the chair, handing Poppy a large glossy pastel pink shopping bag.

The black typeface so clear.

Agent Fucking Provocateur.

Chapter 14

Normally when I am sick, retching is followed by alcohol or the remains of an undigested cheat meal. Today there is nothing but pain in my neck. That thing that dangles down the back of your throat, I feel like forcing it up and out. My knees are wet and the gravel is causing a sharp, necessary pain. I dream of his heart attack. I stare with intent, hoping it will happen before they hit the lobby.

I drag the stone down one side of the car, reaching the front head lamp.

"Oi, bloody oi! What the hell are you doing!"

I see them coming towards me. They have to be in their eighties; a couple of old codgers heading my way, one waving a golf club. I calmly back off. They have no realistic chance of reaching me before I reach the car. I close the glove box, start the engine and pull away. Through the rain I see the same old death-dodger pointing his golf club in my direction. He points as he talks to a younger, fitter couple of guys. I put my foot down and cut across the grass, narrowly avoiding them.

He ruined my life at twelve when he screwed Poppy's mother. At twenty-six he has ruined it again by fucking her daughter.

The rain is lashing down. I want to be driving fast, pounding music, tears of rage streaming down my face. The traffic is not moving. My tears are the pathetic kind, sobbing, quivering lip, a migraine so painful that after I close the glove box I have to turn off the radio.

The couple in the middle lane are smoking. I am sure it is them; their car looks Korean. They are laughing.

Time has passed, hours rather than days. I park the car half up on the curb and buzz the intercom just hoping Cate is there. I pause before opening the door. She is no doubt having a great time in Germany, treating Theo to one of her speciality vice-like-grip handjobs.

Just one solitary text from Clarke:

Don't forget to bell me, bro.

"First thing tomorrow, bro, first thing tomorrow," I think out loud.

The water from the shower beats down on me. I alternate between scalding hot water and freezing cold. Tears, mostly of disappointment, get caught up in the stream of water pouring off my face.

The hot stings; the cold helps provide some clarity. Of course James Danbrook wanted me out of the company; of course it had absolutely nothing to do with my business acumen or apparent indiscretions. The sneaky, lying old bastard pushed me out for the sole reason of keeping me away from Poppy. In the most underhand way possible he thought he had eradicated the competition.

You silly old fool.

I embrace the scalding hot water. It burns my skin as I accept full responsibility for failing to notice the old man

146

in all of this. I accept that this was never meant to be easy. Life is a challenge, according to most of my books, and a challenge is only an obstacle if you bow to it, I knowingly recall.

I notice the sofa is somewhat empty without Cate next to me. I feel a sense of gratitude as the cat appears from behind and curls up on my lap. Relaxed as it purrs and I gently stroke him head to tail. I come up with a viable plan of action and then dismiss it. I come up with a couple of less conventional ideas that I decide to keep on the back burner.

The pain is sudden; his claws dig into my forearm. I let out a sharp scream. It drops onto the floor and leaps up onto the kitchen side.

There are markings, three distinct, bloody scratches two inches long. I walk towards him. There is no fear on his face.

"You deserved that, loser," it snarls, as it cleans the offending paw.

I swing at him but miss.

"Do not show weakness, always be prepared and even in moments of unadulterated pleasure remember pain is sure to follow," he hisses as I feel a sharp claw-like pain tear at my skin just above the pulse.

He scarpers into the bathroom. I follow. He is hiding, maybe injured.
I drop the bread knife.

"That's enough for today," I scream and wash my arms under that icy-cold shower.

The phone beeps, a message. It rings. I let it. It rings again but cuts off before I can reach.

Hi handsome, sorry I haven't been in contact all day, we landed, went to lunch, had a meeting with Hoffman associates, on a f@ckin Saturday. I love you. Just heading out for a late dinner. Thai. Call you when I get back to hotel xx

I opt not to reply.

One of the wounds on my arm is still bleeding and open, but it is not deep. I rinse it off and put on a long-sleeve top. Out of sight, out of mind.

The cat sits next to me on the sofa. We both seem a little surprised and embarrassed. I answer the ringing phone.

"Oliver, Ollie darling, finally you have answered. I must have called one hundred times. Anyway, it doesn't matter, it doesn't matter, I am speaking to you now. Dad had said that apparently you hadn't been feeling yourself again, ignoring his calls. How are you doing? Please talk to me?"

How am I doing?

Well, Mum, I was doing okay. Everything was going swimmingly. My tennis was coming along nicely. Then one day Dad inserted his penis into a low-income carbon copy of you and that pretty much put an end to the good fucking times. My cat died, in pretty horrendous circumstances if I remember correctly. You died, Mum; well, you may well have drowned in your own self-pity

148

and a vat of Cabernet and a little piece of me snuffed it. Then just about the time that I start to see a smattering of light, less therapy and less medication, she strolls into the office. Things have spiralled slightly out of control since then, Mum, but here's the thing: I was dealing with it, I really was. Today has been a slight backwards step on the path to normality, mind you. He's bloody done it again, putting that cancerous cock of his back where it doesn't belong.

"Everything is okay, Mum. I have a new girlfriend; we have pretty much moved in together. I've bought a new car, looking at a few business opportunities. We even have a cat. Have you spoken to Dad recently?" I say confidently.

"Yes, Ollie, I just told you, I have spoken to your father, earlier today in fact. He was concerned. However, it sounds like you have everything sorted. Is that why you have not been attending therapy?
Linda called me, six weeks in a row she said, no calls, no replies to emails; she was worried, that's all. I know client confidentiality and all that nonsense but she only wants the best for you. Mind you, they called your dad also to see if you were okay and he didn't have the decency to reply either. So how can I be surprised? Like father, like son. I'm coming over next Friday, just for a week, going to stay at the Mandarin, the suite. I'm going to bring Charlie."

I stop aggressively picking at the red raw hangnail on my index finger. For one moment, she has my attention. Then I realise she means the kid, her kid with another man. I yank off a piece of skin at least half a centimetre long.

"It will be good for you two to meet. Don't worry, though, Seb, well, he will be staying out in Spain. We would love to meet your new girlfriend. Maybe we can go for afternoon tea. What did you say her name was?"

Mum had spewed out a lot of information and I am not prepared for the question.

"Pops. I have got together with Poppy, Mum. I guess this is why I didn't call. Wasn't sure how you would cope with it all. I can't wait to meet Charlie. How old is he now, four? Five, maybe?" My tone is remarkably even considering the enormity of the lie.

"Nine. Charlie is nine and you know she is a girl, a beautiful little girl and so was Poppy. Oliver, I am friends with her on Facebook; you would know this if you had accepted my invite. She is happily engaged to that lovely boy at Danbrook, Theo something. I have nothing against Poppy, with everything she has been through.
If your father has done one good deed in his life it is helping her get back on track. So please, enough – unless you meant another Poppy, perhaps?

"Anyway, I will come straight to the apartment next Friday. We can go for dinner somewhere nice. I will get something booked, in Mayfair, maybe.

"You know, Oliver, you can always come back to Spain with me. They say sunshine is the best medicine. In addition there are some great specialists and medication is much easier to come by; fewer rules and regulations," she says hopefully.

Her voice falters. She is struggling to hold it together.

150

"Mum, I meant a different Poppy. She's a model. I am going to sell the apartment, no doubt will double my money, a great piece of business, and I am going to move out to the countryside, Berkshire possibly. It is great for Heathrow. She flies to New York a lot." I feel drained and sound unconvincing.

"Don't be silly, sweetie, the apartment's in my name. Perhaps moving to the countryside would be good for you, though. Let's discuss this all next week. Do you want to talk about anything else? I am always here for you, if it's all too much. You know we love you, Ollie." Mum has tears streaming down her face. I can feel it; her voice is soft and concerned.

"See you next week, Mum. I love you too. I will invite Poppy for dinner also."

I do not want to put the phone down.

"Okay, sweetie, I will see you soon then. I will text the flight details. Bye, son." She sounds tired. A ten-minute conversation that has zapped the life out of her.

I have to get out of here.

Chapter 15

I grab the cat under my arm. He wriggles away, but I hold on as he tries to slither from my grip.

I place Rocky – no, not Rocky, on the passenger seat. He stays put.

I close the glove box and take a moment. The scenery, it is always the same. Well-heeled gents helping blank-faced ladies into taxis, the taxi drivers spewing their stories of discontent. Grubby pubs full of twenty-somethings forcing smiles as they pretend to enjoy the company of others, they spill into the road, the same old doorman trying to usher them into the designated area. The homeless surrounded by sandwiches and mineral water kindly gifted to them when all they really wanted was a couple of quid towards some scag. They all want it to be their last winter; you see they have no goals, no destiny to fulfill.

I carry the cat, using his fur to warm my hands. He wriggles out of my arms, awkwardly hitting the floor, but doesn't run away. He sits perfectly still next to my feet. I bash the numbers again on the graffiti-stained keypad. It's dark outside the apartment. Surely I can remember the entry code. 0404, 0440, fucking hell.

A group of young girls walk towards me. I glance down. By pure chance I have put together a well-co-ordinated outfit. I smile. The cat meows, scratching at my leg in the exact place I had an itch.

The ringing phone. Dave. What does he want? I do not answer. It continues to ring twice as loud.

I bang at the keypad. His cheap cologne gets my attention. He is not alone. I have to crane my neck to make out the face of what surely must be a colleague.

"Dave."

"Ollie, that debt of yours is starting to get out of hand. Don't take the piss, mate. Shall we take a look in that safe of yours?" Dave asks in a rhetorical manner.

The cat weaves between us and starts entwining between all six of our legs.

"Stop," I hiss.

"There is nothing to fear here," I think to myself.

I see Dave on a regular basis. We chat about the gym, my appreciation for hip-hop, and then normally he would hand over enough cocaine to see me get a good couple of years in prison. He would then get into a rental car of some description and drive off.

But I do feel nervous. It could be the cat; it could be his block-headed colleague, with his imposing aftershave and almost comical-sized fists.

"I'm a bit busy at the moment." I look at the spot on my wrist where an expensive watch should be.

"I'm working on a project of sorts. Come over in the morning, I'll sort it all out then. How much was it again?" I say, genuinely without any idea what is owed.

Dave and his colleague move out of the way as a pretty but studious-looking girl buzzes herself into the flats. She smiles at me and seems to say hello. I am distracted watching Rocky run up the stairs in front of her.

"£2,000 tomorrow or the debt goes up," he says in a confusingly threatening manner.

I do not point out that the debt could go up a hundredfold and it would still be pocket change to a man like me. There seems to be less and less room between myself, Dave's accomplice and the front door that I am propping open with one foot.

"You need any more? Surely a party boy like you has gone through the last lot." Dave is now smiling as he says this, hand on my shoulder.

"Yeah, sure, I think it's all gone, or maybe not. It's not really my thing anymore, Dave; I just get it in for the guests at my house parties most weekends. You really should come by."

I have no idea where the rest of that coke is or how much is left. Maybe Cate took it, or the cleaner, or maybe I did have a party at some point.

"Did I mention, Dave, that I am going to need something else from you? A new project I am working on. Cool if I call you later?" I say, unsure of exactly what it is I am going to need Dave to contribute.

154

"No problem. Just don't forget that money, though, time to pay up," Dave says, still smiling, still with his arm on my shoulder.

The controlled squeeze his thick hand is giving my trapezius is actually releasing some tension. I would not mind if he continued, maybe worked the other shoulder slightly. I will not ask; it doesn't seem appropriate.

At some point, Dave stops kneading me. He slaps my back and then we say our goodbyes with a variation on the handshake that I never seem to get correct.

I then limply grab the fingers of his accomplice and loosely shake at his mitt, maintaining zero eye contact.

I half jog up the stairs after Rocky.

Flat Six. Top floor. The penthouse.

The place smells remarkably fresh. The cat seems to have beaten me in and is already relaxed on the sofa. On the table there are several letters stacked up, a pile of magazines and a note.

Hi Oliver, sorry to write but you owe me for 16 days' cleaning. Please could you leave money or tell me if not need. I did call you many times. Sorry to disturb. Katia.

The bathroom is spotless, magazines stacked neatly next to the toilet in chronological order. Good girl, or maybe I did this. I pick up a copy of *Flex* and sit on the bath edge. An article outlining the benefits of red meat confuses me; it

155

seems to be a contradiction to a similar feature in last month's issue of *Muscle and Fitness* magazine.

Continuing to read, I wander into my bedroom. The full-length mirror has been polished; it is sparkling. Opening up the main wardrobe I see pressed shirts and jackets, neatly organised shoes, a mini trampoline unused and a shiny baseball bat as of yet unused.

I suddenly have an overwhelming urge to pay Katia, maybe leave her a little extra or wait in for her next visit. A bottle of red, something vintage that she certainly won't have tasted before, soft lighting, maybe see if we can come to a different kind of arrangement. Take her away from a life of clearing up the cereal bowls of wealthy playboys. Probably best I check whether we are aesthetically suited first.

Typing Katia into Facebook brings up more results than I expected. I focus on the two options that catch my eye.

The first Katia's profile picture is set in some destitute Eastern European hellhole. She has sharp features, razor-like cheekbones, no doubt currently being trafficked through Europe as we speak on her way to London to earn £100 a night blowing Stella-fuelled Forex traders. She is wearing tiny hot pants and a sparkly ecru vest that looks like it belongs to a teenage girl. After I see pictures of her smiling on a yacht I presume it is not her.

The other Katia, on closer inspection, may actually be a teenage girl. So I stop my investigation and place a neat pile of twenty-pound notes on the table.

The fridge is completely empty. I pour a glass of tap water and then decide against it, tipping it away and watching it gurgle into the plughole and out of sight.

I collapse into the sofa. I could gurgle into the plughole and out of sight. I am dragged out of my defeatist state by the sound of claw against expensive fabric. Rocky, the cat, whatever his name is, has his paw down the side of the sofa, scratching and creating unnecessary wear and tear.

I grab him under the stomach and gently chuck him onto the floor rug, careful not to catch his claws in the expensive yarn. I push my fingers against the inside of the sofa arm, trying to eradicate any pulls in the designer fabric. I shove my fingers further down. It somehow seems to make the pulls worsen. I seem more frantic as I delve deeper, smoothing away at the catches. I touch something unexpected, cold, textured.

I wedge my hand further down, grab at an object. My fingertips tickle against mottled leather and I sit straight back up. My wallet looks at me, surprised to have been found. I look back confused, disappointed, relieved.

Opening it up I find £190, a debit card, a platinum American Express, a worn-looking picture of me with Mum and Dad, a gym membership card and, of course, the remains of a gram.

I waste some time contemplating whether the thieving whore actually snuck back in and returned my wallet after realising who I was.
I then attempt to masturbate using a sample of fragranced aftershave lotion that, although it moistens, also severely stings.

Books on strategic planning, self-help, motivation, influencing people, getting important things done, are spread across the floor. I start to read.

Chapter 16

There does not seem to be any sunrise.

My mouth feels so dry. I stick on sweatpants, trainers and a musky-smelling hooded top. I change twice. "Presentation is the first rule of successful business meeting."

I peer into the living room. The cat is nowhere to be seen, the scratches on my arms healing.

The rain feels light, refreshing. I breathe in and capture more air in my lungs than normal. I have a positive mood about me. I was wrong about the wallet. Perhaps I could be wrong about the Agent Provocateur bag.

"A good breakfast is the fuel you need for a busy day," I think or maybe even say as I pass a heavily tattooed female holding a long skateboard.

A grubby lettings agency is the only shop separating the two cafés.
One is full of the elderly, infirm and poverty-stricken. Drinking tea from dirty-looking mugs, scooping beans from their plates using what I can only presume is fried bread while simultaneously scanning the pages of the national rag. Who gives a fuck how many immigrants come to the UK. Seriously, if 100,000 Katias want to come and clean up my mess, no questions asked, then who am I to argue. The gut-buster breakfast catches my eye. It is awkwardly scrawled in marker pen on neon yellow cardboard that has been cut with blunt scissors into a star-

like shape. The sellotape is barely holding it up, stained by grease and fags.

Two doors down is a much more inviting space.

Eggs Benedict
Salmon & scrambled tofu
Soaked chia with coconut yoghurt
Acai bowls
Avo on toast

The menu is in a bold yet cosy font on a framed sign, obvious but not obstructing the windows. Inside, men with good hair in New Balance trainers and casual shirts relax on worn-in leather sofas reading *The Independent* while chatting and smiling to pasty-skinned English roses scooping up foam from their coffee and occasionally nibbling at what looks like avocado on toast.

They are laughing and smiling back, young creatives in love. At some point the love will end, the novelty will wear off, she will marry a hedge fund manager and he will settle down with his school sweetheart back in Kent or wherever he appeared from.

I remove my hands from the glass and step back.

Younger girls, in their twenties, are up on barstools facing the window. They look away and then down at their iPhones. Most sip on a green juice; some have black coffee. All with different styles, all impeccably dressed. This is the place for me; I just need to change my outfit.

I march towards the keypad, 7698. Straight through the doors, up the stairs. I chuck on a mid-wash pair of jeans, tapered but not skinny. A lace-up boot, slim-fit crew-neck tee and a 100 per cent cashmere hoody. It does not look particularly expensive but it was. I spend five minutes putting on and taking off an unworn, oversized brimmed hat before deciding against it. I quickly check the flat for the cat – no sign – and then head back to the café.

I turn both phones on, not really sure of the point of me carrying two phones. It hardly ever rang when I worked at Danbrook and doesn't even seem to be connected now.

My personal phone has several texts.

What are you up too? Xx Call me, we have very little on this morning. I cannot wait to get home to you.

Don't forget to call me, mate, I'm free to meet anytime.

I'll need my money today, will be at yours for 10.30.

I text Dave back. *Meet me at the café. Can you make it 11.30?*

I sit down at a corner table; perfect view of the whole place. I made a good call on the change of clothes. A fruit salad, two poached eggs on toast and a bitter-tasting black coffee.

I am desperate for one of the girls to notice my version of the hipster look, then notice our same choice of beverage; it is an ice breaker. It takes me a good ten minutes to spot that the two of them have left and they have been replaced by almost identical clones. They drink calorie-laden coffees and are sharing a pain au chocolat. I down the Americano and order a latte.

As soon as I press the last digit it feels like Clarke answers the phone.

Within thirty minutes he is sitting opposite me in the café. He orders fruit salad, poached eggs on brown toast and an Americano on my recommendation.

I have a large berry juice. I have spent the previous twenty minutes flirting with the Eastern European waitress using only eye contact. She has vividly pink hair and a nose stud. I want to ask her if she knows Katia. Maybe the three of us could hang out, "You know, like you Eastern Europeans hang out on Pornhub."

Clarke wipes egg from his chin and goes to speak. "Ollie, man, about that night." Clarke has dilated pupils, his brain whirring, trying to make sure the correct words come out.

No words come out.

I remain silent. "You learn more from listening than you do from talking," I recall.

Clarke spends an uncomfortable amount of time looking down at his food. He is toying with the poached egg on his plate. Then he looks up with confidence, like he has finally nailed the tricky opener to this life-changing sales pitch and he starts to talk.

I nod enthusiastically.

An hour or so passes. The same clientele come through the café doors ordering wraps, juices, salad boxes. Without breaking eye contact, I scribble on the inside of my palm: *must open a hip café, several hip cafés.*

"So that's how I came to have the flat in Kensington, Ol. Mum and Dad got it as an investment property. I have been round there cleaning it up after work. Hasn't even got a cooker in at the moment. I have been eating sodding Nando's most night. Not sure why I didn't tell you, mate. You've just been a bit off recently. Didn't think it was that interesting." Clarke seems to be more certain of himself with every word.

I am sure there are holes in his story but I can't quite think of them.
I recall to "stay in the present moment", focus, must not drift off in thought.

"So what happened at my leaving drinks, Clarke? Why the fuck were you hiding outside when Theo decided to punch me in the face?" I say this knowing the answer. Does Clarke know I know the answer?

"I let you down, mate, should have stuck up for you. Theo bumped into me on Kensington High Street. He was in a right mood, almost barged me over. I had been at the flat all morning painting. Had nothing else on so offered to take him for a quick pint. Next thing you know he's spouting off about Poppy, fuming, how could she do it with this spoilt little weasel, this loser living off his daddy's money. I put two and two together and realised he was talking about you, mate. You know who told him, mate – it was Cate from the office. She's always had a thing for you and always despised Pops. Guess it was just jealousy." Clarke is animated just like Cate was. He seems to be enjoying this.

His nonsense spills through me. Aside from the words "spoilt little weasel" and "loser", they are Clarke's creation. It is now clear to me what I want to discuss with Dave.

"Excuse me, Katia, what's the time? I have an 11.30 to prepare for," I ask the pink-haired waitress.

"10.32," she says in her sultry tone, pointing at the screens on my illuminated iPhones.

"So I just told him I had no idea but that you did have a bit of a crush on her. That night, the night he hit you, I didn't think he was going to knock you out, just thought he wanted to discuss things, maybe blow off some steam. I didn't want to be in the middle. It's hard, Ollie; you're a mate and he's my boss. What was I meant to do?" Clarke is wearing a smile of satisfaction. He believes his story ticks all of the boxes.

"He didn't knock me out, Clarke." I say this as if I completely accept the rest of his monologue.

My brain is ticking. His story could be true. Cate could be lying.
Hang on a damn second; I know about him losing his phone, that is a fact. I also know that Poppy has been visiting him at this "investment property".

I cannot be certain of anything.

"Okay, Clarke, let's just forget about it. It's my fault for messing around with someone's fiancée." I say this in a nonchalant manner. My face says forgiveness in an easy come, easy go kind of way.

"Just one more thing. Has Theo, Poppy or any of the other guys been round to the new flat?" I slant my eyes and it feels like my ears literally perk up.

"No, mate – not said a word to anyone." Clarke's answer concludes my investigation.

We sit for a few minutes more, talking about meeting up for a few drinks, getting involved in a heavy night out for old times' sake, going to the gym, going halves on some pharmaceutical growth hormone that all of the top UFC fighters are apparently using. I indicate to the girl who works there, or a dead ringer for her, that I will be back shortly to pay the bill, then we leave the café together and head our separate ways.

I excitedly run into the flat, eye-sweep all surfaces on the lookout for the cat, but he is nowhere to be seen. I grab a wad of cash from the safe that I have not been able to lock since forgetting the passcode. I change back into sweatpants and a hoody, putting on the crochet beanie and taking it off again. It is not occasion-appropriate.

As I arrive back to the café so does Dave. He does not want a latte or a green tea. I hand over some money. I detect he is a little put out that I have not made time to count it.

We talk. I mention a project that I wish to discuss with him this evening. I do not mention any potential remuneration, just that it will certainly be worth his while. Now I just need to fine-tune the details.

Chapter 17

It is 7pm and the last few hours have felt like a lifetime. I have paced around the flat, rhythmically tapping on the kitchen island while supposedly deep in thought. I cut my nails to far back with clippers more suitable for toes and then winced at the pain as lemon juice I was squeezing into a cup of hot water sneaks behind my trimmed nails onto the sensitive virgin skin. I have drunk three or four cups of lemony warm water to try to settle my irritated stomach. I am making notes, as many notes as possible, diagrams, trying to put some clarity to the mess in my mind. I have been to some kind of stationery shop and bought A3 paper I scribble onto, a brainstorm, and I Blu-Tack it to the wall. I rip it down suddenly, very aware of how bloody mental it makes me seem. The cat is still nowhere to be seen and I am very concerned.

I have a plan, though – a very good plan.

There's a knock at the door. It is heavy-sounding, made using the side of the fist rather than the knuckles.

For reasons unknown I tidy the coffee table. I purposely open up a 2015 edition of *Flex* magazine, a double-page feature on building thicker calves by world-renowned black body builder Ronnie Coleman.

Neuro-linguistic programming. Find some common ground.

Dave and his Asian associate enter the apartment.

He already takes up too much room in the entrance, annoyingly making my impressive space look considerably smaller than it actually is.

I feel unnerved about how tidy I have made the place. My nose is running. I wipe it on my sleeve.

Ushering them into the lounge I grab my notes and diagrams from the sofa before they sit down.

He notices Ronnie Coleman. The pitch is off to a good start. I contemplate mentioning the cricket to help develop a secondary relationship with the large Asian associate, but for some reason I stop myself.

The sofa is a deep three-seater and this Asian guy is taking up the majority of it. He smells of the gym. He has a white Adidas tracksuit on. It has small black greasy marks over it like he has been working on a car. A heavy gold bracelet is a real contrast against the dark hair on his unnecessarily clenched fist. The matching neck chain worn on top of the sweatshirt suits him.

"Your chain really suits you," I say.

Silence wafts through the room.

He slouches in the chair. I get some small indications that he does not like my choice of decor.

Dave is sat more upright and looking like he has something to say. He looks peculiarly small next to his associate, almost childlike. I struggle to hide my amusement and let out a nervy effeminate giggle.

"Can I get you a tea?" I ask for perhaps the second or third time.

The words come out like a sweet elderly grandma asking her sixteen-year-old granddaughter in the hope she might stay for an hour longer. I am letting myself down. Need to refocus.

"What exactly can we do for you, Ollie?" Dave cuts straight to the point.

"That ginger guy you saw me with earlier; he's been sleeping with my girlfriend." I blurt words out like an unpopular kid snitching on the school bully.

"Ollie, I didn't ask for your life story, pal. I asked what we could do for you." Dave seems keen for me to get to the point.

"Okay, well, I want to pay you some money to get him beaten up. Nothing too bad; just a few cuts and bruises. You could, erm, shave his head also if you wanted?" Uncertainty rises in the pit of my stomach as I say this.

"Actually, don't worry about the shaved head; that will be time-consuming."

"Yes, mate, I can arrange that. £2,000 today, non-refundable, and £2,000 after. Don't make me chase you for the money, though. Just tell me where he's going to be." Dave speaks as he is getting up.

He nudges the coffee table away with his knee, perhaps making room for the Goliath who is hopefully about to leave with him. I disappear and then reappear with what could be £2,000 in neat bundles. Dave again looks furious that I have not counted it. He nods towards his friend, so I give him the money.

"Thanks, Dave. Have a nice evening."

As they leave, the Asian henchman nods at me. He makes no attempt to hide the rolled-up copy of *Flex* magazine he has pilfered from my coffee table.

I smile. Leaving the magazine out has helped create rapport. I close the door, satisfied with how the meeting went, frustrated I have no one to high-five or share a glass of Laurent Perrier with. I ponder whether saying less would make me appear more mysterious and alluring.

Cate is calling. I answer the phone lovingly. We exchange pleasantries. I apologise for missing her calls. The gym, meetings, meetings, meetings, sunbeds to help with my seasonal affective disorder. A very busy weekend indeed.

Chapter 18

I shove clothes into the boot of the car and head back to Battersea. I have less interest than ever before in the beggars, the party-goers, the fashionistas, the tourists, the taxi drivers, the happy fucking families, they blur, they merge, they appear as blinkered lamps as I snake past.

Dave must have been impressed with the meeting. I was warm but focused. He accepted my proposal. I didn't haggle on the price; I didn't need to.

According to her calendar, today is the first day of December. The picture catches my eye: two barn owls snuggling at the forefront of a festive scene. They look content; happy, almost. This could have been Cate and I hibernating through the winter months. I could make it work. She really is quite attractive. Wait, no, that is not the message here. The barn owls represent Poppy and Clarke. That look is not contentment; it is guilt, or is it fear? Maybe Poppy and James Danbrook are the fearful barn owls. I see myself, but they do not. I am making my way towards them, leaving no trail in the snow. I am the python, I strike, squeezing until they are limp.

I fill in every day on the calendar with a workout plan: chest, legs, back, shoulders, bis and tris, cardio, chest, legs, back, shoulders, cardio. This should help emphasise my intensely busy schedule.

My body is becoming stronger. I am noticing a more permanent pump. I wonder whether Poppy will notice the change. Cate will for sure, but I am almost certain I do not care. As my muscles have become larger my erections have become weaker. This is not a problem for now as I focus on the present moment. Her flight lands at 9. I look around the apartment for the cat. Nowhere to be seen. Why would he be? I left him in East London.

One final look at the laptop. Poppy's Facebook status: "can't wait for my fiancé to get home…eek #excited."

This is a lie. Next time I see that face it will be in person. I push down the lid.

I leave a note for Cate, dragging the chalk in thick heavy lines down the cutesy chalkboard.
Gone to the gym – triceps and biceps session (see calendar). Be back tonight about 10pm, maybe later, bye.

I leave the car and decide to get a taxi. The street lamps illuminate the pitch-black sky. The notes I made yesterday seem to make little sense.

"Driver, excuse me, driver, do you have a highlighter pen?" I enquire hopefully.

He doesn't hear me. I decide not to repeat myself.

The heat in the back is unbearable. I open the window and try to gobble up some fresh air.

A small group of students, most probably French, laugh at me as we stop at the traffic lights. I laugh back in the knowledge that I could most probably have them killed by Wednesday for less money than a spa day at the Bulgari.

The taxi pulls in on the corner. I decide to pay him. I tell him to keep the change but maybe for the future to be more considerate of the temperature. He does not hear me.

The shop window provides an extremely flattering mirror. My shoulders appear broad, my waist narrow, my face rugged, focused, and my choice of attire well considered. I will not have the group of pointy-nosed, quaff-haired French students killed. I will instead have the best hair transplant money can buy in the new year.

"What if Theo was on an earlier flight?" I ask myself several times.

"He was not," I answer myself reassuringly.

Cate definitely confirmed they would be getting a car from the airport together. She seemed delighted that I was asking.

What if Clarke is here? Or Dad? Dad. It seemed strange to call him this now. I slow down my walk and consider a plan B.

"If you don't have a plan B, you don't have a plan," I vocalise to the heavily bearded tramp awkwardly half-laying on a small piece of cardboard by the ATM.

We catch eyes as he mumbles back, "expect the best but plan for the worst," or something along those lines.

I look at him a while longer. He is tanned, the kind of tan achieved from a week's skiing in March, his beard thick but not unkempt, his clothes filthy. The plaid shirt may well have human excrement on; maybe it is mud, but his attire is not too dissimilar to the thirty-something hipsters you see occasionally tapping the keys on their MacBooks somewhere in Old Street.

I go to push a twenty into his hand, letting go at the last minute just so we do not touch. I look around. No one saw; perhaps he is just a homeless, not an actor testing the goodwill of the local affluent.

"Call his phone," the rugged tramp eggs me on.

"Do I even have Theo's number?"

"Your old work phone," we both reply simultaneously.

I dial. It does still work. It is off; they are on the flight, he is not home.

"What about Clarke? My father?" I ask.

"On the night Theo comes home, it seems unlikely. Besides, I have been sitting here all day, I would have seen," comes the reply.

I smile and remember the key to clarity is to not overthink things.

"Go get 'em, kid," he says, as he attempts to fluff up several carrier bags he is using as a pillow.

"She will ask how I knew their address," I consider out loud.

"I dropped her – no, him, once in a taxi after a meeting," I reply.

"Which meeting was that?" I probe, aware that she may well ask.

I flick between calendar dates, racking my brain.

Perhaps it would be simpler to admit that on occasion I watch their house. Will it really matter in six months' time?

There is no doorbell. The door knocker is a heavy brass lion's head that looks like it would be heard in Ladbroke Grove. I want to avoid the aggressive, attention-seeking knock of the Asian henchman, so rap out a cheery ra-ta-tat with my knuckles.

Some time passes. I do not knock again.

I hear something, music most likely. It seems to be getting quieter. She is lying alone on a plush velvet sofa – not to my taste but expensive – in La Perla knickers much more to my taste. She wasn't expecting the knock, so is understandably cautious. She slips on her silk robe, also from La Perla, or maybe Dolce, and cashmere slippers as her marble floor is cold, even with the log burner on full blast. A pause as she checks her hair in the antique mirror above the fireplace. There is no need; she will look perfect. Then she softly meanders along the hallway towards me. She opens the door, a slight view of soft tanned breast on show where her gown was tied in a hurry. I am ushered inside.

The meandering down the hallway sounds heavier than I expected. Fuck, it's Clarke. That's what a fourteen-stone footstep sounds like. Before I can pull out my phone to call Dave, the door opens just an inch or two.

"Ollie, Jesus, what are you doing here? It's 8 at night. Theo is on his way home; I am in my pajamas." Poppy has a genuine look of curious confusion on her face.

I feel like that child again. The six-year-old carol singer who has forgotten his lines. I look behind me, hoping to see a smiling parent.
Poppy is wearing some disastrous pink pajamas. There is no way that fabric is not irritating her skin – they are done up so high at the neck that I can just about see her chin, let alone the breast I was hoping for.

She smiles and opens the door further.

"Have you been away? You look tanned. Do you want to come in for a minute? You will freeze on the doorstep," she says with an unusual level of warmth.

The heat hits me as I step inside. The smell of essential oils and the soft lighting do little to improve her choice of loungewear, but her face still radiates beauty, softened by her lack of make-up. She looks petite: it's the high heels, or lack of them. The only other time I recall seeing her without an extra few inches was in Selfridges, seconds after she wrecked my parents' relationship.

The kitchen space is well thought out: a large centre island, polished marble. A double butler sink, Victorian tiling and an unusual fridge unit that seems to have a water dispenser and coffee machine built in.

"He imported it from California," Poppy says.

I ignore her for the time being.

The chilled Balearic beats are pleasant. The Roberts radio they are playing from slightly kitsch in my opinion. I am relaxed, prepared and aware I have yet to say a word.

"I was going to order the fridge freezer myself – good value for money, really. However, changed my mind when I considered my carbon footprint. I mean, all the way from California!"

"Can I get you a drink, Ollie? A glass of red, a tea? It's been odd not seeing you around." Poppy continues with the warm, soft tone.

I can see in her eyes she wants me to speak. What do I say? There is no booming club music to drown out my nonsense, no opportunity to rewrite a confused text message.

I am going to tell her I love her.

"Poppy, why me? Please tell me. First you split up my parents, then you ruin mine and Clarke's friendship – I mean, he could be in grave fucking danger – then you sleep with my dad. What did I ever do?" This is a very different opening sentence from the one I had planned.

The welcoming warmth seems to drain out of her. I feel myself getting pulled into the swirling darkness of her dilated pupils. They have a cat, almost identical to Rocky, but with a more panicked look on his face. He paws at the window blind looking to escape.

"Rocky, is that you? Get down from there now," I hiss.

I look back at Poppy.

"Why not," she says and shrugs.

I am unprepared, completely off guard. I should have told her that I love her.

"I love you," I whisper.

The cat is now behind Poppy on the work surface. Acceptant that there is no escape, he playfully rolls a dead spider along with his paw.

"I slept with Clarke just the once, for your information, not that it's any of your business. He is good to me, he is kind and he offers me unconditional support. Yes, at first he wanted more, but now he knows that we are just meant to be friends," she says in a lying tone.

I gulp. I really need to blow my nose.

"I am sleeping with James, who, yes, happens to be your father," she says truthfully.

"I have a lot of congestion in my face," I murmur and squeeze my nose between thumb and forefinger.

"Everyone lets you down in this life. Everyone leaves you at some point. Surely you realise this, Oliver. Theo will leave me or I will leave him. We barely talk; he is a fucking arsehole, a bore. Your dad, who happens to be my James, he is a good guy. We are having a good time. It isn't love, but he supports me. I am putting money aside, we do nice things together. He will look after me when he is gone."

"Gone," I murmur.

Jesus Christ, how old is he? I would have guessed mid-sixties maximum.

"Do you love your father? Or are we the same? Is your relationship one of understanding? We both get what we need from it. Your nose is bleeding, Oliver; let me get you a tissue."

The noise is excruciating. Rocky's claws leave deep indentations in the glass.

L O S E R, he scrawls.

The piercing sound of claw against glass stops.

I drop to my knees, wiping at my eyes with a tissue.

"Stand up, Oliver, stand the fuck up!" Poppy barks, scaring the cat, who takes the opportunity to scurry past into the hallway.

She hands me more than one tissue. Our hands touch momentarily.

"Stop snivelling. Come on, it's life, what do you want? Us to sleep together? To be together? Your texts day and night, I know you've been hanging around outside, I've told James, he has told your mother."

She holds my hand. It does not feel romantic.

The living area is impressive: reclaimed timber floors covered with scattered thick-pile rugs. She is no longer holding my hand. I sit. The log burner fire is roaring and the expensive antique-looking mirror I anticipated sits perfectly above in pure synchronicity with the fireplace.

This is exactly the sort of home I would love to come home to, with Poppy waiting for me.

"Or even Cate," I surprisingly say to myself.

Giant stone hands are squeezing my head. My brain tries to find a new space within its skull, but there is no room and the pain is excruciating. I opt to only use my right eye and allow my left to close. I use all of my strength to separate the grip, finger by finger.

"I want you to stop fucking my father. I want you to myself," I say, finally.

She sits facing me, perched on the edge of a contemporary coffee table that doesn't actually suit the space. We are close, knee to knee, but close.

"Do you remember that day, Oliver? Do you remember Saturday the 11th of December, 2002? I was so happy then. Life was so simple. You were so cute. A spiky little haircut and trainers that were almost bigger than you. You couldn't stop looking over," Poppy reminisces.

I am sure she is trying to stop her mouth from producing a slight smile.

"Yes, of course, I remember like it was yesterday. I had big feet as a kid, my body had to do some catching up. Anyway, you can talk, you looked like a lollipop with your skinny little legs."

"I wish we hadn't ever seen each other. I wish I hadn't recognised James. He used to treat my mum so well. He would always make sure she had food in the house, always picking her up and taking her to work so she didn't need to get the bus. I never went without. The first time he took us shopping was the first time I remember having something brand new, a pair of sparkly gold trainers. The feeling I experienced watching the shop assistant put them in the box. She came round to the side of the counter and handed the bag to me. I felt so anxious that she had forgotten to put them in I opened it up right there to double check." Poppy does raise a slight smile as she talks.

I want to put my hand on her knee. I do not.

"The day after your mum humiliated and attacked my mother, do you know what happened, Ollie? Do you remember?" Poppy is no longer composed and wipes at her eyes.

Her beautiful eyes. They look wet. A tear forms and drips from her long eyelashes. I pass her my tissue and she actually uses it.
I remember Dad being home earlier for a time. I remember Mum attending more functions with him. There were more babysitters, more expensive gifts for a while, but it was for such a short while.

180

"I don't remember Poppy, I..." My words hardly come out.

For the first time in some time I do not feel like this is entirely about me.

"Your dad stopped calling, Ollie. He stopped coming around. He stopped helping with the rent. He told my mum that when he said he loved her he had been wrong. When he said they would be together soon he was confused." Poppy's voice is raised, tears changing course as they hit her plump lips.

"I didn't know that, Poppy."

"Do you know what happened on the 23rd of December 2004, Ollie? Has your mum living the life in Spain ever told you? Has your dad ever spoken to you about the past? No, they have not, as it's a dirty fucking secret. Just like my mum was before she killed herself. She couldn't go back to a life alone. Couldn't live with the broken promises. Then a year or so later, when your mum found a better option, she decided that she didn't want James. He was spoiled. Family wasn't quite as important as a home in the sun." Poppy is sobbing, her head in her hands.

I want to get up and comfort her, but I do not; I just watch her crying, snot running from her flared nostrils. The little mascara she is wearing starts to slowly slalom down her cheeks. Her positioning allows me a side view of her breast peering from her pajama top and I consider whether this is the most I have ever wanted her.

The crying slowly stops. Poppy lifts her head, looking at me, confused by my lack of reaction.

"I didn't know any of that, Poppy. Jesus. I didn't even know your mum had passed away. They have never mentioned it. Who did you live with?" Everything I am saying is irrelevant.

I cannot help but think how this affects me. Does it change my perspective? No, it does not.

Time passes with very few words spoken. The hardness has washed away from her face. I wonder if she is aware of the time. Maybe she wants Theo to walk in on us in such a tender moment. Part of me feels like it would be for the best, him walking in. I'm sure I could take a weary, travelled Theo.

"An aunt and uncle. A random aunt and uncle who I had seen a handful of times. It wasn't ideal, Ollie; those teenage years weren't the easiest for me. He never tried anything, my old uncle Derek, but he had a bit of a wondering eye." Poppy returns to her matter-of-fact tone.

"I left home, their home, at sixteen."

Poppy is interrupted by bright headlights beaming through the curtains. Taxi headlights, the shuffling of a small suitcase and the slamming of a car door.

My desire to see Theo for round two has suddenly buckled. I feel drained and have the overwhelming need for a hug rather than another punch to the face.

"Oh shit, Ollie. Get in that cupboard; he won't look in there. He will go up for a soak and you can leave. Quick, stop fucking about." Poppy is calm again; well practised, maybe.

Her hand on my back ushers me into the full-height cupboard.

"But your face. You can see that you've been crying." My hands caress her arm as I whisper. I want to pull her into the plughole with me.

"He will not notice, Ollie; he never does."

Through the gap of the door I see her wipe away dried tears and push her hair back. She immediately looks more composed.

The front door unlocks. This cupboard smells musty. I try to accustom my eyes to the dark. It isn't working; they just feel strained. My headache is crucifying.

Whatever it is hanging on the door directly in front of my nose smells like a gym changing room, like an unwashed PE kit. I recognise the handle of the fabric from a brief spell of doing Judo at the age of eight: it's Theo's Taekwondo jacket. I take a crazy risk and, holding my left, less blocked, nostril closed I snot what feels like a full load onto his sleeve. Momentarily I feel delight. Coincidently it seems to have eased the migraine.

I hold the door open, just a couple of inches, and listen. They are louder than I expected.

"Did you have a good trip, baby?" Poppy says.

She is out of sight. I imagine her leaning up to kiss him.

"Have you put any dinner on? Of course you haven't. I knew I should have stopped off on the way home. Useless, utterly useless." Theo's voice echoes through the house.

He isn't shouting, but his voice is certainly raised.

"I didn't. I thought we might get a takeaway tonight, order a pizza in." Poppy voice indicates that she wasn't surprised by his reaction.

I cannot picture her posture.

"Good call; exactly what I fancy after three days of eating out every lunch and fucking dinner, a bloody takeaway. Seriously, you are a waste of space, Poppy. Don't touch me. I'm going for a bath and then I will make myself a sodding sandwich." There is a mixture of irritation and regularity in Theo's voice.

I think back to the day I had called him a cunt. That look in Poppy's eyes had been in agreement.

I creep from the closet feeling sick. Theo has in some way devalued Poppy for me. How dare he do that.

"I'll call you, Ollie, I promise. Now promise me, not a word to anyone. We are friends now," Poppy whispers.

Then she closes the front door and I stand, slightly less alone than before, on the street.

Chapter 19

The taxi drops me just before the bridge. Cate will be in. It is nearly 10pm. I am a little early. I have an hour of free time before she expects me home. I have nervous adrenalin and a constant runny nose, a winter cold. I start to jog across the bridge, halfway crossing the road.

I have so much to think about but my mind keeps wandering to that cat. I just have a feeling Theo is going to take his anger out on the poor little guy.

I could do without making small talk with Cate – her chatting away about long days at dull conferences and whether the breakfast buffet at the hotel was up to scratch. I will nod and hopefully drift away somewhere.

A full moon lights up the sky. I attempt to howl at it but whimper. The wind is bitterly cold yet the river looks completely still. I cannot declutter my mind: nothing has changed, not a single thing. I look at the ice-cold water. Could I just slip in? Perhaps the chill would awaken me, help enlighten me. Perhaps I could sink straight to the bottom.

An elderly couple pass by, well dressed, a mixture of flannels, cashmere and wool. They look well suited to their tall tan and black dog, his fur tightly curled, his greying snout giving away his maturity. He has small, black, glassy eyes, a Steiff teddy bear. His legs stiff, tired to walk, yet too much pride to stay indoors waiting to die.

Poppy is vulnerable. She needs me more than ever.

I get up from the bench. The wise old dog has fallen even further behind. He is looking over his shoulder at me. I recognise that look of disappointment.

"How could you possibly understand, Dad?" I whisper, or shout.

Kicking a crushed Coke can in his general direction.

Her apartment is warm, the lights dimmed. Her suitcase is spilt across the floor, the bathroom door open and the shower on.

"Hi, baby, I'm in the shower. Come in, the door's open," Cate shouts lovingly.

I wander into the living room. In the duty-free bag there is a Toblerone, a 100ml bottle of the new Chanel men's fragrance and a bottle of Moet. I put the Toblerone in the bin and hope the fragrance is for someone else.

The shower stops.

"Ollie, come in here! Can you bring me in a clean towel and some slippers?" Cate shouts far too loudly.

It is impossible for me to ignore.

Her body really is quite nice. She has a long slender neck, a small frame, her shoulders are weighed down by her large breasts. Her stomach is flat. She does yoga and Pilates and you can see some definition on her upper abs. There is some fat around her lower stomach and hips but this is acceptable and adds to her femininity. Her legs are slim and toned and there is a clear line from when calf turns into ankle. Soaking wet and possibly a little cold, she has scrunched her cute little feet into the plush bathroom rug. The hair above her pussy is light blonde and wispy. Even though she does regularly wax she could probably get away with leaving it.

"Are you just going to stand there and stare at me? Do something. Get me a towel, say hello, give me a cuddle, fuck me on the bathroom floor, I have hardly spoken to you in days." She is smiling and steps towards me. Her nipples harden within two paces.

As she kisses me on the mouth I move her head to the side, put my arms around her and hug her, trying to pass the tension from my body into hers.

"Ahhh, now that is a sweet welcome home. Have you missed me?" Cate's chin nuzzles into my neck as she whispers in my ear.

I choose not to answer, squeezing harder. I toy with the idea of squeezing the life out of her and tipping her top-heavy body into the Thames.

I do not.

"Ollie, are you on some kind of new protein diet? Or have you brought us a new addition to our happy little family?" Cate temporarily moves her head away from mine

I look down into her vast, sopping cleavage.

"What are you talking about?" I ask without hiding my agitation.

187

Her smile is endearing in a sickening sort of way and before speaking she pushes her hand down to my groin.

"The twenty cans of cat food in the back of the cupboard, silly. Have you got me an early Christmas present? A little moggy of some kind?"
She squeezes my penis playfully. Her voice is excitable and she is wide-eyed.

"No, Cate, I have not," I reply.

"You are a strange boy, you really are. I am going to need to keep my eye on you," she says, sliding down my body onto her knees.

I lift her back up. My mind is still processing today's events and I really have no time to decipher what Cate is talking about, so I just purposely frown, kiss her on the forehead and squeeze a little bit harder than before.

Chapter 20

I wouldn't like to guess at how many days have passed. I hear nothing from Poppy.

I stop watching their house. I sit in the car but cannot bring myself to drive. I cannot help but look at her Facebook, the last post: "So glad my fiancé is back."

I hover over the request from my mother.

Clarke calls and texts. He just wants to meet for that pint. I promise him as soon as I have my agenda set we will get a date in the diary.

I keep the curtains pulled shut and sit on the floor, back against the sofa. I have on the same sweatpants and hooded jumper as yesterday and perhaps even the day before. The winter flu has taken me hostage. My nose streams and my body aches, my head is pounding and screaming at me repeatedly to stop letting everybody down. There is no medication in the apartment.

At some point, I uncurl from the foetal position I have taken up on the bespoke timber flooring. Through the fibres of the thick pile my phones flashes. Poppy; it must be her. Not wanting to risk trying to stand and failing, I drag myself across the lounge.

I do not recognise the number but choose to answer. It is Dave.
A car pulls up. Two sets of eyes on me from the interior of what looks like a Volkswagen. The skin on my face is

tight, dry from hours old tears. My nose crusty from the winter cold. I am forced to try to grab breath through my mouth.

We talk. Dave talks and I listen. I hand over a wad of notes, which I again forget to count. He asks me if I want any coke.

The hardwood floor once again cools my head. I will just lie here for a minute or two and then get into bed. I cannot help but notice the same motivational video on loop on YouTube. I throw a book entitled *The Art of War* at the TV, hoping it will turn off the overbearing narrators voice. It misses by some distance.

"Hello, Oliver, I haven't seen you for some time. Your mother tells me you have girlfriend. Good for you. I have cleaned your bathroom, it was very dirty. I need you to buy some Viakal or I can buy, but you must remember to pay me. Anyway I leave now," she says.

"Have you seen my cat. A cat?" I ask.

She must have put the heating up high. I am sweating and march into the living room, frantically looking around.

"No, Oliver, I see no cat. Cat food, yes, but no cat."

I offer her money and she takes some and leaves the rest on the dining table.

I sit on the sofa. Closing my eyes, I vision how this week will pan out. I vision how the year will pan out; my life pans out. It's not so clear. They say write it down, write your goals and your dreams down. The deep voice on the

TV tells me not to quit; it tells me I am already in pain, I am already hurt and now I should get a reward from it.

They also say live in the present moment. Right now I have no choice. Right now there is no future. I go back to sleep.

I do not know what time I wake up. It is still pitch black. It could be closer to dusk or nearer to dawn. I start the engine and head towards Battersea.

The streets are not empty enough for it to be the middle of the night. I have that feeling I am being followed. A paranoia I recognise well.

I creep into the apartment not wanting to wake her. Even in the darkness without switching on a light I can see the bedsheets folded tightly to the bed. There is no outline of a body.

I lay down fully clothed, trying to keep my eyes open until she arrives home.

Chapter 21

Today feels like my birthday. The first day of a great new job, that moment when you are in full control of your ejaculation.

It is 6pm on a Thursday. It is halfway through the month. In three weeks it will be New Year. I have already started making notes in next year's diary, as it is going to be my year.

In a couple of hours' time I will be a spectator to a mugging. A guy just on his way out to meet an ex-colleague – no, a friend – he will find himself set upon by a couple of opportunist thugs. Perhaps they are not opportunist; perhaps they have seen him heading in and out of his expensive apartment in his garish clothes. Seen the girl with the designer handbags frequenting his Kensington love pad. Maybe they mistook his Omega for a watch of value. Who knows? He might well fight back and that's probably why they will leave him with a few cuts and bruises. They knock a couple of teeth out due to the lack of respect, the rules of the street.

Oh, if only I had arrived a few moments earlier, perhaps I could have helped. I will of course sprint over, mobile phone in hand, dialling for the emergency services. I will hold Clarke's head, something about stemming the bleeding?

Then I do not know. Maybe I just tell him straight to keep away from Poppy. Maybe as I dab his bleeding nose with my hanky I install in him the importance of being a good friend. Maybe I will just stroke his hair and tell him everything will be just fine.

I pass Cate in the hallway as she comes in from work and I leave for the well-deserved beating of a friend. I had completely forgotten she existed.

"I'm going to the gym, will grab some cat food on the way back," I say as we have a brief interlude on the stairs.

"I thought you were meeting Clarke for a beer tonight? For fuck's sake, Oliver, what's with the cat food? I am getting a little fed up of picking it up and chucking it out every night." Cate has a look of annoyance on her face as she speaks. Not annoyance – a look of sheer desperation would be more accurate.
Her face is covered in too much make-up. Who is she out to impress at the office? It does not hide her tired-looking eyes.

"Oh, yes, that's right. I'm meeting Clarke after, after the gym I'm meeting him." I sound unconvincing. It's apparent to me that I must improve my memory or write more down.

"Oliver, baby, I am worried about you. Your behaviour; you are just so vacant, we need to talk."

She may or may not have finished her sentence as the lift doors close behind me. I will make it up to her. She will be happy for me soon, I am sure.

They say if you love something let it go, and that is what Cate will need to do.

Chapter 22

I stop at the newsagents. They do not stock popcorn, so I grab a generously sized bag of Kettle Chips.

There he is: the hair, disgusting orange hair, clashing with his red hoody emblazoned with some brand slogan most likely from an outlet village or a House of Fraser sale. The high-top trainers and the bleached-out jeans momentarily reassure me that a beating is the best plan of action.

He picks up the phone almost as soon as I dial.

"Hello, mate. Running a few minutes late? Okay, cool, yeah, meet you there…"

A word comes out from his mouth.

Then wallop. I hear the first blow as it echoes through my iPhone earpiece. It must have been the Asian dude as it is identical to the way he knocks on a door.

I slip down as far as possible in the driver's seat, my eyes peering over the top of the steering wheel. I am full of childish excitement at seeing something that perhaps I shouldn't. Frustratingly, the first punch does not knock him down. I feel my fists clenching, mirroring the follow-up blow. It catches us both by surprise, as it is from a second attacker. He swings a punch towards Clarke's face. Instinctively he manages to raise an arm and blocks the frankly weak punch. This isn't what I paid for. I attempt to open the sweet chilli crisps without averting my eyes.

With very little momentum, Clarke throws his head forward and catches a lanky-looking string of piss with a head butt. The assailant falls back. It turns out Clarke is tougher than his cowardly persona suggests. The Asian now strikes again. He manages a run-up and catches him with sixteen stone channelled into a heavy blow. That has got to hurt.

Yes. It knocks Clarke into the building's glass doors. His phone falls to the floor. The wheels are in motion. The second, so far useless waste of money, grabs the phone and cracks Clarke on the back of the head to send him to the floor.
I undo my seatbelt, unsure of why I still have it on. I look at myself in the rear-view mirror. I ignore the unnerving déjà vu, take a breath and get ready to intervene. As I look back over, the scene has changed.

From out of the glass doors a fourth character has emerged, tall, slim, in understated tailoring. He has taken a fighting stance and swivels on his hips, his right foot connecting with the jaw of the gigantic Asian, who topples backwards. Then, in an all-too-recognisable moment, the unexpected partaker rocks back on his heels, and I watch a familiar power harnessed as Theo pushes from the balls of his feet and punches the hired assailant to the floor. Fucking Theo. Why the hell is he here? I put my seatbelt back on and sit upright, intrigued as to how this unexpected twist will turn out.

Theo has spun round to take on the second mugger as Clarke groggily tries to get to his feet.

I see it before Theo but I do not react. The windscreen glass is my television screen. There he is, the narrator.

Don't quit! Don't quit! I could shout, but what would be the point? It is only a film, a very realistic film. My nails are digging into the leather upholstery. The Kettle Chips fall to the floor.

The small shiny blade catches Theo just above the belt buckle to the right. There is no dramatic scream, no valiant fight-back. There is very little noise at all. He just falls to his knees. There is no looking up to the sky, just a sorry slump.

Then the heavy pounding of feet, closer and closer. I do not move. I feel my chin pushing into my neck, the tortoise going back into his shell. I see the wipe of the knife and a glimmer of light as it is tossed into the bushes. They do not look my way and I do not look at them.
How much time passes I do not know. Am I sprinting or walking? I am uncertain. Am I whispering or shouting? I cannot tell.

"Clarke, you okay, bud? Who were they? What the fuck is Theo doing here?" I realise as I speak that my third question must appear a strange one.

Clarke is trying to turn Theo on his side.

"Call an ambulance, Oliver, call a fucking ambulance! They stabbed him, they stabbed him for a shitty iPhone!" Clarke is shrieking at me.

I feel significant in the moment. Theo's loss of blood and Clarke's loss of phone leave them both in need of my assistance.

A teenage girl is screaming and a small group has formed. I see her hardened nipples first, braless and exposed to the cold, hidden behind a flimsy nightdress, then her face, maybe late forties, older than her body suggests, and then I see the phone she is about to use, to steal my heroic thunder.

I am speaking to someone instantaneously. As I say it out loud there is a moment of reality. A stabbing, a lot of blood, a knife wound to the stomach. I don't know if he is breathing. I don't know if he is breathing.

The sirens are loud. They feel very real. An ambulance and then the police.

I stumble away, jogging backwards, my eyes set on the paramedics trying to get Clarke away from the body and into a separate vehicle.

My hand is on the car door. I need to get in, I need to leave now, to fix my story. The police are sure to call. The temptation is too much. I am on my hands and knees, one arm in the shrubbery. I feel the cold metal against my fingertips. Slipping the blade up my sleeve, I am back in the driving seat.

The circle of lights surrounding the body distract any inquisitive eyes away from me as I slip into second gear and away from the increasing crowd of busybodies. I swerve to avoid a Mini Cooper that awkwardly lurches in front of me.

My getaway would have not been as incognito if I had bought the white, slightly newer, model I had first looked at. Decision well made, Oliver.

"Don't quit, I am already in pain, I have already been hurt, get a reward from it."

I park up two roads down from her house. For the entire drive I have been practising my lines, attempting to put a spin on the current dilemma. My main focus is to show myself in a positive light and in no way dwell on the heroic efforts of her current fiancé.
I slow my breathing and hit call.

She answers. I try but cannot imagine what she is wearing.

"Hi, Ollie, I thought you would have tried to call before. I mean, I planned to call you. Everything I said, you will keep it to your self, won't you?"

I put not one second's thought to the question.

"Poppy, do you know where Theo was tonight? Who he was with?" There is a definite seriousness in my voice.

"Theo? He is at Home House, Soho House or Who-knows House, one of the three; drinks with an old school friend, twattish public school friend." I notice the slur in her voice. I can picture her holding a large glass of red wine yet again.

"Did he go to school with Clarke? As that is who he is with, Pops."

There is a period of silence while we both try to digest Theo's need to lie.

"With Clarke?"

"Yes, with Clarke. I was meeting him by his flat for a drink. He has been begging me to meet him. I turned up and saw them both, but it was too late."

"You saw them together tonight? When Theo was meant to be with Rupert at Home House or wherever the fuck they meet? Oh, Ollie, I had a huge row with Clarke two days ago. I told him that we would be nothing more than friends. I told him there was someone else."

My heart flutters.

"Do you mean me, Poppy?"

"No, of course not, I mean James. Well, I mean I was actually just trying to let Clarke down gently," Poppy says, sounding particularly agitated.

It is apparent to me that Poppy has solved the mystery at the exact same time as me.

A heartbroken and dejected Clarke was calling a meeting of colleagues past and present to admit his guilty texts to Theo and explain my innocence, to let his best buddy Theo know that his wife-to-be was actually a little bit of a slut. A commendable move but maybe, when Clarke has the benefit of hindsight, one he will regret.

I fight the urge to smile by focusing on the reason for my call.

"Poppy, I was meeting Clarke tonight – just Clarke, I did not know Theo would be there. He called me over and over again to meet him, had to be tonight, had to be at a certain time, he was so insistent. I had trouble parking, all those residents' permits. It was too late by the time I saw them, Poppy. I saw Theo cowering as the mugger attacked him. Clarke was already on the floor, I sprinted over, maybe just in time, maybe it could have been worse, much, much worse. Theo was bleeding, whimpering. They stabbed him, Poppy, all for an outdated phone. I called the ambulance, maybe saved his life, who knows? Clarke was crying, a useless wreck. As soon as the ambulance arrived I knew I needed to call you. I guess Theo will be at the Chelsea and Westminster. I can pick you up, we can go up there together. Maybe get a bite to eat en route?"

My story sounds plausible. I sound heroic.

"You go," Poppy says immediately, with a coldness in her tone. "You go. You have been so brave, but you should go and make sure Theo is okay. I mean a stab wound – a few stitches, right? You should go and make sure he is on the mend, make sure Clarke is okay, that you know. He realises that telling Theo would just complicate things. Look what's happened! It could have been avoided."

At this exact point, if I had not have known differently, I would have suggested Poppy as potentially the main suspect in this slightly-out-of-hand situation.

She is right; I should go and make sure Clarke is okay, make sure that he saw me arriving just a few moments too late. I should make sure Clarke doesn't tell the recovering Theo that it was him texting Poppy, him fucking his fiancée and not me, make sure Theo doesn't find out what Poppy and my father are up to.

"Remember, we are good friends now, Oliver, here for each other."

Something does not seem quite right, but Poppy continues: "And then, by the time Theo is all fixed, I will have finished the bath I am having and can meet you there, all freshened up," she says, remaining cold but adding a sultry tone that sends a shiver down my spine.

"Are you sure I shouldn't come round, Poppy, make sure you are okay? Maybe you are in shock?"

"No, Ollie, I will see you later, at the hospital, like we just discussed."

The phone clicks and I am sitting in the car confused and on edge. I frantically root around in the glove box, then stop. I stare blankly at the unknown number flashing on my phone. The number may be unknown but that caller is not. It has to be Dave. I choose to ignore it.

Chapter 23

I pass obese people quaffing quarter-pounders, watching their chip packets blow away in the wind, complaining about how long they have had to wait, bloody foreigners taking hospital beds and the lack of real quality English food in the canteens. Sickly, cancer-stricken patients listen on, barely able to nod in agreement but still mustering the strength to lift a cigarette to the rotting holes they call a mouth.

I weave around them, not sure who I need to speak to and what exactly I need to say.

The stench of the hospital, even when it is in Chelsea, repulses me. The overbearing waft of cleaning products tries and fails to mask the smell of the unfortunates in the waiting room.

The tramps already bandaged from previous injuries, the odours that leaks from their decomposing bodies battling against the hydrogen peroxide. Crackheads pacing around the room with no visible issues aside from addictions. One smiles at me, nodding enthusiastically. Snotty-nosed kids coughing and spluttering while their parents take turns to go outside and smoke. The gaunt guy, balding, the remains of his hair scraggly and greasy, his oversized leather a reminder of better days, leaning on a crutch. If he's not at the hospital he is in the bookkeeper's praying that the 1000-1 comes in. You're all fucked.

I find myself pacing around, fidgeting, trying to make eye contact with any member of staff who passes.

"Can I help you, young man?" someone asks.

"Yes, yes, I have a friend here. He was attacked, beaten up. I called the ambulance. His name is Clarke, Clarke…"

I forget his last name.

"Okay, let's get you to the reception and we can help find your friend."

I nod enthusiastically, catching the eye of a crackhead, who nods enthusiastically back. His mirroring technique makes we wonder whether we have read the same book on neuro-linguistic programming.

I stand in the lift, repeating "Floor 3, Clarence Ward" over and over. I watch the lift go down, the doors open in a basement, nobody gets in and I go up again.

What will I say? I imagine Theo is already telling the nurses the story of his fight with two knife-wielding assailants, showing them his wound, telling them all about his karate with delinquents program. Poor old Clarke will be forgotten about – just the guy who got punched. No one will mention his fairly valiant effort to fight them both off. I certainly won't, as I was not there; I was struggling to find parking – hellish, bloody residents' only everywhere.

"I turned up, I saw the attackers. They were black or brown and probably on drugs. It was definitely a mugging. They were wild-eyed, high on drugs. No, I couldn't see their eyes, I was too far away, they had hoods on. They were most likely high on drugs. If I had to take a stab in the dark. Not a stab in the dark, that is inappropriate. If I had to take an educated guess, I would say they were high on drugs and saw a couple of soft targets so decided, impromptu, to steal their phones. I arrived on the scene and called the ambulance. Now, please, I do not want to hear the term 'hero' used again. I did what anyone else would do."

The lift is somehow full. A porter asks what floor I want to get out on.

"Floor 3, Clarence Ward," I say with confidence.

I march with intent, full of beans and feeling like the hero I am.
Left, right, right again and then straight down the corridor. The nurse asks for me to wait outside. I take this opportunity to practise a more sullen appearance. "Yes, I am a hero, but look what they have done to you." I drop my shoulders.

There he is, in his own private room. I hope he has had to pay for this.
The doctor is giving him what looks like a final check-over. He has a split lip, a closed right eye, a lump on the top of his forehead, some lacerations above his collar bone and, according to Dr. Singh, a mild concussion.

The doctor says he is a lucky boy and then repeats it to me. Often mugging victims end up much worse off.

Clarke has yet to face me, but I can see he is not in a good way. He looks bruised and battered. In that respect, this was a well-organised and carried-out plan. Although it ended up a bit of a fiasco, I must give myself some credit.

"How is Theo, my friend who was stabbed? Can I see him? Can he leave with me?" Clarke is speaking to the doctor frenetically; he has yet to look in my direction.

"I am sorry, there is nothing new to report. The last update I have is that he is in theatre. The entry wound was small but it punctured his liver. He lost a lot of blood. Stay here, relax. You need rest. I will come back in a while. If I can I will discharge you and I will also get an update on your friend." The doctor has a gentle, kind voice with a soft Indian accent. He seems weary.

I still seem to have gone unnoticed by Clarke.

I feel a presence behind me. I smell the unpleasant aroma of stale coffee and hear a deep male voice. This catches Clarke's attention.
We make eye contact. He knows. I know he knows. I look down. What seems like a hell of a long time passes and when I look up he is still staring directly at me.

"Hi," I say.

"Where is Dr. Singh? We are here to get a statement, if the patient is well enough to talk. We really need to get some ID kits out to help catch the men who did this."

I swivel my head to see a portly police officer. He has several chins on a youngish face. He is four stone overweight, but a good height helps conceal some of the extra lard. Behind him, hidden away, is a small female police officer, again a little rounder than she should be but with a pretty, bird-like face. They are talking to a nurse who doesn't look old enough to be here.

Clarke's eyes stay firmly on my face. His voice is directed to the imposing police officer.

"Yes, officer, I am ready to talk. I want to get every detail down on paper, while it is fresh in my head." Clarke's voice is worryingly decisive, his face red and swollen.

"Err, officer, I saw some of the incident too. Should I sit in on this also? These arseholes need catching." It feels and sounds as if my voice is breaking as I offer my input.

I awkwardly step backwards to put some distance between myself and the fleshy giant. I glance back at Clarke, who has yet to avert his stare.

"And who are you?" booms the officer.

I crane my neck to look up at him. My eyes are in line with his police number, 0404. Fat squeezes through the gaps like Play-Doh through fingers. He seems to be getting bigger.

I reach out a hand, waiting less than a second before putting it back in my pocket and then linking it with my other hand behind my back. I must stop fidgeting.

"Danbrook. Oliver Danbrook. I am a good buddy and ex-boss to both of the attackees. Is that what you say? Is that a word, attackee? Anyway, I was just parking up and I saw these two dark-skinned muggers attacking my friends. Just about ran over and chased them off, probably from that big estate, you know the one." The words come out too quickly for everyone in the room's liking.

I must get control, stay in the present moment. Like the book says.

"They were not black. Perhaps you couldn't see so well from behind your car. They were Pakistani or Indian. I am sure I recognised one of them, big rope chain hanging off his neck. Did you recognise them, Ollie?"

He doesn't know. He doesn't know how long I was there.

"Are you sure, Clarke? I am sure I saw a dreadlock."

I can feel a reddening warmth spreading across my face.

"Often there can be some confusion. Let's get statements from the pair of you individually and go from there. The one thing we do know is that they definitely were of colour. A good starting point. Mr. McGinley, we will get all of your information first. Mr. Danbrook, perhaps we could conduct your interview at the station afterwards."

McGinley. I didn't even know my best friend's last name.

"No problem at all, officer. I didn't see much. I was chatting to my girlfriend on the phone, just parking up, but I understand the importance of getting my statement separately, so I am just going to wait around here. Hopefully I will be able to see Theo. Take him some grapes, a couple of magazines. He's into his kung fu; still, I suppose all of that goes out of the window in a street fight. You know, just in case he is in overnight." I feel fortunate as the doctor steps back into the room and interrupts my rambling.

"Mr. McGinley, I am really sorry to tell you this, but I have just caught up with my colleague and Mr. Egerton-Jones didn't make it through surgery. Initial details look like he just lost too much blood. Unfortunately, he passed away at 11.15pm."

The officer moves me aside. He suddenly has a bigger case on his hands. He rubs his palms together, possibly thinking of the overtime, just in time for Christmas. I momentarily consider that I will have helped contribute to this lardy underpaid copper being able to buy his teenage daughter a pair of real Ugg boots, her piggy features breaking into a smile as she slips a trotter into one – so much better than the fakes he stole from the evidence room last year.

Their sad silence drags me back into the room.

Clarke just stares blankly, like he is taking in the space, the air between him and the doctor. He glances towards me but this time with no emotion behind the eyes.

I feel my heart rate pick up. A tingling in my arms. I just about fight the smile, but the corners of my mouth are turning up slightly. I try to feel down to fit in with the rest of the room. I feel light, that euphoric moment when the drugs kick back in for a second round of high.

Poppy Egerton-Jones. What a pompous-sounding name it would have been. I am adding this to my list of positives in the face of apparent doom and gloom, along with the fat police officer being able to treat his unfortunate child.

How will she take this? I am sure she will be delighted. She wanted out. Could I tell her it was me – well, my doing anyway? No, maybe it's best to keep quiet. I am guessing Clarke didn't get to tell Theo about his Christmas fling with Poppy as I am guessing that if he had, Theo wouldn't have come to his aid. So in a way Clarke has to take some responsibility for this tragedy.

A plastic chair skids across the floor in my direction. It grinds to a halt in front of the officers. A thud echoes through the room as his fist dents what must surely be partitioning. He drops to his knees sobbing, sobbing really loudly.

I just cannot share in his despair.

The police officers usher me out of the room and close the door.

His sobbing, the wailing I can hear as I wander the corridor confirms to me that Clarke is no longer a stepping stone between Poppy and I. A broken man crying at the death of a colleague rather than an opportunist man realising that there was now one less obstacle between him and the prize. A delightful second wave of euphoria surges through me.

In the bathroom I stand and stare at myself in the oh-so-delightful mirror. The lighting is harsh and yet I still manage to appear radiant, my skin basked in glory. I run this evening's events through my mind. The positives seem to outweigh the negatives.

My phone rings, private number. I reject it. I am sick on the floor. I blow my nose and exit.

The female officer is waiting outside for me. She is much prettier when separated from her gargantuan colleague, her skin brown and flawless.

"Mr. Danbrook, how are you feeling? You look a little off-colour. I know how hard this will be but speed really is of the essence, so if you can come to Kensington Police Station in an hour's time, we can write up your notes while they are still fresh. Such a tragic incident. Please do continue to think of anything else that may be relevant to solving this horrible crime," she says in an unexpected accent with a sympathetic tone I do not quite trust.

"Okay, officer got it, see you there. Here's my mobile number, just in case you need it beforehand."

The constant ringing of my phone is a mood killer.

The hospital corridors are maze-like. On the way out, the lift keeps bringing me back to Floor 3, Clarence Ward. I press the assistance button repeatedly. A man who looks poorly paid in a grubby white uniform assists me to the car park exit. He looks surprised and I feel bewildered as I push a five-pound note into his hand.

There are twenty-six missed calls, mostly from an unknown number, although I know who it is, interlaced with calls from Cate, my mother and Poppy. I want to call Poppy first but also last. I want the excitement of waiting, but the anticipation of her response is killing me. Perhaps she will be sad initially – it is a natural human response – but she should be fine by the weekend. Then I will move in, perhaps literally; I mean, I am not sure I can go back to my Shoreditch pad.

A message comes through from Mum.

Don't forget we land tomorrow at 5pm. Meet you at the flat. Hope you've had a good week. Mum x

I am near certain I did not agree to this.

A message from Cate reads:

WHERE ARE YOU! Call me xxx

Poppy has sent a series of messages:

No updates?
How is he?
Let me know if he is coming home.
Let me know asap.

I call Cate. The aim will be to have her off the phone by the time I reach the car.

"Ollie, where the fuck are you? Still at the hospital? You need to come here now, please, Ollie, come home." She is hysterical, her voice shrill and broken up by an offensive snorting.

How does she know I was at the hospital? Perhaps Theo's parents? BBC news? Does it even matter?

"Cate, you heard? About the attack? Who told you? It was so awful. A mugging. For some reason Theo was at Clarke's flat. They got attacked, robbed by some street kids, teenagers, they are both in hospital. Well, Clarke is in hospital, I am not sure about Theo now, they probably needed the bed. How did you hear? So quickly, I mean."

211

My story and thought process have been knocked off track by Cate's knowing my whereabouts.

"That does not matter, Oliver. I just know. Where are you going now?"

"I'm just at the police station, about to give my interview. The officer said I was a bit of a hero as I chased them off. I am not sure my bravery is really relevant right now, though. Hopefully I can just remember something important. I am really very tired, shouldn't be too long, although it could take all night, so don't wait up." Once again I am rambling rather than speaking coherently.

"Are you sure you don't want me to come to the station? At least pick you up? It will be the middle of the night, are you okay to drive?"

With all of these questions, I am starting to wish I had just sent her a text.

"No, no definitely do not come down here. It's all a formality. Besides, there's not really anywhere for you to sit." My rambling has been replaced with a desperate need to end the conversation.

"Is Clarke okay? He told me he was meeting Theo. He convinced Theo to come down and make it up with you, apologise for the accusations. Clarke called me to ensure you met him, said he was going to fix everything. I wanted to tell you but you were just so, well, vacant." Cate reveals another fact that I could have done with knowing just a few hours prior.

"Oh fuck, why didn't you tell me? Why is everyone so bloody secretive? I've got to go, the detective wants to see me. Won't be a moment, detective."

"I love you, Ollie. I'll wait up."

I hang up before she can finish her sentence.

Why can't everyone be honest? If it wasn't for Cate and Clarke's lies Theo would quite possibly still be alive.

I arrive at Poppy's house, unsure of how I am going to tell her, optimistic that she will share in the positives. Outside sits the empty residents' space that belongs to Theo. A warm feeling of satisfaction drifts through me as I parallel park first time into his space, warm and cosy.

I ring the doorbell, then knock at the door. There is no answer. I call her phone; it is switched off. I bang on the door with the side of my fist over and over again, at an enthusiastic pace.

I move away back to the car and call again and again. She must have heard, made her way to the hospital or maybe to the police station.

"Remain calm, focus on the positive and do not presume the worst," is a mantra I cannot adhere to right now.

The waiting room at the police station is full of the same characters frequenting the hospital. Every woman, whether fourteen or seventy, seems to have smeared eye make-up. There are a lot of unkempt men with their heads in their hands.

213

My phone rings. I don't recognise the number but I know who it is.

I step out of the station into the icy winter's night.

"Hello," I whisper, entertained by the smoke ring I blow in the chilled air.

"Remember that was a mugging you saw tonight, remember that. Nothing more. You turned up too late and saw the attackers running off. You didn't get a look at their faces. They're going to have to disappear for a while now, so the price has gone up by three bags. Understand? Don't fuck up."

The phone hangs up. I see car headlights turn on and then off in the distance. He is just letting me know they are there.

I carefully place two pieces of toilet paper on the seat and sit down. I relay the story over and over in my head. I lean forward and put my hand in my trouser pocket and search around for something to ease my nerves.

The man mountain sits me down. I opt out of the foul-looking cup of coffee that reminds me of his stale, acidic breath. A male colleague sits alongside him. The female colleague, the slightly cold-hearted girl with the accent, is nowhere to be seen. Perhaps taken off the case due to the brief moment we shared.

"I am Sergeant Paul Willis and this is Detective Constable Groves. All we need from you is as much information as you can recall on tonight's tragic events. Walk us through

214

what you saw. There's a good chance these boys will be local lads, so any minor details might help."

The story flows perfectly.

"I was running late to meet Clarke, something I will never recover from – if only I could have been a moment earlier. On the phone to my girlfriend, she had just got back from being abroad. I was parking the car, really looking forward to meeting my buddy for a bite to eat, no beers as I was driving. Then I saw two guys, average height, average build, I'm sure they looked black, of Caribbean descent, hitting Clarke and really pounding another man. At this time I didn't realise it was Theo. Apparently Theo was joining us, very last minute. He was more Clarke's friend than mine; I just knew him from work. He worked for me; nice bloke. I am surprised he couldn't fight back as I am sure he was a karate expert, spent a lot of his time with vulnerable kids. Could that be connected? Who knows? Hopefully not. I mean, he was touchy feely with the women in the office, but nothing to suggest he had any unhealthy interests, you just can never be one hundred per cent sure, can you? I can get you his laptop if need be. Anyway, I get out of the car, duck down and just check up and down the street to make sure there were not any other gang members lying in wait. Then I run over. There was a scuffle between one of the guys and Theo. I didn't see what happened but saw him hit the floor. I shouted running towards them – stupid, really, as they could have jumped me. It was the adrenalin and the knowing a friend needed my help. They both kept their heads down and ran off. I really can't be certain but, as I mentioned at the hospital, I feel like I saw a dreadlock under one of those beanie hats. I don't know the area well, but it looks like they ran in the direction of that tower block, something estate."

The detective nods and makes notes. I am feeling calm about the whole situation; chatty, almost.

"So Paul, Christmas is coming up. Time with the family. Any kids?" I say knowingly.

"A teenage daughter, and I'll be lucky to get much time off with our workload. Anyway, I really just need you to focus on today's events," Officer Paul says.

I knew it. I do not disguise my smile.

The detective breaks the silence.

"Okay, all very helpful, Oliver. Now this seems most likely to be a mugging that got out of hand and unfortunately led to the murder of your work colleague. Those phones nowadays have a high resell value. All of this really aligns with the information Clarke could provide. Although he is adamant the attackers were Asian, we do have a female witness yet to see. She has just come forward, so hopefully we can add another layer of detail." The detective stands up from his chair as he speaks and hands me papers to sign.

I am shown out of a side door.

"Have a good night's sleep. You seem like you are in slight shock still. It all might hit you in the morning. If you do think of any other relevant information or need to speak with somebody – a grief counsellor, maybe, just call me." The sergeant rests an arm on my shoulder. "Really, I am

216

sorry. We will do our best to catch these scumbags." The sergeant seems to squeeze me as he emphasises the word "scumbags".

I get in the car desperate to find Poppy. I call. There is no answer. I park again, this time with less enthusiasm, and knock on the door.
I drive aimlessly back past the crime scene before heading to Battersea. The traffic is slow and I use this time to try and get my thoughts together.

I hear the sobbing and snorting before I even reach the front door.
As I enter she wraps her arms around me.

"It could have been me." "I was so brave." She begs me to be more careful, to make sure "I don't have my watch on display." "These people, they despise hard workers."

She repeats herself, how lucky I was. I feel like telling her, literally, it couldn't have been me. Then she asks if there was traffic as I had left the apartment in such a rush, why it took me so long to get there.
I find myself pushing her away, my palms applying pressure to her shoulders.

Now the problem with maintaining any sort of relationship with Cate is that I do not really like the face she pulls when she cries. Her chin presses into her neck, giving the impression of several chins, which is now, of course, an unpleasant reminder of Officer Paul Willis.

As she forces a hug from me I again imagine crushing her ribcage, just to remove any potential enjoyment from this situation. I look over her shoulder to the clock. It is 3am.

I sit on the floor, back to the ottoman at the bed end, looking at my phone.

"What are you doing, Oliver? Are you okay? I can join you," she whispers tiredly as I frantically search social media for Poppy.

"I'm just looking at pictures of me, Clarke and Theo from the golf day at St Andrews a few years back. Good times," I reply, unsure of whether Cate knew that not once was I invited to any sort of social event.

My eyes are heavy, my mind is still racing, dreading tomorrow, having to meet my mother, having to make small talk, explain what's happened, fend off any potentially unanswerable questions she may ask. All of this while not being there for Poppy when she finally reappears.

The sun breaks through the bedroom blinds. I am tightly tucked under the covers. Beads of sweat break down my forehead. I am uncomfortably warm.

I look around the bedroom. She is nowhere to be seen. Bloody awesome; my day has got off to the best possible start.

Then Cate appears, cup of tea in hand, fully dressed and made up.

"Off to work?" I ask hopefully.

"Don't be silly! I am looking after you today. My brave, brave hero. I wonder if a hero's blowjob would help you feel better?" She is using her slightly grating cutesy voice.

"I don't think so Cate, thanks, though I might have a tug in the shower. You are more than welcome to watch. I have a lot on today, need to squeeze in back and shoulders after missing yesterday's workout. I also need to sort out the apartment. My mum's over tonight and I have a feeling the cat may have made a mess." I hop myself out of bed sweaty but motivated for the challenges ahead.

"Count your blessings and not your problems," I cheerily and loudly repeat to myself in the mirror.

My face is blanched from the heat in the bedroom, radiators on full blast. I look skinnier than usual, too much cardio. I am surprised at my own nakedness. I do not remember getting undressed last night. I glance down at my cock, looking for any clues that Cate may have taken advantage of me yet again. I feel blocked up, a winter cold. I make a mental note to buy additional vitamin C.

An unnecessary noise indicates that my spirit is about to be dampened.

"Your mum is over? The mum who lives in Spain? The one we have spoken about so much recently and you failed to mention her visit? You would prefer to touch yourself than to be with me? And a colleague has just been murdered and perhaps the only friend you have beaten up and you are heading to the gym? I am a little confused." Her tone and posture is more irritated than confused.

"And you or we, whichever one it is, do not have a fucking cat."

I look her dead in the eyes.

"I am fairly sure that I have never mentioned my mother to you and yup, she's over all right and it is going to be horrendous. Your teeth tend to grate against the underside of my penis so, for my own enjoyment in this stressful time, I would prefer to attend to myself, and although it is unfortunate that Theo is dead and Clarke has superficial head injuries, they did however both recently fuck me over so the level of sympathy I have is drastically reduced. Also, as I am sure you have noticed, prior to this week I was starting to see some real muscle gain and therefore training consistency is vital," I say, in an extremely assertive tone.

I strategically decide to ignore the cat statement, as it was not a question, and slither past her chin, which is resting on the floor, and into the bathroom. I lock the door, close my eyes and try to unsee the horror on her flustered face.

I half-heartedly tug at my uninterested penis.

Neither of us speak as I get dressed. She is just sitting on the bed. I do not want to be haunted by her sad, teary face so I reach over and stroke her hair while putting my sock on.

I check out my shades in the mirror as I leave the apartment. It is definitely a morning for sunglasses. I carry my new peacoat underhand just in case the opportunity arises to wear it.

"I'll text you later, I promise," I lie as I pull the door behind me.

Chapter 24

The bright sunshine dazzles from the metallic paint of the car. As I get closer a figure walks towards me. I instantly recognise the swagger of his silhouette, his hat pulled down low and a face scarf pulled up high.

I do not feel in danger; he just wants his money. Inhale confidence, exhale doubt.

I unlock my car. He climbs in and slides low into the passenger seat. I look up to the sky and see Cate looking down from her balcony. I wipe my runny nose on my sleeve, get into the driver's seat and start the engine.

"No problem getting you that cash, Dave, no problem at all," I say with my hands at ten to two on the wheel and my eyes fixed but not particularly focused on the road ahead.

His silence fills the cold interior of the car. I'm driving towards East London hoping this is the direction he wants to go.

He leans in to turn on my low-tech sound system. Celine Dion's "Think Twice" blares out of the speakers. Is there any chance he will mistake my CD for the radio?

"Fucking hell, bruv. I knew you was a bit odd but what the fuck," Dave shakes his head.

"This isn't mine, Dave, I promise. It's some girl I've been seeing, borrowed my car last night."

Although the subject matter isn't ideal I am glad the icy silence is broken.

"Ha, you're lying, bruv, you know me and a pal of mine have been watching you since yesterday and the only man who drives this car is you. It's disgraceful." Dave smiles a genuine smile.

I feel reassured that he is not going to kill me.

"What happened yesterday was fucked up, bruv, you know that. You've got to understand the blame lies with you. Only the one man was meant to be there, one man. Then everything would have been sweet. I'm taxing you the five grand not because I want to but because those boys need to disappear for a month or two, you get me?" Dave speaks and I fully get him.

"Yes, Dave, I understand that, it's no problem – the money, I mean. Listen, I just want to reassure you that I won't mention a thing to anyone."

"I know you won't. In fact I can guarantee you won't mention this again. Drop me down one of those side roads. I've paid those boys so I need you to drop the five bags into the Chicken Cottage on Well Street, after 6pm, this week. Carl – he's the only white guy working there – give it to him. He doesn't need you to speak. Just hand him it in a carrier bag or something."

With that I pull in and Dave gets out. He leans back into the passenger door.

"I know I don't need to tell you this, bruv, but I hear a whisper of you talking then I'm going to pay one of my boys to come and hurt those two pretty girls you're banging."

The door slams shut.

I drive around the block twice before parking. I can't think of my next move. I am delighted that Dave thinks I am "banging" Poppy but creeped out that he has clearly been watching me. Who does that?

I wonder what Poppy is going to do. I mean, I seem the obvious choice but she seems to make some bad life decisions.

She's definitely not marrying Theo, that's confirmed. I cannot imagine that continuing to spend any time with the guy who was less than a metre away from her murdered fiancé is all that appealing right now either. So Clarke could well be out of the picture.

So it's just my dad; my wealthy old pops. He is actually a good-looking old boy – weathered but evenly tanned, which helps hide his thin wispy hair, a strong jawline covered with tautly pulled skin. He looks full of vigour. The PT trains him most days for an hour in the mornings, cardiovascular with some resistance work chucked in. No sign of flabby arms or a paunch. Dresses exceptionally well, always trousers, never denim. Brioni, Zegna, Armani Black Label, occasionally Tom Ford loafers, John Lobb or Churches brogues, a sporty Rolex or a dressy Patek. He knows all the concierges at the finest restaurants and members' clubs. The ballet, the gee-gees, a concert; he never has to book in advance.

But Poppy, darling Poppy, he is old, closer to death by the day. Poppy, think about it for a moment. All of that money, the wealth, where it will end up? With me, Poppy, that's where. Death could be just around the corner. Being a CEO is stressful, takes its toll on the body. Jesus, he nearly had a heart attack just the other week when I was with him. The skin cancer, that'll get him, all of those holidays, all of that sun, and did you know every time you eat French food it takes a day off your life? I will have that money without the stress and I have been using anti-ageing moisturisers since my early teens.

It will all be mine. She needs to see that, to understand it. Mum has already had her share, so what will I get? £10 million, £20? I'll spend it all on her, every penny. I will make up for all of that hurt.

"How many pairs of very expensive shoes does it take to forget a dead fiancée?" I ask Siri.

Siri does not have an appropriate answer.

Perhaps I could do us all a favour? Help speed up the process? He isn't the sort of guy who will want to spend his later years in a nursing home. Once the deal's gone through, I imagine he will start to wither away. Work was his life. You sometimes have to be cruel to be kind.
£5k? £10k? £100k? That's not even a percentage point of what would be coming my way. I am sure Dave would organise it. I mean, the drugs market is so saturated, he is going to have to pivot at some point.

Not a stabbing though, he doesn't deserve that, too many questions asked. Maybe rat poison in his Earl Grey or on an umbrella tip. I recall him doing some business in Moscow in the mid-noughties. This could be viable.

My eyes feel incredibly dry, like I haven't blinked in some time. I zone back into my surroundings and decide to go indoors. Practise answering my mother's questions; perfect any stories I might need to tell. I search the medicine cabinet for Valium or anything that might calm the nerves. I'd better be nice to her. Who knows, maybe we will live in Spain one day. Poppy would like that, I am sure of it.

I browse the web, unsure of the extradition treaty in Spain. That is where all the gangsters go on the run, right? Apparently not anymore; I might need to buy slightly further afield.

The apartment is tidy, the fridge empty apart from some milk, actual cow's milk. Who the hell drinks that nowadays? There is bread, nasty white bread, and teabags on the side counter. A note peers from underneath:

Mrs. Danbrook asked me to get milk and tidy. She ask me to remind you that she arrive to you at 6 please leave my money £30 and I will collect next week thanks, Katia

The cleaner doesn't seem to know my mother's married name and neither do I.

The hours are passing slowly. I almost call Poppy. I almost call Clarke and my dad. I do call my mum in an attempt to cancel but it rings out to voicemail.

Cate's name flashes on my screen. I ignore it. She then follows up with a text that I don't read.

Occasionally I do pity her – Cate, I mean. In a different time she would have been acceptable, done the job. Nowhere near perfect, but who is? At least she isn't sleeping with one of my close relatives.

But every time I see Poppy, hear Poppy, think of Poppy, or her name is mentioned, everything else fades to this kind of sixties grey – the colour of those buildings in irrelevant new towns you drive through outside London.

The door buzzer startles me and I look on the camera to see Mum and a tanned little girl with brown hair and a gap-toothed smile looking in.

Did I find any medication? Something to calm my nerves. I can't quite remember. Will they take the stairs or the elevator? I close the bedroom door and root through the kitchen drawers looking for something – anything.

Chapter 25

Before I can get any words out, she has her arms around me. I had forgotten how tall my mother was, especially in block heels. My nose is running. I can't be certain that I am not crying.

The hug lasts forever. She smells of the sun, of coconut and sweet almond. She looks as glamorous as I always remember. Her neck looks tighter and her lips plumper. I have seen her handbag advertised in the *Sunday Times* style magazine. A Gucci bag from their spring cruise collection range, very tasteful indeed.

The small girl is standing awkwardly in the hallway looking up at me. Her eyes scrutinise my face. Inevitably she reminds me of Poppy all those years ago.

"Come in, Charlie, come and say hi to your big brother Oliver." Mum ushers her inside and simultaneously looks me up and down.

"You look shattered, Oliver. Your face looks so drawn; you look like you're wasting away, son," Mum says empathetically.

"I know, Mum, I've been up late working on new projects, networking. I haven't even had time to see my girlfriend." I walk into the living room and talk. I can't remember the exact details of my girlfriend.

I draw a surprisingly grubby nail along my cheekbone, not drawn out or gaunt, just chiselled.

She makes enough tea and toast for three. I turn my nose up at the translucent toast, aware of the havoc it's about to cause my blood sugars.

Charlie asks me who my favourite band is. Do I like Little Mix or Justin Bieber? Do I have a cat? Where is he? Why hasn't he eaten his cat food? Her English is perfect with the slightest accent. I enjoy the questions. Her constant chatter alleviates the awkwardness and stops Mum from discussing more pressing issues.

"Justin Bieber. He is more urban, more my vibe." I aim to answer every question accurately.

"What is urban?" Charlie asks.

"I don't know," I reply.

"Do you like the *Hunger Games* films? I have watched them all on Netflix," Charlie asks.

"I have only seen the first one – watched it one morning at work. Yes, I liked the idea of it – actually think it's a good idea every so often having a clear-out of the working classes," I reply.

I take a moment. Clarke left Theo's decaying corpse to the crows some time ago. He plans to outwit my father and then come after me.
His ginger hair makes him an easy target to spot. I perch high in the branches of the tree. I watch them tire. I watch Clarke bludgeon him to death with a rock and then I load the arrow into the bow.

"Do you have a cat? Where is your cat?" She looks at the bowl of untouched cat food and ceramic water bowl.

"Yes, Oliver, what's with the cat food? You never mentioned buying a cat," Mum contributes.

"I'm not sure. I mean, I thought I had a cat but I guess he's not around." I look at Mum and at Charlie, suddenly feeling like the child in the room again.

"Oh well, I am sure he will turn up, although you don't have the best track record with cats, do you, Oliver?" she says in a patronising tone I haven't missed.

Mum has a shower and I sit with the kid on the sofa. The questions have finished and we both relax, watching music videos on TV. A rapper with ill-fitting jeans and a Hermès belt similar to one I recently gave to charity makes his fingers into a gun and points them at me through the screen. I keep my hand to my side but point back. I pull the trigger.

She emerges from the spare room, dressed in a knee-length dress with embellishment on the capped shoulders and a pair of sky-high heels. She has an expensive-looking purple gem necklace on, highlighting her starved collar bones.
I decide to get changed into something a little more fitting. Black slim wool trousers, a textured white shirt and a dark charcoal blazer. I fish out a leather patent lace-up shoe that I haven't worn for some time.

It feels pleasant to be stepping out. My anxiety levels are low; even the incessant lyrics from Big Thugga's latest track gyrating inside my head doesn't spoil my mood. Charlie really isn't a bad kid.

I chuck my black beanie hat, black jacket and the binoculars into the boot at the same time as explaining to my mum the reason behind my newly acquired, second-hand BMW.

"I just don't understand, Oliver. Six months ago you sell the Range Rover at a loss after having it for less than a year because you just weren't using it. Now all of a sudden you have bought some rust bucket surely only suitable for a travelling salesman. It just seems, well, a bit strange." Mum sounds and looks slightly disgusted as she sits in the passenger seat of my perfectly acceptable car.

"That's it in a nutshell, Mum. When all I was doing was going to that damn office every day I really didn't need a car. Now I am out and about doing my own thing I need a set of fuel-efficient wheels. I can park it up around the corner of the restaurant if you're embarrassed." I load their suitcases into the already cramped boot as I speak.

"It's fine, Oliver, it is just fine. Let's just get to the restaurant, please."

The place is packed. The maître d' doesn't smile. He doesn't need to; the restaurant has been booked out since its opening. The decor is dark and broody, its clientele the super-rich. Overweight slobs of men shovelling food down as they ogle groups of young women. The divorcees vying for position, their fantastic tits and designer dresses that strategically lift sagging arses. Only occasionally do they nibble at the expensive entrées. Maybe they do not want the calories; maybe their overpriced chemically cut coke has numbed their hunger.

Part of me feels this really isn't an appropriate establishment for a nine-year-old. The other part really fancies a quick line. I scan the room for a potential supplier. I am not looking to buy, just a little freebie. It's been a while, hasn't it?

Mum has marched ahead, leaving the kid and me trailing a few tables behind. She is in her element. I imagine she misses this in Spain. Charlie is holding onto the sleeve of my jacket. Definitely an odd choice of restaurant for a child – the second youngest person in the restaurant is at least twice her age. She totters past in slightly too big Louboutins and a tiny silk playsuit. She has a look of determination on her face but is new to all of this.

We order the same appetiser and entrée. The portions are small. I fill up on warm bread; I keep eating just to ward off conversation.

Mum hardly touches her food. She wants to say something but doesn't. By the time her main dish arrives she has necked near half a bottle of champagne.

"I'm moving out, Oliver. I'm moving out to a dingy villa that doesn't even have a heated pool. I'm leaving him." Mum slurs her words just slightly and gazes at a young attractive couple on the next table as she talks.

"Bloody bastard was cheating on me with the hired help. She wasn't even attractive, had dirty-looking skin, scraped-back hair. Apparently they're in love. All my stuff is in storage." Her wayward stare momentarily moves towards Charlie.

Charlie doesn't look up and continues to pick at the side of her thumb.

"She knows. She saw them at it. He wants to keep her, really not sure what is for the best. Twice in my lifetime. What did I do to deserve these bastard men?" She finishes the bottle and waves it around, looking for the waiter.

I briefly drift away. I couldn't imagine cheating on Poppy, even if her neck started to droop and her arse started to sag. Cate, on the other hand, I would cheat on tomorrow, without a second thought, just to keep myself sane.

The second bottle is more than half empty. I pour a glass just so she cannot. I delve deep into my trouser pockets, looking for something, just a distraction. The kid looks at me. She needs me right now. Bringing my hands back to the table I softly punch her on the arm and point out a man or perhaps a woman who could well be Bruno Mars.
Mum flirts with the sommelier, patting his pert arse cheek at one point. I show Charlie pictures of Poppy on my phone.
Our drunk mother makes a lurch towards a Middle Eastern man with greasy slicked-back hair. He has a sweat-drenched shirt unbuttoned to his sternum and the exact same patent lace-ups on as me. The escort with him takes pity on the elderly drunk and pushes her back into her chair.

Charlie shows me pictures of her dad's new love interest on her phone. She looks exactly like my mother twenty years prior.

Three sorbets arrive at the table. Charlie and I finish ours and watch mother's melt on the dish. She left for a bathroom break some time ago.

I hear her first – incoherent rambling, bleating out orders – then I see her. Two well-built waiters who could easily pass for twins struggle to carry the dead weight of my mother up the narrow marble stairs. She is hanging off them like Jesus on a cross. Every other word is "fucking" or "outrageous."

Charlie looks up, takes in the mortifying sight and, unexpectedly, just laughs.

"This is why Dad is leaving her." Her smile is bewildering.

I get up and head to the front desk manager.

"I really am ever so sorry about this horror show. She is on antibiotics, shouldn't have had that glass of bubbly. If the guys would kindly get her into the car I will pay the bill." I poke an American Express in his direction, meekly hoping he will accept my excuses.

A familiar paranoia sweeps through me, like I am the one on drugs. He looks me up and down.

"Cocaine is what she is on, sir. One of our other patrons found her kneeling, face resting on the toilet lid, gently snoring alongside a neatly cut line." He looks like he wants to laugh but instead sneers and puts through payment on my card.

234

The kid opens the back doors of the car and the two waiters help tip her in. They both look at me, embarrassed and unsure of the correct tipping protocol for this situation.

As quick as a flash, Charlie unzips a hidden pocket on the sleeve of her quilted Moncler coat and pulls out a twenty-pound note.

"Here you go, Oliver, you can give them this. I don't need it." She pushes the perfectly folded note into my hand.

"Sorry about all that, guys, appreciate your help." I shake both of their clammy hands.

I put the car heater on. She puts her seat belt on and I start the engine.

"See if you can find a good song on the radio and I will find us a Happy Meal. I'm still starving." I smile and instinctively rub the top of her head.

As we drive through the dark streets I turn up Bruno Mars, or maybe it's Ed Sheeran, just to help drown out the snoring of my passed-out mother.

The headlamps and street lights seem so bright, they hurtle past my eyes like one of those old arcade racing games. I notice Charlie holding tightly onto the door handle and consider slowing down.
We pass McDonald's and I do not stop.

We arrive at the Mandarin. Her snoring is muffled by the fur throw that is now blocking her nose and mouth.

The bellhops dash over to the car and open the door to help the kid out. I turn off the engine and smile a fake smile. We are all equally embarrassed by the filthy car.

One of them goes to the boot and brings out two suitcases. I snatch my holdall off him and place it carefully back into the corner.

"Before you head inside, guys, we made need an extra helping hand with a particularly delicate old piece of luggage." I point into the back of the car while addressing the main bellhop.

Charlie giggles. I feel smug and then downright miserable as she turns and waves goodnight, following the four men and my mum into the hotel lobby.

"Wait up, Charlie – here, take my mobile number. Maybe tomorrow if Mum is, well, too sick to take you places, we could wander over to the Dinosaur Museum, or even the ice skating."

There is an anxious wait. She scrunches up her face while deciding. Surely she wants to spend the day with her cool older half-brother?

"Well, I would like to go to the IMAX," Charlie suggests.

I feel something real for the first time in a while.

"Okay, coolio. Are you going to be all right getting Mum into bed? Sorting yourself out, whatever you need to do?" I ask, hoping she will just say, "yes, fine."

"Yes, fine. I'm used to it. See you tomorrow." Charlie half skips and half runs to catch up with her mother and their luggage.

I get back into the car and spend a few minutes enjoying the feeling of warmth I have right now. My mind slows down to a manageable pace. The lights seem to dim. Although I do not recall drinking I have that feeling of utter relaxation.

Engine off, I let Celine Dion play. I wind down the window and empty whatever was in my pockets outside. I want to remember how this moment feels, as even I know it will be short-lived.

Chapter 26

I manage to ignore the ringing in my ears three, maybe four, times. Cate. Why won't she leave me alone?

I grab the phone.

"Ollie, why the fuck are you ignoring my calls?"

I look back at the phone. It is not Cate at all.

"Hello, hi, Poppy, how are you doing? All considering." This might be the first time she has ever called me.

"I had to give a police fucking statement. They asked about me and Theo's relationship, my friendship with Clarke, whether we – me and you, Oliver – were close friends, all just standard enquiries, apparently. What have you said to them? I fucking hope you didn't mention your visit," Poppy says accusingly.

"No, I didn't say anything about us, of course not. I just said what I saw, the mugging, the stabbing," I say, completely unsure of what I actually said.

"Okay, I believe you, I think. I am just depressed. I have nobody to talk to. Perhaps I should come and see you. We can be there for each other," Poppy says softly.

"Yes, yes, I can come to you now. I'm only ten minutes away," I blurt out excitedly.

"Not tonight, Ollie, I'm tired now. I'm in the bath and then I'm going straight to bed. I will come to yours tomorrow morning around 11. Tell me the address."

"It's East London, Pops, just by Shoreditch, a really cool area, loads of edgy types, you will fit in. I will message you the address, it's top floor."

"Just tell me the address, Ollie, and I will see you then."

This is turning out to be some night. I have no time to savour it as a reminder appears on my phone. Chicken Cottage.

I park on double yellow lines and breathe. There is one white guy behind the counter. He is tall, six foot five, and wiry.

"Carl?" I ask.

"Take a seat. I'll bring your food over when it's ready."

He hands me a takeout bag and points to a small concealed table hidden slightly by an arcade machine.

The cash is all in twenties and although I cannot recall how much is there I remember nodding in agreement as the bank teller handed it over. I tip it all into the bag and keep it well hidden on my lap.

"Here's your food, mate. Give me that rubbish. I'll bin it for you."

Carl takes the bag from my quivering wreck of a hand and walks away.

I stand up to leave, almost forgetting to take whatever Carl has just served me. I stumble around the corner, keeping my tongue at the roof of my mouth in order to stop the sick coming up. I throw up into an open bin already spilling over with rubbish. My stomach is cramped and it hurts to stand up straight.

As I try to breathe, a wino, who I am sure I recognise from the hospital, leans on the bin and points to the food I have left by my feet.

I kick it towards him. I climb into the back of my car and curl my knees to my chest.

Chapter 27

Without reason I press the buzzer to my apartment in the hope that someone will answer. They do not.

I look into the distance. There they are, the headlamps that have been watching me, the car that has been following me, they click off.

I take the stairs, hoping to meet a friend, a neighbour, just somebody to talk to. I try to think back to the fun I had with Charlie, but I cannot.
The sheets feel cold on my body as I realise that Cate's company is better than none at all.

I reach my hand over the bedside table, grabbing at a container of tablets. I take three, maybe four. I do not attempt to read the label in the pitch black of dark.

I wake up feeling sluggish. It is a struggle to unglue my eyelids, and my stomach feels bloated.

Something is happening today. I check the time. 10.15am. I see a message from the kid.

Hi, Ollie, are we still on for today?

I feel poorly, run down. I barely know her. Besides, she isn't my responsibility, I keep telling myself as I type.

Sorry, Charlie, something to do with work has come up, a business meeting, might be able to do late this afternoon. Is Mum up? Call me if you need me.

241

The reply is instantaneous:

Ok. Mum is asleep. I'll just watch some TV.

I feel relieved. That was easy. Why can't Cate be that accommodating?

Then a message comes through from Clarke:

Would be good to meet up, mate, need someone to talk to, can't clear my head, are you about?

This is almost immediately followed by a text from my dad:

How are things, son? Haven't heard from you in a while. Terrible business with Theo.

I have never felt so in demand. I ignore both. The less conversation I engage in right now the better.

The bubbles wash down my torso, my mind so separated from my body I wash myself over and over again, unsure of what parts I have already covered.

The intercom shrieks at me. I ignore it several times. It's the police or maybe Cate.

Leaving a soaking trail behind I pick up the receiver. Maybe it's Dave. He's got the money and still wants me gone.

"Ollie, it's me." Poppy sounds somber.

I look into the camera just for a few seconds. She has a knitted hat on, not quite a beret but that kind of look, and a navy trench coat with a sloppy rollneck spilling over the top. The sort of outfit my mum would have modelled thirty years ago.

The door buzzes again.

"Ollie, are you there? Come on, let me in, it's freezing out here." Her teeth chatter as she talks.

I watch her for a moment, then she disappears from sight. I hear her tap at the door as I pull on cashmere sweatpants. I pick a navy Sunspel tee from the wardrobe and pull it over my head. Looking in the mirror I tie a sweatshirt around my waist to disguise my sore, bloated gut.

She taps against the door again just as I open it.

We awkwardly greet each other, confusion over one kiss or two. She glides into the living room. The apartment looks great and I look suitably cool, although inside I am anything but.
I excuse myself. Leaving her in the living room I make a dash for the ensuite. My nails are filthy. I scrub them and then clip them, too short as always.

"The apartment looks great, Ollie, really great, very nicely done. I didn't realise you had a cat, where is it?" As she talks she removes her hat and tresses of blonde hair float to her shoulders.

"Oh, I don't, not anymore, he died. In fact I really must tell the cleaner to stop leaving food out." I let the agitation at the cleaner's incompetence show in my voice while scooping the food bowl, mat and water bowl up and pushing them down into the flip-top bin.

"That's sad, so much death," sighs Poppy.

She sits on the sofa, not completely comfortably. Knees close together, hands on top.

I should offer a drink but do not.

"I was wrong to say all of what I said, Ollie, all of that about your dad, Theo, Clarke. My life is just all a bit of a muddle. I have been seeing a therapist, a few therapists, to try and find out what is wrong with me."

"There's nothing wrong with you, Poppy. You're perfect."

It doesn't feel right sitting next to her, so I perch on the arm of the opposing chair.

"How can you say that? Perfect? You are delusional, Oliver. Perfect to who? To the dead fiancé I cheated on with his boss? To the dead fiancé who I cannot even mourn? I don't even miss him. Perfect to your dad? Who I fuck for money? Who pays me a salary way above my pay grade to keep him company? Perfect to Clarke, to someone who every time I need him I use as an emotional crutch, who tells me he loves me on a weekly basis? Who genuinely believes and still believes that I intended to leave Theo for him." The tears are streaming down Poppy's perfect face. She is shaking and the words tremble out.

I had planned to stay silent but the words will not stay inside.

"You are perfect to me."

"Agggh!" She screams. "Perfect to you? Ollie, how can you say that? For how many years have I watched you follow me around like a little lovesick puppy? Your pathetic attempts to woo me, my cruel teasing, the pleasure it gave me to ignore you in public, to watch you crumble as I pass out your champagne and then leave with other men. The only reason I ever paid Clarke any attention in the first place was to watch you squirm. I AM FUCKING YOUR DAD!" Poppy shouts, her body still shaking, tears escaping down her cheeks, her make-up staying firmly fixed to her face.

I attempt to enjoy the certain delight that her and Clarke's relationship is now only an emotional one. Like a homosexual and his girl pal. They probably topped and tailed in bed. I am also a little surprised that he has been so downbeat about the whole Theo thing. I mean, if he really thought she was going to leave him then surely I only helped speed up the process.

The situation with my father I don't feel so comfortable with. There is a certain above and beyond level of deceit about that scenario for sure.

"None of us are perfect, Poppy. All of us have dirty laundry; we have all made mistakes. I just know we have a connection. I can see past your faults. Could you ever see past mine?"

Poppy reaches out her hand and places it on top of mine.

"The only mistake you have made, Oliver, is falling for the wrong girl." Poppy's eyes are dragging me in.

"No, no, I have made other mistakes, bigger mistakes."

"What other mistakes have you made, Oliver? I feel a connection too, but I think it is important that we are honest with each other, like I have been with you," Poppy says, touching one hand against my face.

"Oliver, I didn't love Theo. Tell me what happened."

She temporarily breaks eye contact, slightly clumsily placing her phone on her lap.

I feel comfortable. This is all I have ever wanted.

As I finish telling what I am fairly sure is the truth, I feel lighter, a real weight off of my shoulders. I made it very clear that murder was never the game plan, how I pivoted, embraced the change and am now steering the ship in the right direction.

She wipes my eyes with a tissue and puts her face to mine. I cannot help but notice as Poppy pauses and puts her phone into the Céline bag.

I watch her mouth shaping to speak. Her lips pursed, she leans in and presses hers against mine.

I feel her pulsate through my body. A kiss. Her lips taste slightly salty, or maybe it's my lips. She is leaning her weight into me, pushing onto me, one hand on my chest as her other hand squeezes mine. I push back; I want to dominate our first time. Surely she isn't the sort of girl to just want a kiss. The girl seeing men behind her fiancé's back surely follows a kiss with wild-animal-like sex.

Her hand grips the back of my right arm – the tricep, she went for the tricep, a much bigger muscle than the often-overtrained bicep. I am pushing her into the corner of the sofa. It doesn't look comfortable. I pull back slightly just to check if it looks like she wants me to stop.

"Ollie, I just need a moment. I just need to go to the bathroom."

She sidesteps away and picks up her bag.

"You can leave those here," I say suggestively.

"Oh I need to, you know, powder my nose."

"You could leave your phone."

"Seriously, Ollie, I am meant to be meeting an old school friend for lunch. I need to use the bathroom and I am going to message her to cancel. Relax, I won't be long," Poppy says somewhat nervously.

Something isn't quite right.

I hear the door lock and the seat go down. I slither across the marble floor, I open the cutlery drawer and take out a teaspoon. Treading around the edge of the hallway floorboards I creep to the bathroom door. The taps are running but she has not yet flushed the chain.

I take a deep breath in. I have no plan, no strategy. Sometimes you just need to go with the flow.

The narrow edge of the spoon twists in the lock and with my left hand I pull down the handle. She is standing well away from the running taps, phone in hand. I grab at it. She throws it to the floor.

I grab Poppy's face and pull her towards the door. Unexpectedly, she leans into me. The momentum pushes us against the wall.

I try to push her away, to pick up her phone. Who was she texting? Her lips press against me again; her hands separate my fingers, she kisses at my neck. I grab her hair and tug her head back. The look in her eyes is fear.

She pulls my T-shirt over my head and kisses down my chest, dropping to her knees. I lift her back up by her hair. I undo her blouse and unhook her bra while gripping her wrist. Her breasts are as beautiful as I imagined. I lean down and bite at her nipple.

There is a distraction on the floor. The bra, the Agent Provocateur bra. I kick it away with my foot. I tug down the waistband on her jeans, my fingers on the outside of her knickers. I pull my hand out and push it back on the inside. She is kissing me, on the neck, towards my ear. Her hand is rubbing me, cashmere against cock. She strokes me stomach to tip.

"Take me to the bedroom," she whispers in my ear.

I ignore her, pushing her back onto a recently purchased vanity chair. I grip the waist of her knickers and yank them down her legs. She sits naked with her jeans and Agent fucking Provocateur underwear at her feet. Her pussy is immaculate, hair-free, neat. She leans her head towards my crotch, she attempts to reach her phone with her foot.

I push her back against the chair and separate her legs with my knee. Our eyes meet. She is not in the moment. She is not in the fucking moment.

I pull her to her feet. She manages to cover the phone with her jeans. I was honest with her. She said we needed to be honest with each other.

"Who were you messaging?" I edge her forward and stand behind.

"My work friend, I promise. Afterwards you can check, don't ruin this."

I rub against her exquisite arse cheeks, more perfect than I imagined, and bend her towards the sink.

She puts her hand on my cock.

"You've gone soft."

The tears are not relieving my disappointment. I shouldn't have told her.

"You said it was an old school friend," I say, as I twist my hand around her hair.

"You're hurting me."

"I should not have told you. You tricked me," I say, aware now that there is no turning back.

249

I hold her head under the taps and push the plug down.

"You said we needed to be honest with each other," I repeat again and again.

Her knees give way. I let go of her hair and she slumps to the floor. I turn off the taps and join her.

Chapter 28

It sounds like a police siren but it is not; it is just the buzzer. Who would want to disturb me right now? I have a lot on.

As I look into the camera at a long, tear-stained face that repulses me more than ever, my immediate urge is to scream FUCK YOU at the speaker.

But I do not.

"Hello, who is it?" I ask.

Of course I know who it is.

"You know who it is, you stupid wanker; Jesus, Ollie, what are you up to? Let me in. It's humiliating. Do you know how many times I have called you? Okay, someone else has buzzed me in, I'm coming up." Cate's last few words sound distant as her face disappears from the screen.

I have about two minutes to create a fathomable story. I tuck Poppy into the covers and rest her head on the pillow. I check one final time, hoping she might still be alive. No breath, no time to Google bringing a loved one back from the dead. I use her jeans to sop up the soaked bathroom floor and kick them into the corner.

Banging on the door. It is either the massive Asian dude here to throttle me, or Cate. I have no preference.

251

I could kill her? It wasn't so hard. I can see why these lunatics end up getting a taste for it.

"Poppy, sweetheart, stay here for a minute, now Cate is coming up. I have sort of been seeing her on and off. She isn't going to be too pleased you are here, so I'm just going to pull the door shut, okay?" I don't turn the bedroom light on, leaving her dead but cosy in my room.

"Hi, how are you? You look smart," I say, desperately trying to find a mirror to check my own appearance.

She looks nice, presentable. Her make-up is slightly smeared but her hair is bouncier than normal, full of volume.

I can see how she thought this was going to pan out. I would explain my strange behaviour. It could be something to do with my mother's visit, the death of that guy from work, or a career-related issue. She would lovingly accept my excuses, really showing her sympathetic side. We would have one of those special hugs and then she would force me into having sex.

The problem right now is that she could have walked in here naked with the keys to a speed-boat in one hand, a rose-gold Rolex sea-dweller in the other hand, with a Victoria Secret's model attached to her arse by her lube-coated fingers and the situation wouldn't have changed.

I need to get her the fuck out of here.

She walks into the living room. Her bottom does have a nice shape. How can I word this? "It's not me, it's you." "You'll never guess who I bumped into today."

She is shouting, loudly, too loudly. I can barely make sense of the muddled words, her hands picking up things, putting other things down.

"What the fuck is that? Who the fuck does this belong to?" Cate is shrieking and waving Poppy's beret and coat about.

"It is my beret and my coat, Cate. It's known as Parisian chic."

The lie is bloody desperate. The jacket looks tiny; even before I had started my anabolic steroids stage it would have been too snug a fit.
The beret alone may have been passable.

"It was a rhetorical question. I know who they belong to, that mental slut from the office. I saw her come in here."

I take a deep breath. This moment, or a slight variation of it, was always going to come.

"Cate, you need to understand…"

I catch a glimpse of the cat's tail as he squeezes himself out of the closing front door. I really feel the first blow. Christ, right in the middle of the face. My vision is blurred.

I wince ready for another. I can't quite find my bearings.

"Where is she!" Cate bellows.

My nose is pouring with blood. Apparently by wiggling it you can tell if it is broken.

"She went down as you came up. She is scared of you, your angry face is intimidating. She left her coat and her hat and ran down the stairwell."

This sounds plausible.

"I love Poppy dearly. You, Cate, on occasion I find tolerable."

She raises her open hand but drops it back down, wailing at me. I am not convinced I would win a fistfight and the whole hitting her on the head with an object is just too much of a bloody mess. I am already in a bit of a pickle.

"Cate, please calm down. I apologise; I have been insensitive. However, seeing as you have assaulted me for the second time in our relationship, I think we should discuss this in a public place. No more lies, I promise." I lead her back to the front door, forcefully ushering her out with a palm to her lower back.

"I need a tissue, Oliver, please give me a moment."

I look at my face in the hallway mirror. I wipe away speckles of blood from my moustache and drag my sleeve under my nose.

I chuck the top I had just put on into the linen bin and stick on an identical one. I jump out of my skin as I spot Poppy motionless in my bed. A shiver runs through me and I quickly close the door behind me.

"Come on then, Ollie. Let's go and work this out," Cate says.

"How come your bathroom floor was so wet?" she enquires as we step into the lift.

Fuck, Cate had just traipsed through a crime scene. Please, please, dear God, don't let her have spotted the jeans.

"I left the shower running for a very long time, Cate."

"Why would you do that?" she probes.

"Do you remember me mentioning a potential business trip to Argentina?" I ask speculatively.

"No."

"I mentioned it. I have a potential business trip to Argentina that could be quite interesting. Anyway, it is going to be extremely warm and obviously I could not possibly wear a wool suit. I pulled out a Paul Smith from the wardrobe, very nice, cotton, very appropriate but creased to fuck. So I decided to hang the suit up, run the shower on the highest possible temperature and steam the little bastards out. Then of course Poppy turned up and – well you know, I'm sure you don't want the gruesome details," I say, pleased that it is not all a complete lie.

"Sounds plausible," Cate says acceptingly. "So why were Poppy's jeans and knickers screwed up on the floor? I mean, I know she is a slut, but I'm presuming she wore something out onto the streets of Hackney."

"Shoreditch," I correct Cate.

"She's in your flat, your grubby little den of deceit on a dirty street in Hackney."

I slam the front door behind us both.

"She has a change of clothes here, Cate, an entire capsule wardrobe."

Cate lets out a scream of pure rage.

I let her step out onto the street first. I am prepared to use her as a human shield. It seems busy but I only spot hipsters, no hitmen, just overprivileged fools with scruffy beards and ugly little bulldogs.

"You want a coffee, Cate, or shall we just walk? We could walk you back to the station and chat at the same time," I say, crossing the road in the direction of the station.

"I drove, Oliver. That's my car right over there outside the café."

She points at a navy blue Mini Cooper. I recognise it.

"No, Oliver, you have never seen it before. I've only just picked it back up from my parents' house. I'm sure I told you that."

I shrug, certain I have seen the Mini before but wary of pushing the point.

"I need a cup of tea. We need to talk this through," she announces.

I disagree but once again opt out of arguing.

I do not want to take her anywhere we might be seen. Unfortunately, I am a free agent now and a potential life partner might be on my doorstep.

The dirty little greasy spoon; that will do the trick. The artery-clogging menu is now at a slanted angle halfway down the window, missing the Blu Tack previously holding it all together. The windows a tinted yellow from grease and most probably cigarettes; I doubt a no-smoking policy is in place. What would be the point?

Yes, this is the perfect spot for a quick, neat break-up. Deflect her questions, explain with certainty that Poppy and I are a couple, insist that Poppy shot home to get her yoga stuff, something about a couple's class she wants us to do late afternoon. Maybe mention something about Theo being in debt, a crack habit maybe, hence the withdrawn features. Perhaps that is why Theo was stabbed. Poppy fears for her life. Let's hope they don't get to her.

"Good thinking, Danbrook," I say hopefully, quietly to myself.

"Let's go in here, great little spot. They do a cracking all-day breakfast, black pudding, the lot, a cup of tea's 80p. Perfect." I again gently assist Cate through the door; the enthusiasm in my voice doesn't waver.

Two tables of six working men, all in those high-visibility jackets you associate with struggling to make ends meet. I

257

am fairly sure there are no coal mines in Shoreditch, but these chaps have dirt all over their faces, and the bags under their eyes have bags. They are hunched over and, as they mop up their plates with the whitest of bread, I cannot help but notice the thickness of their wrists.

They are all speaking at the same time, all with different accents, but generally they seem to be in agreement.

On the other table are an elderly West Indian gentleman, impeccably dressed, and a white woman of around the same age. She is ever so slim, a sagging jowl, yet ageing gracefully. Pearls sit on top of a red cashmere jumper.

They sit in silence, simultaneously sipping tea.

The fourteen customers and the sweating hippo of a woman behind the counter all stop what they are doing. They stare at Cate and then glare at me.

"Are you alright, love?"

I look at her face. It is still long and sad but tears are streaming, running down her cheeks and launching like lemmings off her quivering chin. Her bottom lip is trembling terribly but no noise is coming out.

"We are splitting up. Terrible time. Do you have a private booth or something similar we could utilize?" I interrupt, trying to seem upbeat and cheery.

"I was speaking to the young lady. Everything okay, sweetheart? What's he gone and done? Take a seat and I'll bring over a hot mug of tea and some tissues." The woman's face is sweaty with broken veins on her bulbous nose. She has a raspy common voice and tattoos on both of her thick forearms. If lung cancer doesn't get her, diabetes will. I opt out of interrupting for a second time.

"I'm okay, thank you for asking. We'll just sit in the corner over there. He's right, we are having relationship difficulties, lots to talk about and sort out. Could I get a pot of tea? I am just going to use your toilet to clean up my face a bit." Cate manages to hold her composure as she speaks.

I admire her for that. This cannot be easy.

While she is gone I order a chicken and mayo cob, which she assures me is pure chicken breast and not filler, and avoid making eye contact with twelve probably ex-offenders while wobbling my nose left to right, re-checking it isn't broken.

I find myself tapping both feet on the floor, left foot, right foot, right foot, right foot, and looking at the time on a stainless-steel Rolex I do not remember buying. She has been six minutes. What the hell could she be doing? I vision her taking a woefully sad dump. This disgusts me and also assures me I am doing the right thing.

"Do you want anything to eat? A bacon and egg roll? Don't you think it's great they serve breakfast all day? Would you say I have overly skinny wrists?"

I wipe at my nose. Maybe this cold is the flu. I must check the symptoms. I am sure I read once that a severe case of influenza can cause psychosis.

For the briefest of moments reality rears its ugly head. I have to get rid of a fucking body, a beautiful body that I love.

"Cate, I am sorry that..."

"Ollie, let me speak first, please. I am so sorry for punching you. You need help. This Poppy thing, it needs to stop. Please stop with Poppy. What you're doing is unacceptable. It's hurting people who care about you."

She takes a breath.

"Besides the damage you are doing to our relationship, I love you. I accept the feelings you have for her. I thought, I still think, you can change. You will need to change."

Four of the builders get up and leave. One of them purposefully knocks the back of my chair as he walks past, spinning me to a 45-degree angle. I stay put, like if anything he has done me a favour.

I am starting to feel quite sick. I am sure there is medicine in my bedside cabinet.

"I am going to fuck her again, Cate; and again and again. In fact, I plan to finish up this conversation by the time you've finished up that cup of tea and get back over there and give her one." I wouldn't, couldn't actually do that.

"I need to go to the bathroom. Do not let anyone follow me," I whisper more loudly than expected.

I notice Cate and the eight remaining workman and the overweight café owner watch me as she buries her head in her hands. Her sobbing seems well paced and thought out.

Keeping my foot against the door, I push the powder into my nose. It falls back onto my hand. I snort into the sink and splash water around my nostrils. I need to clear out debris, make room for the new. How long it has been since my last line I could not possibly know.

"Cate, Cate, Cate, I don't really have anything of value at your house: a pair of Nike trainers, the black knitted ones, a watch or two and January's issue of *Esquire* that I have yet to finish. You could bike them over. Otherwise I think that's us done." I am now standing and talking, aware of the remaining workmen who look like they would happily rip me apart limb by limb.

"Why did you do it?" she wails.

"Cate, please understand your part in this. You were a comfort to me. I will treasure those moments. I have to go." I have one foot out of the door. I leave a two-pound coin. It should cover my part of the bill.

What am I thinking? I follow up by chucking a wad of notes, mostly twenties, onto the table.

She separates her head from her palms. She has two almost perfect imprints on her forehead from her index fingers.

"Why did you do it, Oliver?" she asks again as I lay down another twenty onto the table.

"I see you more as a friend, Cate, a really good friend, who maybe I just need a break from."

"That guy in your car, the black guy, outside of my house, I think you call him Dave, don't you?"

I sidle back in to the café and take my seat, raising my eyebrows to the remaining workmen and let out a nervous giggle.

"Say again? Black man? Seems quite unlikely. Really I only know one black guy – well, mixed race. Goes to my gym, think he boxes, name's Lennox or something like that. I try and steer clear as potentially he could be a homosexual, imagine."

This is a truth of sorts. I have no idea of his name but he has the lean muscle tissue of a hundred-metre sprinter and is more than comfortable drying himself within my personal space.

There is no way she has any idea who Dave is. Wait, she saw him that night? I will say it was a guy I buy some weed off, some coke off. For when Poppy and I want to go all night.

"Oh, do you mean the black guy who dropped that coke off to me a couple of days back?"

"Yes, I mean the guy who came to your car. I am fairly sure his name is Dave and I am fairly sure he wasn't only dropping coke off." She is comfortably matter of fact.

"Some odd things have happened in the last week or two. Just before I was away, just after I got back," she slurps her tea.

I hope it is stewed, leaving an even more bitter taste in her interfering hole.

"I went on your laptop. Mine was doing some kind of update. I was just looking at holidays, shoes, girly stuff, and you hadn't closed down your browser."

"Was it porn? I do watch quite a lot of porn and some of it leans towards the hardcore side," I say hopefully.

"There was some porn, but it was the other pages that disturbed me. Poppy's Facebook page, Poppy's Instagram page, even her sodding LinkedIn and the timetable of the gym that I was fairly sure she went to." Cate is chewing the corner of her lip.

It is starting to feel like she is enjoying this, the sick twisted individual.

"Can I make a quick call?" I take my phone out of my pocket.

"No, you'll want to hear this. So, very aware that you did have an obsession with Poppy and aware that this could have a detrimental effect on our relationship, I decided to keep my eye on you."

"You followed me?" I ask knowingly, remembering where I had seen that navy blue Mini.

"No, not at first. Initially I decided to just watch and wait. You were in the shower. You were an awful long time. Probably tugging away at your depressed little member."

I nod acceptingly.

"Your phone beeped. I couldn't help but look. The name came up as Dave: 'all set for Thursday, you sure you want this?'"

"Ah, I see," I say.

I remember that message as I had been towelling off after my shower and wank. I really do not even recall Cate being in the apartment.

"At this point in my mind I had decided that Dave was probably a made-up name, a pseudonym for a girl you were meeting up with on the side, most likely Poppy. So guess what, Ollie, I followed you on that Thursday night. I had gone back to my parents and picked up my runaround and I followed you on your journey. Sitting fifty metres away from Poppy's gym I watched you. You told me you had gone to meet Clarke, but I didn't want to jump to conclusions." Cate gulps as she speaks and goes to take a mouthful from her empty teacup.

"I had gone to meet Clarke. He has a not particularly nice flat there; I should have told you that." Physically I am motionless but emotionally I am slipping down into my chair and onto the floor.

"I was holding back tears. I was convinced you were meeting Poppy. I thought I had fixed you, that we could still be together. I called Theo, just to ask him if he was with Poppy, if he knew her whereabouts. He said he was just leaving Clarke's. She was at home, he thought. He had to go as he could hear Clarke shouting. He cut me off. I could hear the shouting too."

"You were there?" I ask. I feel sick. I also pick up her teacup hoping to find some kind of moisture.

Had I mentioned Theo's debt yet? The crack? Poppy scared for her life?

"Apparently Theo had a lot of debt, Cate – crack, it's the new craze among stressed executives. Poppy is scared for her life; they'll probably kill her next." I reach for her hands, speaking through gritted teeth.

"Correct, I was metres away, Ollie. I got out of my car before you. I froze. But unlike you, I froze unintentionally. I wasn't watching Clarke, Ollie, I was watching you, on your phone, ducking down behind the car. You knew exactly what was happening." Cate was now in full flow. She was composed. She was the other bloody witness.

I look around. The café is now empty. When did they all leave? The brutish café owner inconveniently mops around my feet. A waft of bleach and dank water clears my nasal passages.

"I watched and you waited. If you had diverted your eyes for even one millisecond you would have seen me. You waited for the attacker – Dave, or whatever his real name is – to stab poor Theo and then you ran over." Cate has a tear rolling from that left eye of hers. She stops for a breath.

265

"That's not accurate, really it isn't." I had been lying so much recently that even being able to tell another half-truth felt like a weight off my shoulders.

"It was not Dave," I say truthfully.

"I saw it with my own eyes, Ollie. Just like I saw you get into the car with Dave the other night; just like I saw you go to dinner with your drunk mum, and then I saw you giving a bag to a man in a fucking takeaway restaurant. It was money, wasn't it? Blood money." The composure has gone and she is struggling to get the words out. A tear also runs down from her right eye.

"I was meeting Clarke for a beer. You knew that. I forgot to tell you about his new place, as it really is quite unremarkable. I wasn't expecting Theo. I was scared, that's why I froze," I say, comfortable that all of this is true.

"I made up my mind that night that I loved you, that once I knew exactly what was going on I could forgive you. Perhaps you needed to see somebody. I gave a statement, Ollie; I lied for you."

"Thanks, Cate – I mean, you didn't need to; you've got it all wrong," I say, with a confused type of relief.

"I called Dave, I saved his number and I called him."

The relief immediately evaporates.

"I called him and told him what I had seen, that I knew it was him, that if he even thought of coming anywhere near my Oliver I would tell the police."

266

I get up, I walk to the café door and lock it from the inside.

"I told the police that I had decided to tag along as a surprise, that these two guys were grabbing at Theo's phone, that the attacker was being overpowered and that's when he pulled out the knife. I got out of my car and saw brave, fearless Oliver running over."

"Theo really was not overpowering the attacker," I cannot help but point out.

"My love for you has blinded me, Oliver. You are just, well, so damaged but so innocent at the same time. All of these years that you've been following Poppy around like a lovesick puppy I have been following you around like one, and I bet you've never even noticed."
Cate stands up, pushes a wad of notes back towards me and leaves £10 on the table. She picks up crumbs of scone and a raisin and delicately, precisely, places them onto her saucer.

"Oliver, you see now why we need each other?"

I nod, realising that in two weeks it is a new year and mine might be panning out differently to how I had planned.

"The phone I found on your bathroom floor – it's Poppy's. She didn't leave your apartment, Oliver, so where is she?"

I look around the grotty hovel of a café. A couple of tasteless Christmas decorations shaped like stars hang from the ceiling in gold and metallic green. A reindeer with a flashing red nose is perched next to the exit, plugged in to an extension lead that has been lazily taped down to the floor. Somehow I missed this on the way in. During brief interludes of silence I had noticed the background music, but only now could I hear it. It will be lonely this Christmas without you to hold, so lonely this Christmas, so lonely and cold. Outside the world passed by, in a rush, excitedly shopping for presents and enjoying festive cheer.

I look at Cate lovingly. "I think I am going to need a helping hand," I say, as I put my arms around her.

"I am glad you two sorted it. She's a stunner; you'd do well to keep her," the greasy-skinned café owner grunts while slapping me on the back and opening the café doors. "And have a good Christmas."

Chapter 29

Dave's phone is off. Permanently turned off. He knows where I live. He knows where Cate lives. He knows people who would happily kill me for less than the average weekly wage. I will need to tread carefully.

Cate lets herself in. She thanks the two homosexuals, possibly my neighbours, for helping her up the stairs. She mentions something about them popping by for a gathering, maybe New Year's Eve, just as long as we have finished decorating. She has four huge Ikea bags full of unsuitable tat.

I hold the door open as she drags them in. For thirty minutes I watch her. She turns on the radio, she opens the blinds and starts placing unsuitable ornaments around the house, hammering in some nails and hanging generic black and white imagery. She places cactuses on the kitchen side and succulents on the window edge. As each bag empties she neatly folds them to one side.

"Right, come on then, we better get this done," she mutters.

Her dead, motionless body feels surprisingly light in my arms. As Cate looks on I do my best to hide the overbearing sense of longing that must be oozing from me.

I lay her on a bed sheet, gagging as Cate hums an Ed Sheeran tune while roughly cleansing Poppy's entire body with a toilet wipe. She dresses her and then wipes the body down one more time. I take one final look at that beautiful face. Cate hurriedly pulls the sheet over before I am finished.

She opens up one of the giant blue Ikea sacks and I lower Poppy's folded dead body in. As I hold the sack together I allow a tear to roll from my out-of-sight left eye, well away from Cate's intimidating glare. She puts the other sack over the top. To any prying eyes the bags just look like unsuitable junk ready to be returned to store.

She watches me; she watches for the neighbours as I carry the bags into the lift. It is dark outside but not pitch black. As I lift her to the boot of the car with ease I imagine for one brief moment that I am carrying her into our honeymoon suite, into the Caribbean sea, anywhere aside from the trunk of a BMW 1 series.

Cate is already in the passenger seat. I freeze as a group of teenagers in identical tracksuits pass me. This is it. Dave has sent them.

"Alright, mate," one of them says.

I ignore him, get in and lock the doors.

"Have you got the knife?" Cate asks.

"Yes, it's under the passenger seat, there in the Paul Smith washbag," I grimace, knowing what lies ahead.

I turn Celine Dion down. We remain silent.

We drive east, through the streets of Leyton and Woodford. We park up. Cate stays in the car. I pop the boot and drag Poppy's body out. She feels heavier than before, or perhaps my arms feel weaker. I drag her behind some trees and poke the knife into her body three or four times.

"I am really fucking sorry," I say as I leave her beautiful, murdered corpse in Epping Forest.

"Well, I'm glad that's done," Cate declares.

I park up and walk to Cate's Mini. We do not speak. She grips the steering wheel with an awfully tight grip. My penis winces. She takes the back route home.

She opens the balcony doors and throws the knife and the phone into the Thames.

I let her kiss my neck. I let her chew my earlobe.

Chapter 30

I am sitting in the lobby of the Mandarin Oriental. I am waiting, not particularly patiently. Right foot tapping, right foot again and then left foot two or three times. Where is she? We had agreed to meet at 9.30am; it is now 10am. Perhaps choked on her own vomit after emptying the mini bar? No, Charlie would be there to put her in the recovery position. Perhaps she is finishing off with the young concierge who had helped her out of the car two days ago, his roaming hands getting a feel of the wealthy cougar. She could have left without saying goodbye, encouraged by Charlie, who now despises her letdown of a half-brother.

"Oliver! Oliver, snap out of it. Always in a daydream." The sound of stilettos on the marble floor echo, as does my mother's raspy voice.

She looks remarkably well. Twenty-four hours of massages and lounging in a spa seem to have worked wonders. A completely different character to the human-sized battered leather holdall two waiters and three hotel staff had dragged from restaurant to hotel room.

"Hi, Ollie," Charlie says.

She plonks down next to me.

"Hi, how are you both?"

"Charlie is fine, such a good little girl. I am better after that awful business on Friday night. I have a good mind to sue.

Manhandled after catching food poisoning in their restaurant." Mum looks around the lobby, whispering in a furious tone.

"So that explains them finding you with your chin resting on the toilet seat," I say.

The kid giggles. I actually manage a smile.

"Well, it must have been my antidepressants, Oliver; Charlie will tell you. I'm depressed. I must have taken one too many. I might have even done it on purpose. You know…" Mum says, in the same whispering tone, as if someone is listening in.

"To commit suicide? Like Poppy's mum? It might have been quicker to swallow twenty pills, Mum, rather than chopping them up with a credit card and snorting them," I whisper back through gritted teeth.

"Is Poppy your girlfriend?" Charlie asks.

"She was going to be," I reply to myself. "I am so sorry about yesterday, Charlie, I really am. I had a few things come up."

"No worries. I know I am only a kid. I went to the IMAX by myself anyway. It was cool."

"Did you know I was depressed? I am getting another divorce. He wants to take her off me. You are not helping matters, all of this nonsense about a girlfriend. Poppy? Grieving Poppy, whose fiancé has just been murdered? She messaged me via the Facebook, Oliver, yesterday. She said you needed help; said you were being a nuisance. He won't take Charlie away from me." Mum's whisper builds to a convincing din at the end that bounces off the lobby walls.

"I want to live with Dad," Charlie states.

Good for you, kid. This woman is a mess.

"Be an angel and go and book us a taxi. Save us having to squeeze into Oliver's runaround. I need to talk to him for a moment." Mum shoos Charlie away.

In her most serious of mother moments she faces me, hands on knees. Seemingly oblivious to the growing contingent of tourists starting to fill the lobby and also seemingly okay with sending her child to run errands.

"I spoke with your father. He is concerned," Mum says.

"About your second divorce? The coke in the cubicle incident? Both?"

"No, Oliver; he tells me you are not taking his calls. He tells me that there are rumours of your colleagues owing money to crack dealers. You're not doing crack, are you, Oliver? He tells me you are not answering your friend Clarke's calls either."

"Rumours?"

"Yes. Your father spoke to Clarke. The police have a lead on the case. Apparently Theo had an addiction; he owed quite a lot of money."

"I had no idea, Mum. I mean the haggard, withdrawn face should have been a giveaway, I suppose."

"Yes, apparently while Theo was in Germany he confided in a colleague that the stress drove him to drugs. The shame of it," she says, comfortably ignoring her own addictions.

Good old Cate, I think to myself.

"This is why I want you to stay away from Poppy, just in case the police get the wrong idea."

"Good idea, Mum," I say almost in disbelief.

I am hugging Charlie.

"I am going to miss you, kid," I whisper, pulling her head close to my chest.

She giggles, a giggle that I don't want to let go.

"Come to Spain and visit us in the new year. I am going to tell my dad what a great brother you are, Ollie," she says sincerely.

"I could be a great brother," I say to myself.

"Oliver, come and see me in Spain, please. I think I need my son back," Mum says. We hug less awkwardly than normal.

Chapter 31

The phone rings. Cate is asleep, so I edge out of the bed, wrap a dressing gown around me and go out onto the balcony.

"Clarke, sorry I have missed your calls, I have been super-busy."

"She is dead."

And I had completely forgotten. Most likely it would have been temporary, but for that brief moment my conscious was clear.

"Ollie, mate, are you there? They found her murdered out in the woods in Essex, stabbed, like Theo. Mate, I am devastated. I loved her."

My silence is good; it suggests shock when really I just have very little to say.

"We all loved her, Clarke, every single one of us," is all I manage to get out.

Chapter 32

The police interview goes swimmingly well.

The rumour mill is in full swing. They found a secret phone at her home with messages to another man. They found a secret phone in his gym locker with messages to several other women; he was even a member of a high-class dating agency. They found coke, weed, uppers and downers in a shoebox in the walk-in wardrobe. If I had to guess I would presume it was a Louboutin box.

The crack surprised everyone. I feigned surprise. We were close. I acted as a confidant to Poppy while she struggled to deal with her cheating fiancé.

The only mention of my father was of him working them both to the bone, even at the weekends. Perhaps that pushed them to drugs.
I had the car valeted twice, then sold it for ten thousand pounds to a suspicious-looking Eastern European who looked vaguely familiar.

I watched him pull up the shutters, his lanky frame instantly recognisable. I follow him in.

"Give this to Dave. Tell him I am sorry," I say, chucking the bundle of money behind the counter.

Carl looks uninterested, unfazed.

"Sure," he says while tipping an Ikea-sized sack of frozen chicken into a vat.

I am hardly surprised at the amount of interest my apartment on the border of trendy Shoreditch and Hackney has received in just two days. I decide to show a few couples around myself; let them know exactly how lucky they are to be renting this exciting space.

I am more surprised at the turnout for Theo's funeral. I attend with Cate. We hold hands for most of the ceremony. I mask my smile and she overdoes her tears. I shake hands with Clarke, who apologises for the way he treated me at the hospital. I assure him I have no idea what he is talking about and reassure him that I won't mention his fling with Poppy to a living soul.

I recognise the security guard, and the fat receptionist temp – they gave her the full-time job. I nod at Glen, who is apparently actually called Andy. He nods back. I notice a group of kids who look like delinquents, some of whom have turned up in Taekwondo gear.

He is nowhere to be seen though. Good old James Danbrook hasn't shown up. People ask and I make excuses for him. A business trip, skiing or an unavoidable lunch with one of President Putin's ex-associates.

His mother gives a heartfelt speech about her honest, hardworking, kind and loving son. I spot Andy hiding a snigger, which catches me off guard.

Cate does not say much that night, or the next few nights. She shows people around her place, pointing out the spectacular views across the river, noting the underfloor heating, the en suite and separate wet room.

I count eighteen people at Poppy's funeral, and that includes her uncle with the wandering eyes. Clarke sobs most of the way through his speech. I proclaim myself too sad to make one, which maybe I am. Cate doesn't look happy as such, just more uninterested. He stands next to me, Mr. James Danbrook. There are no tears. I feel his hand squeeze my forearm and then he lets go.

He has been kind enough to put on a wake. Someone, most likely the housekeeper, has made enough food to feed eighty, let alone the handful of people who drove out of London to attend.

I leave Clarke and Cate talking, confident that they will just be reminiscing about those who have passed.

Darkness is all my eyes can see. The dusty darkness of a room not slept in for some time. I recognise the silence, the creaks in the floor, the anticipation of the front door opening. I listen just like I used to, straining my ears for an argument disguised as a discussion. There is nothing.

I reach for the side table lamp and the dull light illuminates my old bedroom. Everything is the same: my three lonely-looking trophies evenly spread out on the second shelf of the bookcase. A calendar on the wall with a menacing-looking shark for the month of April 2010. Not one event seems to be scheduled in. Nothing has changed, like a shrine to a person who died too young.

At first I see the pictures and my eyes avert but curiosity drags them back. A silver frame with five pictures: two of a kitten, three of a slightly older-looking cat. Rocky, poor Rocky. It was an accident. After Mum went I thought he had run away. I thought maybe she had taken him to punish me. I was so sad. Poor Rocky. And then when he came back I felt so angry, I threw him, I didn't mean to. Turns out cats don't always land on their feet.

The door creaks open and my father is standing there, two whisky on the rocks in hand.

"So you and Cate are moving to Spain, to be with your mum," he says, swishing whisky over ice.

"Yes, looking forward to it. 22 degrees in January – just what I need," I say.

"Make a new start for yourself, a new life," he says, picking up the photos of Rocky and laying them face down on the desk.

"That's the idea, Dad. Maybe open a restaurant, or a gym with yoga facilities."

"Stay off the drugs, son."

"I will, Dad."

He gulps down a mouthful of alcohol.

"I know what you did, son," he says calmly, accusingly.

I take a moment. I swish the tan liquid around its glass, choosing to pause and contemplate what I may have done.

"But do you know what you did though, Dad?" I retort, as my life to this point passes through me.

"So let's consider my silence your very final Christmas present," he says, shaking his head and ensuring our eyes meet for perhaps the last time.

I nod. I nonchalantly swig back the last of his rare single malt, pick up the framed pictures of Rocky, squeeze past the old boy and willingly leave the rest of my mess behind.

Printed in Great Britain
by Amazon